SOMEWHERE
IN THE
SUNSET

SOMEWHERE IN THE SUNSET

ESTELLE MASKAME

INK ROAD

First published in the UK in 2024 by Ink Road

INK ROAD is an imprint and trade mark of
Black & White Publishing Ltd
Nautical House, 104 Commercial Street, Edinburgh EH6 6NF

A division of Bonnier Books UK
4th Floor, Victoria House, Bloomsbury Square, London, WC1B 4DA
Owned by Bonnier Books
Sveavägen 56, Stockholm, Sweden

A CIP catalogue record for this book is available from the British Library.

ISBN: 978 1 78530 493 4

13 5 7 9 10 8 6 4 2

Typeset by Data Connection
Printed and bound in Great Britain by Clays Ltd, Elcograf S.p.A.

www.blackandwhitepublishing.com

For C.

GRACIE

Maybe I should burn down the apartment.

Pile his clothes high on our coffee table, soak them in gasoline, and set them ablaze.

Maybe I'll stand and watch this place burn. Watch as the flames spread to the rug, tear across the couch, soar up the curtains. They'll spread quickly, I imagine, and soon our home will be nothing but crumbling walls, burnt furniture and belongings turned to ash, all blanketed by toxic smoke. And if I haven't passed out by that point and the door hasn't melted, I'll maybe even slam it shut as I walk away from the wonderful life we'd built together.

But we are also on the fourth floor of this apartment building, with the most amazing neighbors either side, and I suppose it wouldn't be fair to risk their homes and their lives because I can't get a grip on my mental state.

I light the orange and vanilla scented candle that sits on the electric cooktop and then bury the lighter deep inside a drawer, safe from my dangerously intrusive thoughts. This is *not* me. My mind doesn't unravel like this. Never, ever, ever.

So, fuck him.

Fuck him for having me question my sanity.

Deep breaths, Gracie. You've already cried a thousand tears over him. He doesn't deserve a single drop more.

I polish the kitchen sink until it's sparkling, water the gorgeous arrangement of lilies my mother sent over earlier in the week, even stand on a chair to dust above the refrigerator. But there is only so much I can do to keep my hands busy – the apartment is the cleanest it has ever been, and that's saying a hell of a lot. I am undeniably a compulsive clean freak. If my home is cluttered, so is my brain. Maybe that's why I have convinced myself cleaning the bathroom three times a day might help me feel better.

Well, no.

I admit defeat and grab a bag of chips from the cupboard, then settle on the couch in front of the TV that I don't turn on. I wrap myself in a blanket, prop the bag of chips between my crossed legs, and allow myself to feel the insurmountable weight of my broken heart nestled deep in my chest.

And it is agonizing, feeling it. Every time I sit down and focus on the hollowness inside of me and the echoes of a thousand memories, I lose my breath. My lungs constrict, my stomach twists; it is so tangible, so real. Pain. That's what heartbreak is: insufferable, physical pain.

But there's no Band-Aid to fix it. No pills to soften the blow.

You just have to carry it. Maybe even forever.

And I can't handle that. This throbbing ache, this piercing agony, this breathlessness ... I can't feel this way forever, because if I do, it will kill me.

A whimper escapes my lips and I punch the pillow next to me. Whoever said crying is therapeutic is a liar. Crying hurts like a bitch. That lump bulging at the back of my throat, the sting at the corners of my eyes, the tension in my shoulders ... It all hurts. And it is so relentless.

We were supposed to have forever. We were supposed to *want* to have forever.

And a week ago, I would have never spent a Saturday night alone eating chips on the couch. I'd have been bent over it, his mouth hot against my ear and his hands pulling at my hair.

A thunderous knock at the door shakes away that image.

"Open up!" Elena's voice pulses through the apartment. "We're here for an intervention!"

I wipe away my tears with my blanket and carry my chips to the door. My best friends have had to deal with my unwavering lack of self-care all week, so I'm no longer ashamed to open the door and reveal myself. My apartment may be a show home, but I look like a slob who's broken in.

"Oh dear," Madison says.

She and Elena pityingly tilt their heads in sync before pushing past me into the apartment. I survey them in alarm. They are dressed to go out. Mini dresses, five-inch heels, volumized hair, strip lashes. They are dressed to go *out-out*.

"I thought I made it clear the last thing I want to do tonight is go out," I say as I click the door shut. My voice doesn't even sound like my own anymore. It's so flat, quiet, void of my usual liveliness.

"And you think this is better? Eating junk food in your sweatpants and crying?" Elena asks, pursing her glossy lips and daring me to deny that that's exactly what I've been doing. "It's your birthday!"

I glance at the birthday cards I made an effort to line up on the coffee table. She and Madison already came by this morning to drop off gifts and give me hugs that were tighter and longer than usual. More meaningful. That's all the celebration I need. This is not a birthday I wish to remember.

Madison waves the bottle of wine in her hand. "We thought about it all day. Should we do what you want, or should we do what you *need?* And what you need is to get out of this apartment, let down your hair, and have a good time with your friends. We aren't leaving

4

you here to mope on a Saturday night. Birthday or not. Where's your corkscrew?"

"Guys. Guys!"

The pair of them ignore my pleas as they search through my kitchen for wine glasses and a corkscrew. I knew I should have burned the apartment down while I had the chance. As I approach, Elena pulls the bag of chips from my hands and replaces it with a glass of white wine. My glass is noticeably fuller than both of theirs. Clearly, they think I need it more than they do. And they're right.

I take a sip. More than a sip. A gulp.

"See?" Maddie says. "You need this."

"I do, but . . ."

"A toast," Elena interrupts, holding out her glass. Maddie copies her and the two of them stare me down until I reluctantly hold out mine too, the three of us in a perfect circle. "Here is to Gracie, for being an amazing person who doesn't deserve to have her heart broken. Here is to girls' night. To being single and independent. To accepting drinks from sexy bachelors, because we do *not* date pathetic little boys. We only want *men*."

"Here, here!" Maddie cheers, and they clink their glasses hard against mine.

I force a small laugh, but I'm doing it again. Focusing too hard on the cutting edges of my heart. I suck in a breath. Elena is right – I do need this. A night with my girls, giggling over cheap wine in the club as the deafening music drowns out every painful thought. By the end of the night, I'll be hugging a cheap pizza in the backseat of an Uber.

"I haven't washed my hair in five days," I admit.

"We can tell. Shower. Now," Elena orders. She puts a hand on my shoulder and turns me toward the bathroom. "We'll go through your closet and find you a dress. You just . . . get those sweatpants off." She wrinkles her nose teasingly and shoves me into the bathroom, shutting the door on me.

I tap on my smart watch. It's only eight. My birthday isn't over yet, and if there's a chance to salvage the day, I have to take it. Elena and Maddie are trying their best to make me feel the slightest bit more human. I have to meet them somewhere in the middle, and that requires effort.

Discarding my sweatpants on the floor, I turn on the shower faucet just as I hear Taylor Swift's "22" blast through my apartment. Of course. What else would my friends play over my speaker on my twenty-second birthday?

All of Taylor Swift's albums, apparently. "We Are Never Ever Getting Back Together" blares next, and both Elena and Maddie scream the lyrics at the top of their voices. I imagine them now, dancing in my living area, wine glasses held high.

Maybe tonight is *exactly* what I need.

WESTON

I hate Zeitgeist on the weekends.

It deserves its reputation as the most popular dive bar in downtown San Francisco. It's grunge as all get-out, rough around the edges, and has the most bizarre rules. If you've never been grabbed by the scruff of the neck and dragged out by a bouncer, then have you ever truly visited Zeitgeist? It's a rite of passage, given it's famous for kicking people out over snapping a photo or sitting on a table. But it's exactly the kind of rowdiness I need tonight.

It's nearing ten and the patio is packed. Every single picnic table is overflowing with boozed-up patrons and there's not much standing room left, either. I keep my head down as I navigate through the thick crowds and squeeze back inside the bar. Punk rock roars in my ears and I keep on pushing, past the long bar with endless beer on tap, past the pinball machines, and out onto the street. There's now a small line to get in.

I stumble off around the corner and find a quiet spot. Leaning back against the graffitied wall, I sink down to the ground and draw my knees up to my chest. Out here, alone, the beers rush to my head. I blink away the stars and fish my phone out of my pocket.

There is a severe lack of notifications on my home screen. Not one single text, missed call or voicemail. Just a resounding silence in response to my pleas.

And I know I shouldn't do it *again*, but my desperation only grows stronger, consuming all of me. Her number sits at the top of my call log, emboldened in red, and I ignore the fact that I have (apparently) already called it nineteen times today. I dial it again.

It doesn't even ring. It goes straight to voicemail. Am I blocked? Did her phone die? What the fuck?

I suck in a breath of fresh air, and tell her voicemail inbox: "Hey, listen, I'm a little drunk now. But I just . . . I just really want to hear your voice, babe. Please call me back so we can talk about this. I love you. *I love you*. Okay? Are you even listening to these or are you just deleting them as soon as they hit your phone? Because I wouldn't mind if you deleted the voicemails I left around lunch. I was a crying son of a bitch then. I had a moment. I'm sorry. It's just that I really do love you. I can be better."

"Man, you really are scaring the fuck out of me. You are *whipped*."

I pull my phone away from my ear and look up. Cameron has followed me outside and now stares down at me with furrowed brows. Did he listen the entire time? Probably. I'm too drunk to have noticed.

I stand from the ground and stuff my hands into the pockets of my jacket, shaking my head helplessly. "What am I supposed to do?"

"For starters, you need to stop harassing her," Cameron says, lighting up a cigarette as he leans against the wall next to me. He takes a drag and exhales a plume of smoke into the evening air. "Stop blowing up her phone. It's been one day. She needs time before she can even *think* about reconsidering her choice."

"But shouldn't I fight for her?"

"Not like this," he says, waving his cigarette at me as though I'm some sorry excuse of a man. Cameron is my closest friend, and that means he always tells me things straight. No bullshit. "And I'm not telling you to take Adam's advice of flying off the rails, because that won't help either, but you need to relax a little, man. Things happen for a reason, Weston."

We don't say much more as he smokes the rest of his cigarette. I stare at the sidewalk, at all the gum embedded in the concrete, and can't possibly imagine *ever* getting over her. She has been a part of my life for four years and

I took it for granted that she always would be. She knows it too. It's why she left.

We head back through Zeitgeist to rejoin Adam and Brooks at our table in the beer garden, where a new round of tequila shots is waiting for us. Adam is wasted already, but he's also superhuman in the way he can drink to obliteration every single weekend and not even have so much as a headache the next morning. His body is that of a sixteen-year-old. For me, one beer too many results in a very fragile experience the next day.

"Did you sneak off to call her *again?*" Adam asks with a roll of his eyes. He slides one of the tequila shots across the picnic table toward me.

"Nah, he just needed a second to himself," Cameron answers, and we exchange a glance. I'm always grateful he has my back. Not that Adam and Brooks don't, but Cameron is always the one I go to with any worries. The one I can talk to without fear of judgment.

I take the shot of tequila without hesitation. Maybe if I get blackout drunk like Adam, I'll forget about her. The others follow, slamming their shot glasses down on the table.

Brooks involuntarily gags. "It's official. I can't drink like I used to."

"I'm just glad you're here," I say, clasping his shoulder. Brooks is now the only one in a committed relationship and he only ever joins us guys for beers on special occasions. He's a hard guy to pin down, because his girl comes first. Mine didn't.

"Hey, you need us for moral support tonight. I had to be here. But you." Brooks raises his middle finger to Adam across the bench. "Stop buying goddamn shots."

Adam grins in that usual, overly confident way of his. "Oh, baby, we're just getting started! The night is still young. Temple is calling our names!" He turns to the group of college girls sharing the other half of our picnic table. "Where are you girls heading later? Wanna come with us to Temple? Our buddy right there" – he points to me – "is heartbroken because his girlfriend just dumped him."

"He's so insensitive sometimes," Cameron mutters, and Brooks nods in agreement.

The girls let out a chorus of "awws" and pout their lips at me in sympathy. "Sorry about your girlfriend," one of them says, and I only offer a tight smile in return before chugging the remainder of my beer from earlier. It's warm and gross.

"So where do you guys go to school?" Adam proceeds to ask the group, getting up from the bench to walk down to the other end of the table. I stifle a laugh at how predictable his moves are. He just wants to be closer to the little brunette on the end.

And then he does it – he sits his ass down on the corner of the table. A Zeitgeist sin.

"Ah, fuck," Brooks says, smothering a hand over his face.

A nanosecond later, the bouncer is grappling with Adam to remove him from the patio. Cameron, Brooks and I calmly finish our beers, grab our stuff from the table, and then follow Adam out onto the street. This is the only way we ever make an exit from Zeitgeist – following in the wake of Adam's careless behavior, and as always, not one apology leaves his mouth. He wipes his hands on his jeans and points down the street, muttering something about the club we're heading to having a hotter crowd anyway.

I trail a little behind until Cameron waits up for me, syncing his steps to mine. "Head up, Weston. You've still got us, even though Adam's value is questionable." He scoffs and nudges his elbow into my ribs. "Shake her off and try to have some fun tonight for your own sake. You'll feel much better if you can get through the rest of tonight without thinking of her."

I tilt my head back to the dark sky. Cameron's right, but he so often is. I'm already out and I can either continue to be miserable, or I can push her to the back of my mind and start embracing this new life without her. Even if I have to fake it at first.

I glance at Cameron out of the corner of my eye and force a smile. "The women at Temple *are* hotter."

He thumps me on the back of my shoulder and says, "Attaboy!"

I can survive without Charlotte.

I have to.

I will.

GRACIE

It's a breezy, chilly evening in San Francisco and as I step out of the Uber, I grit my teeth and hug my arms around me. I never want to give in and wear a jacket, so I suck it up and bear the chill in the air to avoid the inconvenience of checking in a jacket at the door.

It's how you know who's local and who's visiting from out of town. The locals? We're cold, but we don't complain. The visitors? They stand in line for the club, teeth chattering in confusion. They think: *California? In July? It'll be ninety degrees!* And so they step off the plane at the airport in their shorts and sun hats and immediately rush to the first store they find to invest in some jeans and sweatshirts. They can blame the Bay Area's marine layer. It's why we have so much fog.

I nervously adjust the hem of my dress. I go a little too hard on leg day at the gym, but it pays dividends – I *like* my legs, even though they are three inches shorter than I'd like them to be. The dress Elena and Maddie picked out for me is of course the sultriest dress I own. Flatteringly tight fitted with spaghetti straps and a cut-out just below my breasts, revealing a flash of skin. All black, because is there anything sexier than a black mini dress to boost your confidence when your self-esteem is on the floor? My feet hurt in my heels already. But they make me five foot seven instead of five foot two, so the blisters are a fair trade-off.

"Where are you going?" Elena asks, clutching my elbow.

I point down the street, beyond the general admission line that snakes all the way down the sidewalk and around the corner. Cheat Codes is the guest DJ tonight. We probably won't even get in. "The line starts back there."

"Standing in line? On your birthday?" Elena says with a snort, and Maddie grins as though they're dangling a secret over my head. "This way!"

They fall into step either side of me, locking their arms with mine, and guide me past the general admission line, the line for those with tickets, and toward the bottle service entrance. We walk straight up to the suited VIP host.

"Hi, ladies! Do we have a table tonight?"

"We do! It's under Elena Morales. The rest of our group should already be inside."

I narrow my eyes suspiciously at Elena, who makes a conscious effort to completely ignore me as the host checks his tablet, so I turn to Maddie instead, who can't wipe the giddy smile off her face. "What the hell have you guys done?"

"You need this to be the best birthday *ever*. We just want you to have a night you'll never forget." She squeezes our arms tighter together then lets go to search her bag for her ID. I mimic her, handing over my state ID. The older I get, the more embarrassing it is that I don't have my driver's license yet.

"Happy birthday!" the host says as he hands back our IDs, then unhooks the red rope blocking the door. "Come with me, ladies."

My stomach somersaults with apprehension. Bottle service at Temple is ridiculously expensive. Like, a thousand bucks *minimum*. I know it's my birthday, I know the love of my life just left me, I know I'm having an existential breakdown, but I can't believe my friends splurged so much on me. Thank God I pulled myself together enough to come so this surprise didn't go to waste.

Inside, the club shakes with the heavy bass of EDM and the neon glow of a thousand LED bulbs flash erratically to the beat of the music. Temple is our favorite club in the city and we've spent countless Saturday nights packed onto this dance floor since we all turned twenty-one last year, but we've never experienced the luxury of a VIP package. The host escorts us along the edge of the packed dance floor and it feels pretty damn nice not to be one of the poor souls buried among sweaty strangers for once. Then we arrive at the elevated, private booth where five of our mutual friends yell, "SURPRISE!"

"Enjoy your night! Your waitress will be over soon," the host says, but I see the amusement in his eyes as he walks away. I'm frozen in shock, my shoulders drawn in tight. The sight of all my friends here, the deafening music, the bright lights . . . It's too intense after feeling like the only person in the world all week.

"Told you guys we'd get her here!" Elena cheers, and she pulls me up into the booth where I'm immediately enveloped in hugs and kisses. The *happy birthday*s are mixed with condolences.

I pull myself together, barely, and let the sympathetic frowns go over my head and focus instead on the fact that it *is* my birthday, my friends are all here, and they've splashed out a ridiculous amount of money to make this night special for me. I feel so lucky to have people around me who go to such lengths to bring some joy into the tragedy that is currently my life.

"I hate *all* of you!" I joke, laughing as I bury my head into my hands to hide my blushing.

We snap some pictures of the eight of us together while we're all mostly sober and before someone inevitably spills their drink and ruins their outfit, and then settle into the comfort of our booth. All this space, all to ourselves. No strangers breathing over my shoulder. No inhaling someone's BO. Why have we never tried this sooner?

Camila scoots up close to me, leaning into my ear so I can hear her over the music. "I'm so sorry about Luca."

My body tenses at the sound of his name. It used to feel so warm and comforting and safe; it used to feel like home. Now it feels like freshly sharpened knives.

"I can't believe someone can just change their mind like that after so long. You'd think he would have realized sooner," she continues, but as her words echo everything I have already thought of myself a thousand times over, I stare at Georgia across the booth.

Her engagement ring glistens under the lights. She only met David two years ago, and already they are planning their fall wedding. Seven *years*, and instead of an engagement, all I got was a broken fucking heart. Did he even wish me a happy birthday today? Oh my God. He didn't. Does Luca even care about me *at all?*

"I'm not thinking about him tonight," I tell Camila, cutting her off politely. I don't want to discuss my wrecked relationship in the middle of this club. I want to get drunk. So drunk, in fact, that I'll text Luca at four in the morning and give him a piece of my mind. That's why I've given in and come out tonight. To give him a giant metaphorical middle finger, to prove I can survive perfectly fine without him.

But I also really, really don't think I can.

Oh God, my chest hurts again.

Elena plops down on the other side of me and gestures out over the packed dance floor. "If anyone catches your eye, I'll get out there and invite him over here for you. And hopefully he has some hot friends, one of which can take me home tonight if he plays his cards right." She wiggles her shoulders, her brunette curls bouncing. Unlike Maddie, who dates and dates and dates but never finds the right connection, Elena is perfectly content with being single. She *chooses* it.

And maybe it's because I've been in a relationship since the age of fifteen that I can't fathom choosing to be alone. I've never been on my own. I was always a package deal. It was never just *Gracie*, it was always *Gracie and Luca*. I don't think I even know how to navigate life as an entity that exists all on its own.

My breathing grows labored. I'm having another crisis. I feel so out of my depth, trying to tread water when I've never been taught how to swim. I'm going to drown. I am literally going to drown without Luca holding me up.

"She looks terrified," I hear Camila say.

"I was just kidding! Well, a little," Elena says with a wink. "I know, I know, getting with someone new is the last thing on your mind right now, blah blah blah, but the option is always there if the desire just so happens to arise. Look how badly they want us." She nods toward the men desperately hovering around the edge of our booth, sipping on their drinks while they leer at us, begging for one of us to give them some attention. Little do they know, flirting is Elena's favorite sport. She blows one of the guys a kiss, and he leans against the side of the booth and seductively motions for her to come over. "A free vodka soda awaits," she trills, and heads off to entertain him.

I check out the club from this new, heightened position. It looks so different when you can see something other than the back of someone's head. The DJ tonight is indeed Cheat Codes, and the trio throw themselves around inside the DJ booth up front as the crowd surges forward to get closer to the action. At the back of the club, the line for the bar is three people deep. It's really going off in here tonight.

I run my eyes through the crowd, picking out individuals to focus on, all men. Even the hottest, most attractive, Greek-God-like man I can find, I don't feel anything for. Is there something wrong with me? Why can't I even *appreciate* a hot guy? I'm almost concerned by how disinterested I am, but how else am I supposed to feel? I've never once looked at another guy. It has always been Luca. For seven years, since we were both fifteen and sophomores in high school, he is the only person I've ever had eyes for. He was all of my firsts, and he was going to be all of my lasts. We were going to be together forever. It was *always* going to be him.

But what if that's still the case? What if, despite him walking away, my heart will always choose him? I thought my future was set in stone, so it will take a lot of time to undo everything I thought I knew, to rebuild a new life without him in it.

Fuck. I'm screwed. And not in the way Elena wants me to be.

WESTON

I can't believe we just stood in line for forty minutes, paid fifty bucks cover, and now can't get anywhere near the goddamn bar to buy a beer. I normally love hitting the clubs at the weekend, but when there's a famous DJ on the decks and the room is dangerously packed from wall-to-wall like this? Yeah, forget it. This place is clearly at capacity, and I make a mental note of where all of the emergency exits are located. This isn't enjoyable. It's like a hundred degrees in here, Brooks keeps stepping on my foot, and I can't hear a damn thing. For the sake of the guys, I try and convince myself this is so much fun.

"We should have gone to DNA instead," Cameron yells into my ear, and I nod in defeated agreement. We should have, but we didn't. And now we're stuck like sardines making no forward progress toward the bar.

Adam tries to push his way through but rightly gets put back in his place by a guy double his size. He groans with frustration – he hasn't had a drink in an hour, and he gets impatient when he feels his buzz fading. "Plan B," he says.

Considering this is the only bar on this floor, Brooks seems skeptical. "What exactly is your plan B, Adam?"

Adam stretches up to point over the heads of those around us. We follow the direction of his pointed finger, all the way to the VIP booths on the edge of the dance floor. Some of them are occupied by groups of guys in expensive shirts and designer watches, but most of them are full of women. And they probably all look like super-models, because it's *always* the gorgeous girls who have bottle service, but every girl's face in this place is a blur to me. I don't notice the detail of their eyes, the shape of their nose, the color painted on their lips. Every face is nondescript. I don't see supermodels, I only see people who *aren't* Charlotte.

"We find some girls to invite us into their booth and we use their bottle service," Adam explains. "We get chicks *and* booze. Win-win. Brooks, don't mention you're wifed-up already. Cameron, flex your biceps. Weston, make it known you own handcuffs. Some girls like that."

I cock my head to the side. "And what about you?"

"I'll use my charm, obviously."

Cameron rolls his eyes. "What charm?"

"You think it's this nose of mine that gets me all the girls? It's my endearing charm that does the hard work."

He bats his eyelashes romantically at the three of us in turn, and I do laugh. I'll give it to him, he *is* hilarious. He hasn't cut his hair in months, his nose is crooked from when he broke it during a fist fight in high school, and he's about ten pounds underweight. But his confidence is through the roof, and that makes all the difference. He has the most game out of all of us.

"Whatever. I'm sick of standing here, so let's try it your way," Brooks says, anxiously rubbing his neck. I'm not sure his girlfriend will like the idea of him spending his night in the company of other women.

Charlotte never did.

I spent more time being Adam's wingman than I did treating her right. I should have stepped up and been a man, put her first before even myself, and loved her harder than she ever thought possible. A few weeks ago, she was passed up on for a promotion at work. She was upset that night, and I *knew* she was upset, yet I still went out because Adam had no one else to hit up the bars with. I'm kicking myself for that now. Charlotte needed consolation and reassurance and I was the one who was meant to give it to her. I was never there for her in all the ways she was always there for me.

Her words echo inside my head: *I know you love me, Weston, but you don't make me feel loved.*

My throat feels dry, whether from dehydration or guilt, I don't know. But I do know I could really do with another beer right about now.

23

Adam leads the way through the dance floor because he's the only one who has no qualms when it comes to shoving people out of his path. Cameron, Brooks and I squeeze along behind him, our apologies going unheard beneath the thumping of the music as we bump into countless strangers.

A group of hostesses approaches one of the VIP booths closest to the stage, some carrying large signs that say "Happy Birthday", some waving dazzling sparklers, and one has an ice bucket on their shoulder with a huge bottle of Cîroc vodka inside. The women in the booth cheer and dance, the flashlights on their phones shining like a dozen spotlights as they take videos. Must be nice, not being stuck on this sweaty dance floor, unable to even buy a drink at the bar.

Adam abruptly halts. "Her," he says. "Look at *her*. Holy shit."

He doesn't have to point her out. As the hostesses leave, a petite brunette within the booth hugs the bottle of Cîroc to her chest and poses for a photo, her tongue out. I can sense Adam twitching in anticipation.

"Let me talk to them first," Cameron says, nudging Adam to the side. "You'll freak them out if you go over there drooling like that. Weston, back me up."

God, I wish I had a drink. What am I supposed to do with my hands and why am I so aware of my every movement? I follow Cameron up to the barrier around the booth, but there are already other guys hovering, probably with the same intentions as us. This is so stupid. I wonder how much longer I have to show face for before I can slip out unnoticed? Maybe if the club wasn't so packed tonight, I may have found some enjoyment in it.

There are around eight girls partying in the booth together. I gloss over them and acknowledge they're all attractive, but there's no fighting my disinterest. No one can ever compare to Charlotte, and my chest tightens as I realize I may never kiss those lips of hers again.

My hand automatically reaches for my phone, but Cameron nudges my shoulder hard before I can act on that urge.

"Weston, did you hear her? Her name is Elena," Cameron says, fixing me with a stern look for being so blatantly rude and distant. When did he even get her attention? It's the little brunette Adam has his eye on. "Sorry about him. He's got a lot going on right now."

"Sorry. Hey," I say. And because I can't think of a single thing to say to this blur of a girl leaning over the barrier toward us, I default into wingman mode. "You see that guy over there? Busted nose, curly hair? You are totally his type. I promise his jokes make up for that shitty shirt he's wearing."

Elena laughs, but the sound of any girl's laugh other than Charlotte's makes me feel a little sick. "Why don't you invite your busted-nosed, curly-haired, shitty-shirt-wearing friend over here then?"

I turn around and signal for Adam and Brooks to join, and they are straight over here without hesitation. The four of us stand on the other side of the barrier at the mercy of this girl's drunk decisions. Will she let us join them or will she kick us to the curb for pathetically trying to enter their booth?

"Your friends tell me you have good jokes," she tells Adam, crossing her arms against the barrier and smiling down at the four of us.

Adam leans up against the barrier and narrows his eyes challengingly. "Let us join you and maybe you'll hear some."

And clearly there is something about a cocky guy that must be right up Elena's street, because that's all the convincing it takes for her to invite us into the booth. The other girls exchange confused looks with one another as we plant ourselves down next to them all, but quickly warm up to the idea of having some male company. They offer us some of their vodka and mixers, but we already have the privilege of taking up their VIP space and we aren't going to use up their booze too. It's just their expedited bar service we want. We call over a hostess and order a bucket of beers.

"This isn't good," Brooks mutters, pulling at the collar of his shirt, feeling the pressure of being in such close proximity to eight beautiful women. He sits between Cameron and me so that he only risks brushing his hand against *our* thighs, and he locks his eyes on the stage, refusing to make eye contact with anyone. He really is all in when it comes to his girlfriend. My guilt pierces even deeper.

As Adam and Elena hover around the drinks table and chat, a red-haired girl sits down next to Cameron and asks him if we're visiting from out of town. She seems a little too happy when he tells her that we are local (they are too), and he seems even happier to entertain the conversation. Girls always gravitate toward him – he's all muscle. And when they find out he's a personal trainer at a gym downtown, oh boy. They die every time.

The hostess arrives with our bucket of beers and sets them down on the table. I get up to fetch a bottle and as I'm popping the cap, I hear the tail end of Adam's conversation with Elena.

"Oh, he's a cop. He has handcuffs. Are any of your friends into that kinky stuff? He needs to get under someone new to get over his ex. Preferably immediately. He's not usually this boring."

With my free hand, I reach out for his chest and grab a handful of his shirt. "Dude. Stop it."

"Oh, this is *perfect!*" Elena squeals. She stumbles away in her heels, leaving Adam to stare at me with complete nonchalance. He is so blasé sometimes.

He pushes my hand off his shirt. "What?"

"I don't *want* to get under someone new. Maybe if I didn't spend half my time getting wasted with you,

Charlotte wouldn't have left. So how about you shut the fuck up?"

Adam narrows his dark eyes to mirror my glare and for a split second, I consider cracking my beer against his skull. But if there's one thing my field training has taught me, it's patience and remaining calm in high-pressured situations. I relax my shoulders and take a step back from him, but our eye contact holds strong. A threat lingering between us.

Elena reappears, thrusting her friend forward. Adam still doesn't break, and neither do I.

"Gracie, I want you to meet . . ." Elena says but trails off when she realizes she doesn't know my name.

"Weston," Adam finishes for her. The corner of his mouth twitches with a cruel smirk, and he continues to look me straight in the eye as he adds, "But don't get your hopes up, darling. He doesn't know how to treat a girl right. Just ask his ex."

Fuck my patience.

My fist connects with Adam's jaw before his final word even lands. Elena and her friend scream as Adam rocks back against them, knocking one of them to the ground. Under the flashing lights, everything is a blur. Adam lunges toward me and together, in the midst of swinging fists and grappling, we crash into the table in the middle of the booth. Glass shatters around us, liquid seeps through our clothes. All of the girls are screaming now. Brooks grabs Adam, Cameron grabs me. They pull us apart, but our adrenaline is pumping and we are out of control, desperate to get one more punch in. Adam may be fueled by booze, but I'm full of pain and anger.

"Weston. *Weston!*" Cameron hisses in my ear, his huge arms locked around my shoulders as he holds me steady. My chest rises and falls with each heavy breath I take. "You can't act like this."

Brooks has Adam backed up into the opposite end of the booth now, and the distance is enough to snap me out of my sudden rage. There are shards of glass everywhere. The girl knocked to the floor is helped back to her feet while another girl flies off the handle in a fit of rage at the spilled cranberry juice down her white dress. Elena screams obscenities into Adam's face.

Club security descend upon the booth within seconds. One bouncer twists my elbow with such ferocity that if *I* did that to a troublemaker, I'd be accused of police brutality. He hauls me out of the booth.

"Everyone out! NOW!" I hear one of the other bouncers order, and he begins corralling the girls out of the booth too, which of course, they protest.

"This is our booth!"

"They aren't even with us!"

"We don't know them!"

The bouncer snaps, "EVERYONE!"

And it's humiliating, being physically dragged through this club on display in front of the masses who *aren't* losing their shit. Adam isn't far behind me. We are guided to one of the emergency exits I noticed earlier and thrown straight out of it into a back alley behind the club. Cameron, Brooks and the group of distraught girls voluntarily follow.

"You and you," one of the bouncers says, pointing to Adam and me. "Don't show your faces around here again. You're banned."

The door slams shut, the echo traveling down the alley until it fades into the cold night air. No one says a word as we all stand motionless, processing. Cameron sparks up a cigarette and leans against the wall, bemused, and I dare to exchange a glance with Adam.

His shirt is soaked and his jaw displays a hint of redness. The look in his eye makes it pretty clear he'd go for a second round, so I grit my teeth and turn my back on the group to walk away. I should know better than to get into a fight, and now I have something else to be mad at myself for. Why can't I hold myself together?

"You absolute *douchebag!*" one of the girls yells after me. She's not wrong.

I hear heels click against the concrete as someone runs to catch up with me. It's Elena. She steps around me, hand held up to block me. There's lipstick smeared on her chin, and her drunk gaze struggles to focus on me. "Do you have any idea how much that booth cost? You just ruined our entire night!"

"Give my friends your Venmo. I'll pay the bill. Okay?"

"No! You ruined our night!"

"It's not the only thing I've ruined," I mutter, then step around her and hasten my stride.

More arguing breaks out in the alley behind me, Adam's voice mixed with what sounds like every single one of the girls' voices at once. I'm not a total asshole. I do feel bad for getting these girls kicked out of their own booth, especially when it's someone's *birthday*, but Adam just had to push me over the edge.

As I hit the street, I pull out my phone, full of hope that maybe Charlotte will have tried to call me back before she went to sleep tonight. But it's approaching one in the morning, and there are no missed calls and no new messages. My stomach sinks and I switch over to the Uber app.

I'm going home. I'm going to bed, to stare at the ceiling all night, and then I'll deal with this hangover in the morning.

GRACIE

This is perfect. I was praying the club would be evacuated due to an accidental fire alarm. Hell, even an *actual* emergency would have been gladly welcomed by me. There is only so much I can do to ignore the ache in the pit of my stomach, and I was losing the ability to maintain the smile on my face. I wanted the night to end, and thanks to a couple of moronic strangers, I have my exit.

Elena, on the other hand, is jabbing a perfectly manicured finger into the chest of the guy she'd been flirting with, making it known she now thinks he's a jerk. Maddie picks a shard of glass out of her hair, her sensitive disposition meaning she's on the brink of tears, and the rest of the group are crouched around Camila and her white dress, dabbing mercilessly at the stained fabric with handfuls of napkins. Their attempts to salvage that dress are futile. It's cranberry juice! What hope do they have?

I tuck my purse under my arm and take a couple steps to the side. No one notices, so I take a few more. I glance toward the street. The guy who threw the first punch, the one Elena was forcing me to say hi to, has just disappeared around the corner. He has the right idea. I want to get out of here, too.

Discreetly, I slip off my heels and shudder as my bare feet touch the cold, disgusting concrete. If my friends hear the click of my shoes making a dash for freedom, I don't doubt for a second that they'll chase me down. It's after midnight. The night is still young and there are other clubs they can drag me to.

I lower my head, heels hugged to my chest, and make a break for it. Out on the main street, that guy is still here. He paces back and forth directly beneath a street-light, his face aglow, and he glances repeatedly between his phone screen and the road.

I walk up to him and only now, in the fresh air, do all those vodka cranberries hit me. My steps aren't that steady. "Are you waiting for an Uber?"

"Yes."

"Can I share a ride with you?"

The guy lifts his eyes from his phone, his expression more blank than confused as he looks at me. "You want to get in an Uber with me after I just ruined one of your friend's birthday celebrations?"

"Yes."

He doesn't say whether or not he agrees. I press my back to the wall and hug my arms around myself, feeling the cold more than ever. A minute later, the Uber pulls up in front of us, and our silence is broken when the guy turns to me and says, "Fine."

We climb into the backseat together and I'm too tipsy to care that I'm getting into a car with not only a stranger, but that same stranger who just got my friends and me kicked out of the club. He clearly has a short fuse, but I need a ride home and he can pay for it. Also, the Uber driver is a woman, so that always helps.

"One second. I need to add another drop-off," the guy tells her, then passes me his phone with complete indifference and angles away, staring out of his window.

The Uber app looks a little fuzzy as I add my apartment's address as one of the drop-offs. I offer the phone back to my new companion, but when he doesn't bother to take it, I set it down on the middle seat between us. The driver sets off, and clearly the silence in this vehicle is stifling for her, because she turns on the radio.

As we drive through downtown, past the late-night crowds still lining the sidewalks outside of clubs and bars, I study Mr. Fighter out of the corner of my eye. He props his elbow up on the window, resting his head against the palm of his hand, his mind so clearly elsewhere. I can smell the alcohol that's soaked into his shirt.

"It's *my* birthday," I say. Well, it's after midnight, so it's not *really* my birthday anymore.

"Huh?"

"It was my birthday we were celebrating."

He groans and drops his arm from the window, casting me the briefest of glances. "Happy birthday, I guess," he says with not one ounce of a shit to give.

I snort. "Worst birthday *ever*."

"Sorry about that."

"Oh, don't worry about it. I was already having the worst birthday ever." I try to joke about it, even attempt a laugh, but the sound is hollow and suddenly I feel like I am going to explode into the torrent of tears I've been holding back all night.

It should be Luca sitting next to me in this Uber. I have never gone home to our empty apartment on my own before. We did *everything* together, and it seems that was the problem for him. Every drunken Uber ride home, he was by my side, casting seductive glances at each other in the backseat, knowing that soon we'd be in bed together.

"Are you . . . *crying?*"

My lips tremble, my eyes brimming with tears. I'm not the most graceful of criers to begin with, let alone when I'm drunk. I tilt my head down and can't help but make this awful whimpering noise. Everything hurts so, so much.

"Is she okay?" the Uber driver asks.

"What do I know? I don't even know her," the guy mutters, then turns toward me. "What's your name?"

"Gracie. My friend was trying to introduce us when you . . ." My shoulders involuntarily judder as I hiccup, trying to find my breath in between my tears. I just want Luca.

"Okay, Gracie, I'm Weston," the guy says. "I think you're drunker than I am, because you're ugly crying in an Uber with a stranger, so maybe . . . don't do that."

I abruptly lift my head and angrily narrow my eyes at him before saying, very matter-of-factly, "The love of my life left me."

Weston's gaze remains firmly locked on mine. He allows a beat of silence to fill the air before he says, "So did mine."

"Well then, how about some sympathy?"

He laughs harshly and shakes his head. "I don't want to bond with you over your boyfriend dumping you, okay? That sucks for you, and I get it, but I just want to go home. How far is your apartment?"

The Uber driver catches my eye in the rearview mirror. "You guys don't know each other?"

"No," I say, crossing my arms and glaring sideways at Weston. Zero consolation from him. What was it his friend said to make him so pissed? Something about not treating his girlfriend right? If this is his attitude, grumpy and uncaring, then I don't blame her for leaving him.

"Do you feel safe right now?" the driver asks me.

Weston scoffs. "What do you mean, *does she feel safe?* We are going home to separate apartments. I am *not* a predator, like you're insinuating. I'm a police officer."

I tilt my head at him. "The Golden State Killer was also a police officer."

"That's true," the driver agrees with rapid nodding.

"She hopped into *my* Uber!" Weston protests, then points an accusing finger at me. "Maybe you're the predator."

"Unlikely," the driver says, and Weston snaps, "Do you want me to tip you or not?"

The driver focuses back on the road, I resume my emotional breakdown, and Weston seethes with unrelenting anger. As far as Uber rides go, this is the weirdest one I've ever had. When we pull up outside my apartment building, I wipe my tears and step out of the car. My complex, although incredibly safe, feels strangely intimidating in the dark. I've never returned home this late by myself before and my anxiety spikes at the thought of walking through those doors alone without Luca waiting for me on the other side.

I poke my head back into the car. "Are you really a police officer?" I ask Weston gently.

"Yes," he says.

"You promise?"

Weston sighs and pinches the bridge of his nose. "I promise I am a sworn-in police officer of the San Francisco Police Department. Now what do you need?"

"Would you . . . Would you mind walking me to my door?" My cheeks blaze red in embarrassment as soon as I ask the question. My mind is such a jumbled mess. Life just seems so terrifying all of a sudden.

"I already feel dizzy in this car and I just want to get home. You can walk inside your own building, surely?" Weston meets my saddened gaze and, as the seconds tick by, his expression gradually softens and something changes in his dark eyes. "Okay."

He slides over the backseat and steps out of the car, asking the Uber driver to hold on five minutes, and then walks with me to the entrance of the building. We don't say another word to each other as I unlock the doors and he follows me to the elevator. As it climbs to the fourth floor, I realize how stupid this is.

"I'm sorry. You don't have to walk me all the way to my door. I can take it from here," I tell him, trying both to catch his eye and avoid it at the same time. Even with my heels on, he's so much taller than me, but so is the majority of the population.

Weston presses his lips together and leans back against the handrail. "My cop instincts are kicking in now. It's no problem for me to walk you to your door."

"Thank you."

There's a pause in the air as the elevator passes the third floor, and Weston tucks his chin to his chest, eyes locked on the ground. His shirt is still damp from all the spilled drinks.

"Sorry for being a douche in the Uber back there. And for getting you kicked out of the club," he mumbles without looking up, and although he may be drunk, his speech is clear and concise. "I swear I'm usually much nicer. I'm just having a rough night, and I don't mean to take it out on you. Especially when it's your birthday."

The elevator doors open, but neither of us moves. Our eyes meet now; mine blurred from my tears, his bloodshot from however many beers he's consumed tonight. The corner of his mouth twitches with an attempt at an apologetic smile.

"I'll take your word for that," I say, my arm accidentally brushing against him as I walk out of the elevator. "That you're usually much nicer."

Weston laughs as he follows several steps behind me down the hallway to my apartment door. He observes me closely as I jab my keys into the lock and push open the door to reveal the darkness of my apartment. I flick on a light switch, and mine and Luca's home lies bare before me. All of our framed photographs of us together and in love. The couch he always hated, because I wanted fabric, he wanted leather, and so we of course got the fabric. The coffee machine in the kitchen is his. I imagine he'll take it with him when he officially moves out.

I'm never going to return home to him waiting for me anymore.

As I stand frozen by the door, Weston clears his throat.

"Home safe and sound," he says. "Are you good from here?"

My pulse beats painfully, but I force myself forward into the lounge. "Yes," I lie.

The thought of another night tossing and turning because my bed doesn't feel right without Luca next to me is unbearable. I press a hand to the arm of the couch for stability as I slide off my heels again, my feet immediately soothed by the softness of the rug. I throw my bag onto the coffee table next to my birthday cards. I am *so* exhausted. From everything. This apartment doesn't even feel like home anymore, and I still want to burn the place down, more so than I did before.

From the threshold, Weston says, "Okay, well . . . Goodnight."

"Wait," I say abruptly, spinning to face him. "Do you want a new shirt?"

He raises an eyebrow with a sense of amusement. "I think I'll survive the five minutes from here to my place. Thanks, though."

"Okay. It's just that I have a closet full of Luca's clothes and . . . Never mind," I say, but my voice is weary. I cross to my kitchen and turn on the faucet, because no matter how late it is or how drunk I am, I simply can't go to bed with dirty dishes in the sink. In my mini dress, I dunk my hands into the hot water and close my eyes. I've just about got my tears in check.

"Are you okay?" Weston asks quietly.

I grip the edge of the sink, my back to him. "Did you miss the part where I told you the love of my life left me? It only happened on Monday, and I'm still surrounded by all of his things, so no. I'm *not* okay."

"Yeah, me either," he says. "My girlfriend broke up with me last night."

I spin around from the sink with water dripping from my hands. Weston is still at the door, both hands pressed to the frame, expression twisted. He looks just about as broken as I feel.

"You can come in, you know," I say. The distance between us seems too far.

He hesitates briefly, and just when I think he's about to shake his head to decline, he steps forward into my apartment. There is uncertainty in the way he moves as he joins me in the kitchen and leans back against the counter with one foot crossed over the other. He stares down at the vinyl floor, swallowing the lump in his throat.

I haven't really focused on him until now. His jaw is sharp and well-defined, lined by the faintest trace of stubble, and there's a beauty mark right in the center of his left cheek. One of his arms is completely covered in tattoos, from the back of his hand snaking all the way up beneath the sleeve of his shirt, each design intricately woven together.

"Why did your girlfriend leave you?" I ask. There's no polite way to phrase such a question.

41

Weston doesn't look up from the floor. The anguish pulses from him when he admits, "She didn't feel loved by me. But the truth is, I don't think I realized just how badly I loved her until last night. And that's about four years too late. She won't even answer my calls anymore." He clenches his jaw and scoffs to hide his pain as he waves his phone helplessly. The screen is empty of any notifications. He sucks in a breath. "How about you?"

"The opposite," I say, but my voice is breathless. "Luca thinks he loved me *too* much, and now he wants to be selfish. He wants to find himself . . . Whatever that even means." The confusion that's haunted me for days returns, hanging over me like a storm cloud. I still can't make any sense of what it is that Luca wants, and I think that's why the breakup has been so hard. Not because I've spent seven years of my life with this person, not because my future vanished in a split second, but because I don't *understand*.

Weston lifts his head. He fastens his eyes on me, an all-too-familiar pain rising to the fore, and then closes the distance between us. He steps in front of me and pulls me against his chest, arms wrapped around me.

"What are you . . . ?" I mumble against his damp shirt, my arms hanging limply by my side.

"Goddamn it, hug me back," he says.

I press my face into his chest and envelop my arms around his back. He's large and muscular, and as he holds me tight, the ground beneath my feet finally stabilizes. The world stops spinning and I feel steady.

Weston's chin rests atop my head, his soft breaths getting lost in my hair. When the moment lasts a little too long and I try to let go of him, he doesn't release me. He only holds on tighter. "I needed this," he whispers.

And then we unravel from one another and immediately turn away. I dunk my hands back into the sink and Weston retreats from the kitchen. That was too much intimacy to share with a perfect stranger, and now it's awkward. Unbearably so.

"I better grab the Uber," he says, but his voice carries across my apartment and I realize he must already be at the door. "Goodnight . . ." And then with purpose, with *weight*, he adds, "Gracie."

I swallow the lump in my throat. "Goodnight, Weston." The door clicks shut, and he's gone.

WESTON

Fuck. *Fuuuuck*.

I swear to God, I am never drinking again. It wasn't even worth it. Did the tequila make me forget about Charlotte? No, it didn't. What a waste of money only to feel like death has come calling my name.

The bathroom tiles feel like ice as I hang over the edge of the toilet bowl, trembling in my boxers, my insides burning with acid. My skin beads with sweat. Every time I try to move from the bathroom, a new wave of nausea washes over me and I find myself right back in this spot, praying for a miracle. Promising God that I won't ever drink again if he cures me right now.

I manage to hold myself together long enough to have a shower. I pull on a pair of sweats, open up all of the windows in my apartment to breathe in some fresh air, and set a skillet on the stovetop. When I take

44

the carton of eggs out of the refrigerator, however, I gag and immediately abandon the idea of breakfast. Too hungover for that.

It's after eleven and I still haven't found my phone, which is a problem. What if Charlotte is trying to reach me? When I woke this morning and reached out for my bedside dresser, my hand didn't immediately land on my phone. And it's always there, always charging. My eyes shot open and, in a frenzy, I kicked my sheets around, searched through the pockets of my jeans on the floor, and raided the rest of my apartment. And it's a *studio*, so there's not many places to lose a phone in the first place.

I know I left the club with it, because I ordered an Uber. So, if my phone isn't here, then there's only two places it *can* be.

In the Uber, or in that girl's apartment.

God, that girl from last night. I can't even remember her name, that's how drunk I was, but I am haunted by the fact that I hugged her. How pathetic is that? I want to die every time I think about it. What the hell was wrong with me? I couldn't watch her head into that building, alone and heartbroken, when she specifically asked me to walk her to her door.

Because I never walked Charlotte to her door. I'd drop her at the curb, kiss her goodbye in the car. And when I analyze every wrong action of mine that led to losing her, self-loathing fills me when I realize I would

45

never even wait until she got to the door of her building. I would just drive off. I don't think I even glanced back a lot of the time.

So maybe that's what last night was about. A chance to learn from my mistakes.

But that hug. Fuck, that hug. I needed it.

And now I have to go back there.

Between being too hungover to drive and not being willing to maneuver my car out of the parking garage, I find myself on foot in search of my phone. I may not remember her name, but I know exactly which building she lives in. It's in Hayes Valley, which just so happens to also be a neighborhood within the division I'm stationed at for my field training, so I am used to working the beat on these exact streets. When we pulled up outside her place in the Uber, I recognized it. I'd been there a few weeks prior to take a report.

The skies are clear, the sun is out, but of course there's a breeze. I walk with my hands stuffed in the front pocket of my hoodie and when I pass Zeitgeist en route, I think of Adam. He's predictable. He'll wake this morning (feeling absolutely fine), and instantly regret all the dumb shit he said and did. He'll text and apologize. Blame it on the tequila. And I'll forgive him, like I always do. Maybe I'm also predictable.

I find the apartment building. It's luxurious as hell. Modern and purpose-built, some apartments with floor-to-ceiling windows, some with balconies. *Expensive.* I linger by one of the entrance doors and as soon as someone leaves, I slip through into the courtyard. It's well maintained, with a shit ton of shrubbery that most of the apartments overlook, and I flag down a lady heading to the fitness center behind me. Why doesn't my building have its own gym?

"Morning," I say. "Sorry to bother you, but I'm looking for someone. A woman in her early twenties. She lives in this building, but definitely not on the first floor." I remember we took the elevator, but where the hell did we get off? I glance up, counting. There's only five floors.

The lady laughs. "You might need to be a bit more specific."

What the hell happened to my observation skills? It's one of the most important things I've been taught in training so far – memorizing every minute detail of every person I encounter. Their distinguishing features, the clothes they're wearing, their height and weight. But I couldn't even tell you what color hair the girl I'm looking for has.

"She's shorter than me," I say, scratching my head. She folded into my body with ease, fitting perfectly against my chest. "And she lives here with her boyfriend, but they just broke up."

47

"I think every woman in this building is shorter than you," the lady says with a smile, and then pats me sympathetically on the shoulder. "I hope you find her."

As she heads into the gym and I contemplate just buying a whole new phone, a voice calls out, "Are you talking about Gracie Taylor by any chance? And Luca Hartmann?"

I spin around. It's the maintenance guy for the building, so of course I can count on him to know all of its residents. *Gracie.* It settles inside of me, warm with familiarity. "Yes. I think so. Can you tell me which apartment she's in?"

"I'm sorry, I can't give out that information," he says with an apologetic shrug. "Privacy concerns."

I nod. I'd be concerned if he *did* give out a young woman's apartment number to a complete stranger who has wandered into the building complex, so I get it. He continues on through the courtyard, and I wonder how long it would take me to search every floor. Maybe I would recognize her apartment door if I saw it.

"Weston?"

I start at the sound of my name. It doesn't feel like mine. I turn around and she's standing several feet away from me, rooted to the spot and terrified to come any closer. Fuck, she remembers my name, and that's a lot more than I remember about her.

I memorize her now, like I should have done last night. Hair that's copper in the sunlight, bangs framing her face, the rest pulled back. Freckles. A whole load of them, scattered over her nose and cheeks. Lashes so long I'm convinced they're not natural. She is even shorter than I remembered, and I'm amazed at the grocery bags bundled in her arms. If she's managed to hit up the market already, then clearly she can handle her booze better than I can.

"You seem to be feeling a whole lot better than I do this morning," I say, hoping to break the ice.

But the ice remains solid.

She continues to stare at me, emotionless. "Are you here to get your phone?"

I let out an audible sigh of relief. "I don't even remember setting it down."

"Well, you did, and I have it."

"I'm sorry if it's been ringing off the hook. I've been waiting for a call back."

Gracie arches an eyebrow and there's the briefest flash of sympathy in her gaze. "No one has called."

Ouch. Charlotte *still* hasn't called me back? It's another punch in the gut. Trying to get through to Charlotte is like communicating with a brick wall reinforced with steel. But I can't give up. I need my phone back immediately so I can keep trying.

"Can I . . . ?"

Gracie nods and makes for the elevator, still juggling the grocery bags in her arms as she reaches for the button for the fourth floor. Did I ever carry any of

Charlotte's bags for her? There's a lot of things I didn't do, and they all seem so obvious to me now.

"Let me take those for you," I offer, holding out my hands as the elevator doors close.

Gracie eyeballs me, skeptical. "You're just trying to steal my fresh avocado."

"I don't even like avocado," I say, then lift the bags out of her arms. I stand by her side, both of us facing the doors in silence. Out of the corner of my eye, I can tell she doesn't know what to do with her hands now. She begins swinging her apartment keys around her index finger.

The elevator doors open and we retrace our route from last night, only now we are sober. Her apartment is at the end of the hallway, right on the corner. Corner apartments are always the most expensive. She unlocks her door and I follow her inside.

"Just put those bags down there," she says, waving a flippant hand toward the breakfast bar built into the kitchen. I do as instructed, then stand idle as I watch her navigate her apartment.

It's huge. Like, over a thousand square feet, which makes my pathetic three hundred square feet of space seem even more claustrophobic than it already did. Gracie straightens out a crease on the folded blanket on the couch, then moves the potted plant on the coffee table one millimeter to the left. So particular.

"Can I ask what you do?"

She glances up. "What I do?"

"Yeah. For work."

"I don't. I just graduated from SFSU."

"Okay, then what does Luca do?"

She stiffens, her hand on one of her birthday cards from yesterday. Her voice lowers. "You remembered his name?"

"The maintenance guy downstairs reminded me." *I couldn't even remember yours.*

"Nothing. He just graduated too," she mumbles. In one fell swoop, she gathers an armful of birthday cards and dumps them into the trash.

"You're both new graduates with no jobs and *this* is your apartment?" I say in disbelief, shaking my head. "He's a drug dealer, isn't he? You should turn him in to me. I'll get on it first thing tomorrow."

Gracie laughs. It's a gentle, uplifting noise. She steps beside me and unpacks the first grocery bag, waving a giant avocado at me. "He is *not* a drug dealer. We're . . ." She blushes and tilts her chin down, her bangs falling in front of her eyes. "We're influencers."

"You're what?"

"An influencer," she repeats, shy.

"What the hell is an influencer?"

Gracie quits unpacking the groceries and crosses her arms, looking me up and down with furrowed brows. "How old are you?"

"Not as old as your tone is making me out to be. Twenty-three."

"Then you should know what an influencer is," she says. "You know, on social media?"

I shake my head. "I don't use social media."

Her eyes narrow. A pale blue, so much like Charlotte's. My chest tightens. *Why won't she at least hear me out?*

"An influencer is someone who has power over their target audience. We can sway their purchase decisions, for example," Gracie explains, breaking our eye contact. After a beat, she sighs. "Let me show you."

I don't realize she wants me to follow her until she crosses the apartment and gestures for me to join. She pushes open a door, revealing an office. I *knew* this was a two-bedroom apartment. How much money does this girl make? A lot, apparently.

On a huge oak desk that wraps around the room, there's *three* computers. A desktop setup, and two laptops. There's floating shelves on the wall, displaying a range of different cameras. There's a professional ring light on a stand in the corner. And I get it now.

"Oh. You do porn," I state.

Gracie parts her lips in horror. "*No.*" She plops into the fancy swivel chair in front of the desktop and wakes the screen, navigating to YouTube. I lean over her shoulder as she opens a channel that's full of video thumbnails of her smiling, cheek pressed against that of some guy. "We do YouTube. Luca and me. We started it when we were fifteen, just making dumb videos. But they kind of blew up," she explains, stealing a quick glance over her shoulder at me. "Essentially, we just vlog our entire life. We get paid to promote brands. We get invited to cool events. And our Instagram has been doing really well recently too."

I don't get it. At all. The little banner at the top of their account says they have over six hundred thousand followers. "Why would people want to watch someone else's life?"

She leans forward to shut off the desktop and then sinks back against the chair, releasing a loaded breath of air. "Because our life was perfect."

This girl is more heartbroken than I thought. I doubt a relationship can ever truly be perfect, and clearly theirs wasn't, otherwise it wouldn't have ended. She was sobbing in the goddamn Uber last night.

"Gracie, I think you're delusional," I say.

She scoffs. "Weston, I think you're judgmental." She pushes back from the desk, ramming me with the chair, and then pulls open a drawer. "Here. I kept it charged for you," she says, shoving my phone into my hand. "I was going to hand it in to the police station up on Fillmore later. I figured that was my best shot at getting it back to you."

"That's actually my station, believe it or not." I scan my home screen. Charlotte's name isn't there, but there are messages from Adam and Cameron, as expected.

"You work in this neighborhood?"

"For now, yes. I may be moved somewhere else once I finish my field training."

Gracie opens her mouth to say something, but we both jolt at the sound of the apartment door opening. We exchange a look.

"Gracie?" a voice calls. A male voice. It must be Luca.

"Fuck," Gracie says, but her voice is too soft for it to sound harsh. She tucks the chair back under the desk and presses a finger over her lips, instructing me to remain quiet. "Stay in here," she whispers.

I nod while resisting the urge to roll my eyes. I just came to get my phone back. I don't want to get in the middle of this girl and her ex, but now I'm stuck here in this office. He calls her name again and I lean back against the desk, arms folded. Who knows how long he plans to stay?

Gracie makes to step out of the office, but Luca steps in front of her, blocking her exit.

"What are you doing in here?" he asks, but instantly his alarm bells go off when Gracie seems too eager to push him back into the living room. He steps further into the office, and his eyes go wide when he sees me. "What the fuck? Who the hell is this guy?"

I straighten up from the desk and innocently hold up my hands. "Hey, man. I'm just picking up my phone. I got a little too wasted last night and left my phone

in the club. Your girlfriend found it. Or roommate."
I'm rather good at de-escalating situations, even if it
does require twisting the truth slightly. I don't think
it would go down well if Luca knew I was already in
the apartment last night while both Gracie and I were
drunk.

Luca glowers at me with skepticism, then turns back
to Gracie. "You went out last night?"

"It was my birthday. Elena and Maddie didn't give
me a choice," she says, but there's a tremor in her voice
which has me immediately questioning why she seems so
scared. How bad was their breakup?

"Shit. It was," Luca mutters. There's even a flash of
guilt in his expression, but it's quickly replaced with
aggravation when his attention veers back to me, the
intruder in their home. "You've got your phone. Can
you get the hell out of my apartment now?"

"Luca," Gracie hisses, her hand finding its way to his
bicep.

I size him up. He's a slim guy, but athletic. The kind of
guy you'd be able to wrestle to the floor but lose track of
if he took off running. I hate the ones who run. I almost
never catch them.

"Don't worry, I'm out of here," I say. I slide my phone
into the pocket of my sweats and make my way through
the door, though I feel the pressure of Luca's stare burning holes in my skull. As I pass Gracie, I catch her eye
and mouth, "*You okay?*"

She gives me a small nod that is anything but convincing.

Luca follows me to the apartment door and takes great satisfaction in closing it behind me, engaging the chain lock. I stand in the hallway for a second, not necessarily eavesdropping, but just for my own peace of mind. When there are no raised voices, no screaming, only then do I leave. It's not my place to get involved.

GRACIE

"Why are you here, Luca?"

It pains me to look at him, the person I love with everything I have. To look at him and know he wanted anything other than me is agonizing. How can you be with someone for so long and then change your mind seemingly overnight? Why didn't he realize sooner? God, we have wasted so much time. I have invested everything into our relationship, and now I have nothing left. I gave too much of myself to him.

Luca is on edge. He scratches his palm, his anxious habit. "I came to pick up some more of my stuff." He casts a final look at the door, clearly aggrieved at having found Weston in our apartment, but it's not like he'll ever be back.

"So, you're really moving out?" I ask, and my voice immediately cracks. I have so many questions that have been left unanswered this past week, and so many won-derings about what my future looks like now.

"I don't know," Luca says, but his actions say other-wise. He pulls his suitcase out of the storage closet and I blink fast when I spot his luggage tag, because it's the other half of a matching set with mine. We have been on so many trips together, our last being Hawaii in the spring.

Maui was so beautiful. We went on gorgeous hikes, snorkeled in La Perouse Bay, ate expensive seafood, and spent all night every night wrapped up in each other's arms. On our last morning before our flight back to California, we window-shopped in a luxurious jeweler, admiring the engagement rings. Luca was all smiles and I was all winks as I reminded him once again that when (always *when*, never *if*) he proposed, it better be with a teardrop diamond ring.

Because that was the plan. Marriage. Why else would we be dating if we didn't plan for it to be forever? We discussed it a lot in the past two years. Luca promised he would propose after college, and then we would enjoy our gap year in romantic bliss, traveling Southeast Asia and on to Australia. We'd have the perfect wedding on a rustic ranch in Southern California the following year, surrounded by our family and friends who have watched us grow together since we were teenagers, and then we would honeymoon in the Bahamas. We always agreed on two kids, but not until we bought our forever home in the Midwest. We would work for a few years here in San Francisco first. Luca in tech, me in teaching.

Graduation was in May, over a month ago. Instead of the engagement I was promised, I got my heart broken instead. It's cruel, now that I think about it. I was sold a dream that went up in flames.

As Luca heads for our bedroom with his suitcase, I follow close on his heels, pathetically desperate for a sense of understanding.

"Don't you think we should talk about this?"

He doesn't look at me as he slides open the mirrored closet doors. He grabbed a handful of clothes when he left, but now he's grabbing the rest with a sense of urgency. My heartbeat quickens when I realize he's taking *everything*. "Talk about what?"

"About the apartment. The channel. We have your parents' anniversary party next weekend," I say, sitting down on the edge of our bed and watching him with a hollowness in my chest as he fills the suitcase beside me. "You'll need to tell them I won't be coming."

"I assume they already know you won't be coming." Luca leans his head against the wall, taking a deep breath. "For the channel, just throw together some old footage we never used or something. No one will know it's not recent. And you can keep the apartment for now."

"You want to lie to everyone?"

"What else are we supposed to do?" he says, his frustration pulsing between each word. He slides the closet door shut and crosses to his bedside drawer. His departure didn't feel permanent until now. "Our channel is done if we announce we aren't together anymore. Just keep the money flowing for now, okay?"

I don't agree, but I also don't *disagree*. Our YouTube channel has been our source of income for years, saving us from having to work retail part-time all through college like the rest of our friends. It has allowed us to rent this incredible apartment, take trips of a lifetime, and save for the future we were supposed to have. Putting an end to our income stream feels like financial suicide, but it also feels so wrong to lie to our viewers and brand partners.

"Luca . . . I don't want you to leave," I croak. "Can you please think about this some more? You're just having cold feet because we both know what our next step is, and it's a big one, I know, but we can work through it. *Please*."

"That guy," Luca says, slamming the bedside drawer shut. He fastens his eyes on me. "Did you bring him home from the club? Did he stay here last night?"

"No," I say, shrinking under the tone of his voice. We were always so happy, it was rare for Luca to be so abrupt. "You think he went to the club in sweatpants?"

"I don't know, Gracie. It just seems really fucking suspicious that you went out last night, and then I find you the next morning with a stranger in our apartment," he snaps. He zips his suitcase shut and drags it off the bed, standing it upright. "Well?"

I stare silently, shellshocked at just how wrong he is. "*You're* the one who wants to sleep with other people, not me."

"That's not what I said," Luca says with a sigh.

"You said you wanted to see what else was out there, and we both know that means you want to see *who* else is out there." I rise from the bed to stand in front of him, arms folded. I dare him to deny that seeing other people is what he wants. I *dare* him.

His blue-gray eyes set on mine, and I think of how I could paint every inch of him from memory with my eyes closed. Luca Hartmann is all I've ever known.

Those cheekbones that were full and rounded in high school, but then grew sharp and defined throughout college, that I've planted so many kisses on. His blond hair that's been styled in a hundred different ways over time, from the hair-flip to the buzz cut I hated, that I never get tired of running my fingers through. The way he smirks suggestively at me, the birth mark on his hip I always admire, the echo of his laughter.

How do I even begin to forget him?

"Gracie . . ." he says, his voice lowered now, pained. "I just think we owe it to ourselves to live our lives without each other. We've been together since we were fifteen. *Fifteen*. We've never had the chance everyone else gets to find out who they are as individuals, because it's always been *us*. And I'm not saying we are over for good. Maybe I'll come back. But I need some breathing space first. I don't want to propose now and then, twenty years down the line, regret sacrificing my youth."

His words aren't any he didn't already say on Monday, except that final line. That final line is a complete blow. My mouth is agape.

"You think being with me has been a *sacrifice?*"

Luca steps forward and grasps my wrists. "No. But I'm scared one day I'll feel that way, and that's why I need to do this *now*. Please, just let me get everything out of my system and then I think I'll be ready to be with you forever."

"You *think?*" I spit, pulling my wrists free. I don't recognize the person standing in front of me, let alone understand him. "You don't get to do this to me, Luca. You don't get to leave me, do whatever the fuck you want, and then come crawling back. If you really loved me, you wouldn't *need* breathing space. I feel so . . . complete . . . being with you. That's why I can't ever begin to understand why you don't feel that way too."

Luca tucks my hair behind my ears and cups my cheeks, pressing his lips to my forehead. "I love you," he says, then lets his forehead rest against mine and stares deeply into my eyes. "You know I love you. But I have to do this."

I reach up for his hands and push him away from me, squeezing my eyes shut. I can't let him hurt me like this, to walk in and out of my life whenever he pleases, to have me question why I wasn't enough to make him stay. I deserve better than this. I deserve better than him.

"If you walk away now," I whisper, "then you are *not* coming back. And I fucking mean it."

Luca's features twist. He glances at his suitcase, then at me. And just when I think the threat of losing me forever might just change his mind, he reaches for the suitcase, and my heart shatters once more.

"I want you to find yourself too, Gracie," he says, and as I crumple back onto the bed, my chest heaving, he lifts my chin. Kisses the corner of my mouth. Brushes his thumb delicately over my cheek. And then walks out of my life so, so easily.

WESTON

I need to see Charlotte. Immediately. Because I can't take one more second of this silence. She can ignore my texts, my calls, my voicemails, but she can't ignore me when I'm standing right in front of her. There's still so much I have to say to her. So much to apologize for.

That's why, as I'm halfway home to my apartment, I decide to haul ass onto the BART green line. Charlotte and I normally drive to visit one another, but I'm still too fragile after last night to even *think* about driving yet. I find a secluded seat on the train and collapse into it, my hands tucked into the front pocket of my hoodie and my forehead pressed to the window. It's over an hour to North San Jose, and despite how tired I am and how very easily I could fall asleep, I force myself upright and check out the texts from Adam and Cameron.

Cameron just wants to know that I definitely went home last night, and that I'm alive. I text and let him know I'm on my way to San Jose to see Charlotte, and he replies with a face-palm emoji.

Adam, however, I decide to call.

"'Sup, bro? You good?" he asks nonchalantly, answering on the very last ring.

"I'm good. Are you?"

"You busted my jaw. I have the sickest bruise ever," he says with a laugh that very quickly transforms into a sigh. "You know I didn't mean what I said. I'm a horrible drunk."

"Yeah, you are."

"And I'm sorry."

"You should be."

"And I deserved to be hit."

"No, you didn't," I admit. It's not Adam's fault that Charlotte left. I spend a lot of time hitting up the bars and being his wingman, but it's not because I'm doing him a favor. I choose to go out, because I need loud music and too many bottles of beer to decompress after work. I can't put the blame on him for my screwed-up priorities, and I shouldn't have lost my temper the way I did last night.

In the background of the call, I hear a female voice murmur, "Ask if he knows where Gracie went."

I press my phone closer to my ear, trying to hear better. "Who's that?"

"Elena," Adam says, and I have to think hard about it before I remember who Elena even is. She was at the club last night, one of the girls celebrating Gracie's birthday. The tiny brunette Adam had his eye on, and the one who erupted with rage.

"When I left, she was screaming at you."

"That's called foreplay, Weston."

I can picture his smirk right now, and I roll my eyes even though it aggravates my headache. "Remember to get her Venmo username for me. I was serious about paying for the booth." Throwing a punch at Adam last night is going to cost me the better part of a grand, I imagine, which is so not worth it, despite how good it felt at the time. "And also, Gracie got home just fine. I made sure of it."

"You gave her a good time, huh?"

"You're such a dick."

There's some rustling across the line and muffled conversation that I can't hear, and then, "Okay, but *did* you spend the night with Gracie?" It's Elena now, who sounds dehydrated as hell. Adam is the kind of selfish prick who would forget to even offer a girl some water, and I honestly don't know how Cameron copes with having strange girls in their apartment every weekend. It's why I live alone. In a shoebox, admittedly, but alone.

"No," I tell Elena. Is it normal for girls to care so much about their friends getting laid? With Adam, I get it, because he's a fucking Neanderthal. Maybe Elena is too. That's probably how they've ended up in bed together.

"Aw," Elena says. "That's a shame. The guy she's dated since forever dumped her out of nowhere and I've been worried about her all week . . . I think she needs to get under someone new to get over him, you know?"

"That's exactly what I've been telling Weston," Adam remarks in the background, and I roll my eyes *again*.

"I thought you'd be the perfect guy for the job," Elena continues. "Since you're in the same boat and all. Adam says your girlfriend left you this week, so what if I give you Gracie's number?"

"Or how about," I say, "you both leave us alone? Huh? How about that?"

"Whatever. Gracie doesn't like jerks, anyway," Elena huffs, and I hang up the call before she can pass me back over to Adam.

I only want Charlotte. No one else.

By the time the train pulls into North San Jose, I feel only slightly more human after a quick half hour of shut-eye. I sprint up the station stairs and break into the daylight, filled with determination to win back my girl, and navigate the streets on foot.

I won't let Charlotte throw our relationship away. We've spent four years together, and that's too long to just give up like this. I still remember the first moment I laid eyes on her, back in our sophomore year at San Diego State, when she tapped on my shoulder in the library and asked if I had a highlighter. I didn't. She moved on to the next person. Two weeks later, I spotted her at a frat party.

"You're the highlighter girl from the library," I said.

And her face twisted with confusion before she exchanged a look with her friend that clearly meant, "This guy is a creep."

Because for her, that interaction in the library was insignificant and unmemorable. For me, it was the start of a crush. I couldn't help it. She was soft-spoken with a gentle smile, inviting eyes and a gap between her front teeth that was attractive as hell. I never did find her again in the library, so coming across her at that party seemed like a miracle, until I opened my mouth and made it weird.

We found each other again in a quiet corner of the frat house just after midnight. Both drunk with no inhibitions. She told me her name, I told her mine. We talked for a long time, then I walked her back to her dorm. I didn't leave until the next morning.

We had a blast in college. Studying for finals together while fighting to keep our hands off one another, partying with friends, exploring San Diego on the weekends. After we graduated last year, we both moved back home to the Bay Area, and I think that's when things changed.

Life got serious, and maybe I became too absorbed in figuring my own shit out, rather than planning for a future with her. I just didn't know I was capable of doing things so wrong.

I hesitate on the sidewalk outside of Charlotte's walk-up apartment. Maybe I should have warned her I was coming, but I doubt she would have read the message anyway. Her spare set of keys are attached to my own, so I let myself into the building and begin the dreaded climb to the fifth floor, sidestepping around packages scattered over the stairs. I never liked that she lived here. It never felt all that safe to me, but I also can't remember if I ever expressed that concern to her.

Outside of her apartment, I knock on the door rather than barging in unannounced. She's probably not even here. I'm sure she mentioned something about staying with her parents for a while.

"Charlotte?" I call gently, pressing my ear to the door and listening for any signs of life on the other side. "Please open the door if you're there. It's me."

The lock clicks and I jolt back from the door, my body tensing. I rack my mind for all of the things I wish to say to her, but there are so many, the words blur together and I panic that I won't be able to say anything at all.

Charlotte opens the door, but only a crack. She peers through the gap and quietly says, "Weston." My chest seizes at the sound of her voice carrying my name.

"Can I come in so we can we talk?" I ask, though my tone is cautious because, right now, I'm walking through a minefield. One wrong move and she will slam the door in my face.

It's torture, watching her debate whether or not she will let me in. Finally, she opens the door fully and then heads back to the couch, deliberately avoiding eye contact with me as I enter her apartment and shut the door behind me. Charlotte stares at the TV. She's watching *Friends,* her comfort show.

"Don't sit down," she says, holding up her hand as I move to sit next to her. "You aren't staying."

This is going to be tough. I press my hands to my face with a groan and then step in front of the TV so she is forced to look at me. She does, reluctantly.

"I've been calling you. Did you listen to any of my voicemails?"

"Yes, and there's a reason I'm ignoring them," she says, arms crossed and expression impassive. Her blond hair is pulled back off her face and without makeup; she always looks so young. And adorable as fuck. If we weren't broken up right now, I would kiss her until her lips were swollen. "Nothing you say now changes anything."

In frustration, I sit down on the coffee table in front of her and desperately take her hands in mine. "I fucked up, I know. Forget my friends. *You* come first from now on. You're what I want, Char. You've always been what I wanted."

70

"You don't get it," Charlotte snaps, trying to tear her hands free from mine. I squeeze tighter. "You're drifting through life right now without making a single decision, because you *don't* know what you want. You hate your job, but no one *made* you choose it. You just didn't want to let your dad down, so now you'll spend the rest of your life complaining about it rather than *doing* something about it. You get drunk with Adam on your weekends off because you *have* to let off steam, while I'm over here by myself! When was the last time we did something that wasn't just hanging out at your apartment, Weston?"

Each word of hers is so cutting, I almost feel too wounded to think of an answer. "We went to Perbacco for our anniversary meal, didn't we?"

"That was two months ago!" She snatches her hands back from me now and I don't fight her as she shoves me away from her. Rising from the couch, she throws her head back in exasperation. "You need to grow up! We aren't in college anymore! I want someone who knows what they want in life, and that isn't you."

"Charlotte . . ." I croak, but everything inside of me is crumbling. I have never seen such an awful expression behind her eyes, something so pained, ugly, unrecognizable. She means every single word and there's no convincing her otherwise.

"You took it for granted that I'd always be here, and I deserve better than that, Weston," she says, releasing the softest of breaths. As our eyes lock, her voice dips to a whisper. "I deserve better than you."

I spiral into panic. "I'm sorry. I'm so fucking sorry, you have no idea." Fuck, am I crying? I squeeze my eyes shut, my clenched jaw slackening with a tremor.

"Weston," Charlotte says, but the emotions she's been holding back emerge and my name cracks in half. She starts to sob and loses her hands in my hair as she presses her body against mine. Still seated on the coffee table, I wrap my arms around her slim body and pull her closer. I bury my face into her stomach, clinging to the fabric of her T-shirt.

"Please," I beg, but she shakes her head against the top of mine. "*Please*."

"It's too late," she whispers.

My entire body shudders uncontrollably against her as I try to get a fucking grip on these tears, and she holds me steady, soothingly, until all of my regret seeps through me. I have no choice but to allow myself to feel it, the remorse and the guilt. And only once it's embedded in my core does she decide it's time.

Charlotte smooths out my hair as she unwinds her fingers. She steps back, and I let her. My eyes hurt like a bitch as I lift my head to look at her, but I'm not all that sure she looks any better. This wasn't how it was supposed to be, staring back at one another with such heartbreak pulsing between us.

"Go home, Weston," she says, wiping away her own tears. She rubs wearily at her temples and collapses back onto the couch, not quite looking me in the eye anymore. "Please don't call me or come by. I want a clean break, and I need my spare keys back."

I stand up from the coffee table, but my legs are like Jell-O. The ground really has been knocked out from under me. In defeat, I reach for my keys in my pocket and slowly unwind Charlotte's apartment keys from the keyring. My heart is in my throat as I pass them to her.

She hugs a pillow to her chest and nods to the door. "Just go. Please."

But I don't go. I study her face one last time, memorizing every tiny speck, carving her features into my mind, because I never want to forget a single thing about her. I love her, but now I have to give her what she wants, and that is a life without me.

If only I had my shit together. If only I loved her harder, sooner.

I walk away.

I leave her apartment, her building, her.

And then I google the nearest bar that's open this early on a Sunday.

GRACIE

I need to try harder to pull myself together. It's been five days now since Luca left with such finality, and approaching two weeks since he walked out the first time. Things aren't getting any easier. I still can't shake the numbness and I feel stuck in limbo, like I'm waiting for something. But this isn't a temporary glitch in the matrix, it's my new normal, and I need to accept that I'm on my own now. I need to learn how to survive.

"Tomorrow I'm going back to the gym," I announce, cutting through Elena and Maddie's conversation that I lost track of five minutes ago. "Do you guys want to come?"

"On a Saturday? When it'll be packed with cute guys who can watch me deadlift three hundred pounds?" Maddie says with a grin. "Absolutely."

Elena scoffs and adjusts her glasses. "I get my work-outs from men."

"Don't we know it," Maddie says, and Elena flicks her fortune cookie at her.

"I'm going to start eating healthy meals again," I continue with steely determination. Feeling bloated, I push away my container of chow mein and then poke at the leftovers with a chopstick. "Not this junk."

"You say that like there's something wrong with eating takeout every night," Elena says. "I do. And I feel fine."

"I think it's time I learned how to drive too."

Maddie swallows a mouthful of orange chicken and exchanges a surprised glance with Elena. "Really?"

"Yeah. I need to be able to get around by myself. It's time."

There was never any need to get my license until now. The BART is efficient for getting around the city and Luca always drove when we needed to travel further, like whenever I visited my mom. But there is no direct public transit to Santa Cruz, so unless I learn how to drive immediately, it'll be a while before I can visit my mom again. Plus, it might be nice to gain some independence.

"I think this all sounds like a great plan," Elena says, "but it's missing one thing. We need to put you on Tinder. Or Bumble. Or Hinge. All of them, in fact."

"*Elena*," I groan in frustration, reaching for my wine. It's alarming how easily these glasses are going down.

"I'll date again when I'm ready, which will be a long, long, long time from now."

"Can I just reiterate for the thousandth time, I am *not* telling you to date," Elena says with a dramatic sigh, then narrows her eyes at me with a smirk. "I'm telling you to get laid."

"*No.*"

"I'm sure a quick smash in the backseat of a car would knock that stubbornness straight out of you."

Maddie tries to muffle her little puff of laughter. "Sorry, Gracie, it's just . . . God, Elena, you really do have a way with words. You are going to be such an amazing lawyer."

"Thanks," Elena says, shaking out her shoulders. She pouts at me. "Okay, I'm sorry. I'll let you work on yourself for a while, but if three months from now you still haven't gotten laid then I'm going to have to intervene out of genuine concern for your wellbeing."

Elena means well, but there is no way for someone who has never had their heart broken to ever *begin* to know just how much I am hurting. Getting over Luca isn't that easy. I fall backward and let my head hit the pillow, but instantly feel nauseous as the ceiling swirls overhead. We are onto our second bottle of wine.

We've pushed Maddie and Elena's beds together, creating one giant king, and the three of us are sprawled out together in our PJs. The wine flows, the Chinese takeout containers sit in the middle of us, and music plays from the speaker.

Rogue struts into the room, the street cat Maddie found on campus a few years ago and kidnapped, brought home (much to Elena's disgust), and who now lives here. He springs onto the bed and curls his body around my head.

"Ew," I say, moving his tail out of my face.

Maddie gasps and reaches over to grab him, cuddling him protectively and kissing his forehead despite the fact it was once infested with fleas. "Don't listen to her, Rogue. There's nothing *ew* about you."

"I really fucking hate that cat," Elena mutters.

I smile and reach for my wine glass. It's been forever since I had a night like this with my best friends. Weekends have always been spent mostly with Luca, except the one weekend each month where we would both spend time with our respective friends, so whenever I did see Elena and Maddie, we made it an occasion. Now I feel almost mournful over all of the nights I missed, just hanging out, eating takeout and drinking wine in our PJs. Elena and Maddie get to spend every night together, and I now live alone in an apartment with way too much square footage, terrified of every noise I hear in the middle of the night.

"Thanks for letting me stay over tonight," I say, propping myself up on my elbow so I can take a swig of my wine, emptying the glass. "I'm not doing too well living on my own for the first time in . . . Well, my entire life."

Rogue purrs with joy as Maddie strokes the little white patch above his nose. "You're more than welcome to move in. It could be fun!"

"Maddie, we already share the one bedroom this dump has," Elena reminds her. "Gracie, you *are* more than welcome to move in, but you'll be sleeping on the couch."

"It's okay, guys," I say with a laugh, spotting the unopened third bottle of wine on the dresser. Being alone is something I need to adjust to, whether I like it or not. I slink off the bed and grab the wine. "Okay, girlies. It's Friday night. We're having a slumber party. We feel sick from overeating and we're boozy. Now can we play this music louder or what?"

Maybe we shouldn't have ignored the warning. When the old guy in the apartment next door came by at midnight to tell us to shut the hell up, we probably should have. When you're drunk and screaming the lyrics to your favorite songs from the early 2000s, it's difficult to rein it in. And now there's more pounding at the apartment door, although this time twice as aggressive.

"I'm going to kick this guy to the curb," Elena says as she jumps from the bed, fists already clenched and ready to throw it down with an elder. We are all out of breath from putting on the performance of our lives, jumping on the beds, flicking our hair like rockstars, and using the empty wine bottles as microphones.

Maddie pulls the speaker's cable straight out of the socket, and as the three of us move into the lounge, there's another rap against the door, and behind it a voice announces, "San Francisco Police."

We freeze, our laughter immediately faltering.

"Oh no he did not," Elena hisses, features twisting with anger. "The old crank called the cops!"

Maddie, being the more sensible of the two, rushes to the door before it gets busted down. As she opens it, Elena and I stay exactly where we are, our perfectly innocent smiles mastered. Still, it's jarring to see a uniformed man at the door.

He's an older cop, hair grayed, and he holds himself with the superiority of someone who's been doing this their entire life. One hand rests on his duty belt, the other presses against the doorframe as he leans forward to scan the apartment behind Maddie. "We've had a noise complaint," he states, his voice deep. "What's going on here tonight?"

Now Elena, who is the better *talker* of the two, steps forward. "Oh, officer, I'm so sorry. Were we being too loud? It's just girls' night. No party here. It's such a shame there's such awful sound insulation in this building, isn't it? We had no idea we were making enough noise to warrant a visit from you."

The officer doesn't crack. His expression remains expertly neutral. "I believe a neighbor already voiced their complaints."

"Oh? That's news to us," Elena lies.

"Just keep it down. Or better yet, shut the music off entirely. It's late," the officer snaps, and it's very apparent he would much rather be out on the beat doing badass shit than dealing with another boring noise complaint.

"But it's the weekend! You seem like someone who likes to have fun on a weekend, am I right?" Elena smiles wide, sweetening the officer up.

He narrows his eyes and his scowl has yet to show even a hint of fading. "Which one of you rents this place?"

Elena points to herself, then to Maddie by her side. "We do."

"Let me see your IDs real quick."

Elena sighs, deflated that she hasn't won him over, and she and Maddie move from the door to go fetch their wallets. There's a new voice in the hallway now, someone mumbling complaints, and I realize the old man next door has come out to play.

The cop rubs his forehead and turns to take care of the interferer, but also tells someone, "Check their IDs."

And that's when I realize there's a second officer. He takes over at the door, stepping into the space the older officer has just left behind. My jaw slackens in humiliation.

I gasp. "Weston."

It's him. The guy from last weekend. Only now, rather than smashing bottles during a fist fight in the middle of the club, he's in *uniform*. Dark blue pants and shirt, duty belt around his waist, radio by his collar, military boots. His armful of tattoos is hidden beneath the long sleeves of his shirt, but I still spy some ink on the back of his hand. There's a gold name badge that says *W. REED*.

"Hello, you," Weston says, his lips pressed firmly together to hold back a smirk. He doesn't step over the threshold. He can't. Crossing one foot over the other, he leans his shoulder against the doorframe and his eyes dance with amusement at the panic written all over my face.

"You look different," are the only words I manage to gather. At the club, he was soaked in vodka. The morning after, he was unshaven and in sweatpants. Now his jaw is perfectly smooth, dark hair styled with gel, and he looks surprisingly intimidating. It's the uniform.

Weston looks me up and down, his smile becoming increasingly less subtle. "I could say the same about you. Are you a little drunk, Gracie?"

"It's not a crime to be drunk," I remind him, but I also hug my arms around my chest in an attempt to hide from him. This shorts and tank top combo isn't the most attractive sight in the world, especially when paired with a messy bun and a severe lack of mascara. Why does it feel so embarrassing having him catch me like this?

"Here's my ID," Elena says as she parades back into the lounge, "but can I just point out I got that photo taken on a day I was sick with tonsillitis, so that's why

I look pale and malnourished." She halts in her tracks when she looks up from her ID and realizes the older cop she was trying so hard to charm has been replaced with a much younger officer.

Weston furrows his brows as he studies her, then snaps his fingers with recognition. "Elena, right? Adam passed on your Venmo to me. Did you get the money I sent over to pay for your booth?"

Elena stares at him with great confusion, then at me, then back again. It's hard to remember the faces we encounter when drunk. "Wait . . . You're Adam's friend from the club?" She purses her lips at him with disdain. "So, you really *are* a cop, and yet you still got into a fight? Is that even allowed?"

Weston laughs, pretends to check over his shoulder, then presses a finger to his lips. "Of course not," he says in a low voice, then clears his throat. "I do need to check your ID, though."

Elena eyeballs me with a peculiar look as she walks to the door to hand Weston her ID, and Maddie rushes out from the bedroom waving hers. She doesn't recognize Weston at all, but she never interacted with him that night at the club. He scans both their IDs so quickly I doubt he even made it beyond their photos, then hands them back.

"Where did your buddy go?" Elena asks.

"Calming down the neighbor you guys have made irate," Weston says in disapproval, but his relaxed features make it clear he thinks this is hilarious. "And Bill only wanted to check your IDs so he can remember your names if we get called back here a second time. Don't make that happen."

Maddie nods compliantly. "We won't, officer."

"If I do come back here tonight . . ." Weston's gaze moves to me, settling for a moment, and the corner of his mouth twitches. "Then I'll have to fine you, Gracie."

Our eye contact intensifies. Maybe it's the use of my name, maybe it's the teasing smirk, maybe it's that uniform again, but my stomach flips and I don't know exactly why. The stare-off is only interrupted when Maddie wonders aloud, "How does he know your name?"

"Oh my God, Madison," Elena says, whacking her shoulder as though to smack some realization into her. "That's him. The guy who got us all kicked out of Temple. Gracie's . . . *friend*."

"Don't you dare," I warn Elena, glaring fiercely. If she so much as winks suggestively, I'll throttle her right here in the presence of a police officer. I will *die* if she says anything more.

Weston chuckles by the door. "Don't worry about it, Gracie, she already pulled the same thing with me over the phone last week too."

"*Elena*," I hiss, mortified.

Elena shrugs, guilty as charged. "I just *think* . . ."

The other officer reappears behind Weston. He glances sternly into the apartment. "All good here now?"

"All good," Weston confirms. "I'll meet you at the car."

As the officer heads off, the sound of his radio crackling echoes throughout the hallway and we all remain silent and unmoving until he is out of earshot. Then Weston tucks his thumbs into his duty belt and catches my eye again.

"Come out here for a sec," he says – an order, but somehow it's gentle. Hard to ignore.

Elena and Maddie nearly explode. I glare at the pair of them and drunkenly meet Weston in the hallway, nervously standing before him, arms still hugged around my chest. Up close, he seems even *more* intimidating. The San Francisco Police Department patches on the shoulders of his shirt, the gun in its holster in his belt. I swallow hard.

"What?" I force out.

"Consider this a wellbeing check," he says. His smile has lost its teasing and now softens with sincerity. "How are things with Luca? I wasn't sure I wanted to leave you alone with him on Sunday, but it was also none of my business. Are you okay?"

I'm taken aback, for starters, that he even remembers Luca's name, but also because he waits for my answer with an incredible amount of patience. Out of the corner of my eye, I notice Elena and Maddie eavesdropping from inside the apartment, so I pull the door shut.

"It's really over," I say, devoid of emotion. There were moments last week while the breakup was still raw that I genuinely believed Luca would realize what a huge mistake he'd made and draw me into his arms, full of apologies and I love yous, but that all changed on Sunday. The end of our relationship was clear cut, and now that there is no hope left, it's easier to say it out loud. *We are really over.* "I haven't cried this week, believe it or not. But it's also not getting any easier, and those two in there have never had a serious relationship, let alone gone through a breakup, so they don't get it. The wine helps, though. How are things with Charlotte? Did she ever call back?"

Weston's gaze flashes. We may have been drunk when we shared that hug in my kitchen, but it's very clear to both of us now that we were listening to each other that night. "I went by her place and spoke to her. It's definitely over for me too," he says, the words strained. "It's a hard lesson to learn."

"Which is?"

"That I need to figure shit out and stop being so selfish."

"You don't seem selfish," I say. He gave me that hug in my apartment when it was so clear I needed one, and now he's checking in on how I'm doing. He *was* a bit of an ass in the Uber, though. And I've met him all of three times, so I suppose I can't know for sure.

"Well, I am," he says, then reaches for his radio as a voice breaks through the frequency. It's his partner, telling him to hurry up; they just got dispatched to their next call. I'm sure it'll be more thrilling than this noise complaint. "On my way," he says into his radio, then regards me intently. "I get off at seven. I'm going to grab breakfast at Eddie's on Fulton Street before I go home to sleep for an eternity. Meet me there?"

"What?" I take a perplexed step back from him. "Why?"

"You just said your friends don't get it. I do."

"But—"

"But what?" he cuts me off. "It's just breakfast and conversation, Gracie. There's not much to lose, is there?"

And as he walks off, I resign myself to gaping after him. He walks with almost a swagger, his duty belt shifting against his hips. Before he turns the corner, he casts a fleeting glance over his shoulder to enjoy my astounded expression one more time.

WESTON

Maybe I should have made it clearer that I *wanted* Gracie to meet me. It's twenty minutes after seven and there's still no sign of her. I swirl the dregs of my filter coffee around inside my mug, fighting off the exhaustion of working overnight, and then turn back to the window. Working nights always fucks with me. While the city is waking up for the day, I'm winding down. More cars whizz by, more pedestrians fill the streets, and a stream of customers come and go from the diner. Eddie's Café is a tiny, old-school diner on the corner that serves the best breakfasts around here, and their hash browns are the only thing that keeps me going through my twelve-hour shifts. It's not the most glamorous of places, but it doesn't need to be.

I'm tired, and starving, and there's no way Gracie is coming. I tear my eyes from the window and grab the menu, even though my order never changes, and wave over the poor waitress who I've repeatedly told to give me one more second. It's obvious I've been waiting for someone, and even more obvious that they now haven't shown up. The waitress whisks over with a pot of coffee to refill my mug and I order a Denver omelet and hash browns. A filling breakfast is always enough to knock me straight to sleep by the time I get back to my apartment.

I suppress a yawn and take a swig of the fresh coffee, but pause with the mug hovering by my lips. The bell above the door jingles as Gracie enters. She's wearing sunglasses even though it's overcast, but I recognize her petite frame and copper-blond hair. As she scans the small, bustling diner, her shoulders visibly relax when she spots me in a booth by the furthest window.

She weaves hastily through the tables and slides into the booth opposite me. The very first words out of her mouth are, "You are so cruel asking me to meet you here at this time. You remember I was drunk seven hours ago, right?"

"Good morning," I say, keeping my expression nonchalant. I'd rather not make Gracie aware that I find amusement in how terrible she looks. "I'm not the only one who needs coffee right now. Do you want something to eat?" I raise a hand again to call the waitress back over.

"Coffee sounds good," Gracie mumbles, but recoils when I push a menu across the table. She must be really hungover if even *pictures* of food make her queasy, even though she didn't seem wasted last night. Tipsy, sure. Maybe she's just a lightweight. She *is* tiny.

"Coffee for her too, please," I tell the waitress, and she returns with a mug and pours Gracie some much-required caffeine. Gracie grabs the coffee and gulps half of it while I stare at her with one eyebrow raised. "That bad?"

"That bad," she confirms. She wraps her hands around the mug for warmth, brings it to her chest, and relaxes back against the booth. Her sunglasses remain firmly planted over her eyes. "How was the rest of your shift? Catch any bad guys?"

"Oh, yeah, absolutely. Couple traffic citations, threw some woman in the drunk tank, brought a guy in for a warrant. Real blood-pumping stuff," I say with mock enthusiasm. She doesn't know that the noise complaint against her was the highlight of my shift. Watching her squirm at the sight of me as her cheeks flushed pink . . . Incredible.

"Sounds . . . interesting," she says.

"It wasn't." I mirror her actions, leaning back, getting comfortable. I'm still surprised she appeared. It's seven thirty on a Saturday, and it's a lot to ask of a perfect stranger to meet me here at this time. "I didn't think you were coming. I already ordered without you."

"I wasn't going to. I was asleep twenty minutes ago," she admits, pressing her lips to the rim of her mug. Even behind her sunglasses, I sense her eyes locked carefully on mine. "But you made a valid point. You *are* the only other person I know right now whose world has just imploded, and maybe . . ."

"Maybe . . . ?" I prompt.

She sips her coffee purposefully before answering, "Maybe you wouldn't be the worst person out there to teach me a thing or two. In fact, I think you might be the perfect person."

Now I'm confused. "Teach you a thing or two?" I repeat.

Our lives have taken similar turns and Gracie has been the only person I felt comfortable discussing Charlotte with, even though the moments were brief and fleeting. Cameron is understanding in most ways and I have no reason to hold back my feelings around him, but with a stranger, it's just easier. The words flow better. How can there be fear of judgment when you don't even know the person? It's why I invited Gracie here. I thought we could unload on one another, but now she's gone in a different direction.

"You said you were selfish. That you put yourself first," she says, and I narrow my eyes at the reminder. It's true, but I don't want her to believe it. "Well, I need to learn how to do that. I've never put myself first, and it's time I lived for me and no one else."

I squint at her, reading her expression. Her jaw is set with determination as though her mind has been made up for a while. She straightens her shoulders and presses her lips into a firm line. My lack of response frustrates her, but I have no idea what the hell she actually wants from me.

"Well? Can you, Weston?"

There's weight behind my name, and I don't know why I tense at the sound of it. Her voice is sweet, buttery, yet my name sounds fierce. My curiosity about her strengthens. "Why did you say my name like that?"

"You mean the same way you said my name last night? Like a challenge?" She sets her mug down on the table with a clink, then rests her elbows on the table and lifts her sunglasses. Those pale blue eyes so similar to Charlotte's fix on me, but they are unreadable.

The waitress interrupts us. She arrives with my food and places it in front of me, but I am yet to unlock my eyes from Gracie's. A small smile toys at the corner of her round lips and she lowers her sunglasses back down, shielding her gaze again.

"Those hash browns might just make me throw up," she says, wrinkling her nose at my food.

"These hash browns, for your information, are my comfort food," I say, pointing my knife defensively at her.

I am too hungry not to immediately tuck in, and she watches in repulsion with her hand over her mouth.

"This omelet would cure your hangover," I say after a while. I've already scoffed all the hash browns, so she ain't getting those. "And since I'm now trying so hard *not* to be selfish, I'll even let you have some." I suggestively push the plate with half the omelet remaining toward her.

Gracie makes a small *humph* in defeat before pushing her sunglasses up into her hair and pulling the plate toward her. As she lifts the first bite to her mouth, she takes a deep breath. It's like I'm offering her roadkill off the freeway.

"Just eat it already."

She groans, then shoves the forkful of omelet into her mouth and chews at lightning speed with her eyes closed. She gags, and I crack into laughter before pulling my plate back.

"You aren't getting to waste good food, even if you're going to act like it physically pains you to eat it."

"But it *does* physically pain me to eat it," she argues. She shudders dramatically and dabs at her lips with a napkin.

I polish off the remainder of the omelet and the rest of my third cup of coffee, then clear the table to one side. Now that I'm fed and caffeinated, I mean business. I hunch forward and fold my arms in front of me on the table. "Can we rewind a sec? The reason I invited you here is because I feel weirdly . . . comfortable. With you. And I feel like you're someone I can be around without having to act like everything is okay right now. But the reason *you* came is because you want me to teach you how to be selfish?" I raise an eyebrow at her again, waiting for confirmation.

"That sounds insulting, I'm sorry," she says, shyly biting her lower lip. "And also kind of stupid. You know what? Ignore me. I have no idea what I'm even doing right now."

"No, I get it," I say, glancing down at my lap. I always feel bare in my uniform without my duty belt. "You need to put yourself first and I need to put . . . someone else first."

"I'll be your guinea pig."

I roll my eyes.

"I'm serious," says Gracie. Her features sharpen.

"What?"

"You walked me to my door last weekend," she says, "and it seemed like you did care when you asked last night how things with Luca were. That leads me to believe that you're capable of being a decent boyfriend. Whether that's to your ex, or someone else entirely, I don't know. But you can practice with me."

I don't hide my laughter from her, but I do rein it in when her solemn expression doesn't falter. This girl is full of wild ideas that don't make much sense to me. "Okay, I am officially too tired to have *this* conversation with you. I'm going home to sleep."

Gracie clicks her tongue, shaking her head in dismay. "See, this is where you need some guidance. You have a hungover girl in front of you. Think, Weston. What would a caring man do?"

"Take you home to your apartment?" I guess. Where did this examination come from? I don't think I was the worst boyfriend in the world. Selfish, but never callous. I cared for Charlotte – I just didn't show it.

"A reasonable suggestion," Gracie says, then cocks her head to the side, her gaze softly confident. "But I'd much prefer more coffee."

I heave a sigh, still rather confused by what she expects of me right now. I'm too tired to play this game, but maybe it's not the *worst* idea in the world. Surely, I'm capable of putting someone else first.

"Gracie," I say with a smile, "would you like to come back to my place for more coffee?"

"Now you're getting it. Let's go," she says.

As she stands from the booth, she beams with a radiant grin. She's got me right where she wants me, and it's the first time I've seen her smile wide like that. It leaves me dazed in the booth, looking up at her with a sense of awe. She has a gorgeous fucking smile. It travels all the way to her eyes, the pale blue sparkling.

"C'mon, Officer Reed," she says, clapping her hands together to hurry me up.

I glance down at my name badge, like I've forgotten my own last name. I'm just tired. I throw some bills on the table and force myself upright. How the hell am I supposed to get some decent sleep when Gracie is coming home with me?

"I'm parked around the corner," I tell her as we head for the door, and I make sure to hold it open for her. "But if you dare throw up in my car, then you can forget this little idea of yours."

And as she walks outside, she looks up at me from beneath her long eyelashes and says, "If I *do* throw up, just know a caring man would hold my hair back for me."

GRACIE

Weston lives in the Mission District, which isn't all that far from my own neighborhood. We're practically neighbors.

"You should really clean out your car," I say, plucking the empty Starbucks cup from the center console and holding it up for Weston to glower at out of the corner of his eye as he drives. I shuffle my feet around the trash in the footwell. "I don't even have a car, but I know damn well if I did, it would never look like this."

"I didn't force you to take this ride," Weston reminds me, taking the cup from my hand and sticking it back into the holder. "If you aren't happy with the service, get an Uber."

I roll my eyes and keep my focus trained on him as we head underground to his apartment building's parking garage. It's nearing eight in the morning and he's still wearing his uniform, minus the duty belt, and his hair is more tousled now than it was last night. There are lines of exhaustion etched around his eyes. For a moment, I feel guilty. The poor man just wants to collapse into bed and sleep for the rest of the day, but I've forced him into entertaining a complete stranger.

But what Weston said back at the diner struck a chord with me. He feels comfortable with me. And that makes a whole lot of sense, because I feel comfortable around him too. When he hugged me in my kitchen, it was something I was sorely in need of. Strangers be damned, it felt nice. And he didn't judge me for my relentless crying, which is a bonus. So, if he wants to vent about Charlotte, I'll listen.

"I do really need to sleep," Weston says, finishing strong with a yawn. He kills the engine and pulls the keys from the ignition. "But I'll still get you some coffee first."

"I appreciate that."

We leave the car and cross the parking garage to the stairs, climbing them to the second floor of the building. It's not the most glamorous. Older, with a worrying lack of windows in the hallway and only a dim, yellow wall light to compensate. I don't judge, because Luca and I have been blessed with our finances under exceptional circumstances, and I never forget just how lucky we are to have the apartment in the building complex that we do. Or rather just me, now.

As though reading my mind, Weston hesitates with his hand on the handle of his apartment door. "Heads up: it's a studio, and it feels like a shoebox compared to your mansion."

I blink with indifference. "Just open the door."

"And I wasn't expecting to have a guest," he adds, before letting me into his apartment.

It *is* small, but what studio apartment isn't? The kitchen consists of three cupboards, and his bed that's pressed right up against the wall is a mere six feet away from his couch, but the apartment is tastefully decorated and clean, which is way more than I can say for his car. I circle the floor, suddenly feeling awkward.

I can't remember what I'm doing here.

Weston brushes past me to pull the curtains shut, but they aren't blackout curtains, so the light in the apartment only dims. How he manages to sleep in here after working nights, I have no idea. Another yawn escapes him and he moves his fingers to the buttons of his shirt, but stops.

"Gracie," he says quietly. A sliver of light from a gap in the curtains illuminates one side of his face. "I need to sleep . . . And I don't sleep in my uniform."

Heat rises in my cheeks. "Right."

The apartment feels so intensely quiet and still, and Weston's tired laugh is like a breath as I turn my back to him. I pick at my nails and concentrate on the floor as he changes, but out of the corner of my eye, I catch his reflection in the wall mirror. There's a lump in my throat as I watch him unbutton his shirt to reveal a black undershirt beneath. His tattoos are exposed now, that one arm painted dark from his shoulder all the way down to the back of his hand. I never thought I liked tattoos all that much before, but they suit Weston. He kicks off his boots, steps out of his pants, and pulls off the undershirt.

Now I gulp. He stands a few feet behind me, wearing nothing but a pair of black fitted boxers. He is indeed muscular, like I already guessed from the way his clothes fit, and there are lines of definition carved into his stomach that continue into the waistband of his boxers. I am mesmerized, not necessarily by *him*, but at the sight of a very nearly naked male. Luca is the only guy I've ever seen, and suddenly it's like I'm fourteen again, blushing over shirtless boys. Unfamiliar territory.

"Okay," Weston says as he pulls on a pair of sweatpants. "Coffee. Do you take creamer?"

My cheeks are absolutely on fire now as I turn back around, and I'm certain he sees it because his lips curve into an amused smile. I wish he'd put a shirt on. My head spins and my throat feels dry.

"Do you mind grabbing me some water instead?" I say, subconsciously touching my fingers to my throat. "I think I'm dehydrated."

"Yup. Wine will do that to ya." Weston turns to his small kitchen and fills me a glass of water from the faucet. It's ice cold as he slips it into my hand. "You need some Tylenol?"

I shake my head and sip at the water, quenching my thirst. Over the rim of the glass, I watch Weston very forcefully suppress a yawn in an effort to be polite. He's tired; I'm tired. Now is not the time for more conversations over coffee.

"I'm sorry, I should go and let you get some sleep," I say, setting the water down on the coffee table, prepared to make a hasty exit. "I need some more sleep too."

"You're more than welcome to crash here," Weston offers, then after a beat, adds, "on the couch." He smiles shyly.

It's not the worst idea in the world. Weston's couch does look comfortable, and I would much rather be here than heading home to my own empty apartment that bursts with too many painful memories.

"Okay. Thanks."

Weston grabs a blanket from inside a storage ottoman at the foot of his bed and hands it over. The close proximity nearly makes me die as I fight to keep my eyes from dipping to his bare chest.

"I'm going to grab a quick shower," he says, then disappears off into the bathroom.

I blow out a puff of breath, compose myself, then get comfortable. I take off my Nikes, curl up on the couch, and pull the blanket over my body for warmth. I'm wearing yoga pants and an oversized sweater, because I had every intention of meeting Weston at the diner then dragging myself to the gym where Maddie will scream at me to lift heavier weights despite my arms resembling pool noodles, but napping here is a much better use of my time.

I shoot Maddie a quick text to reschedule our session until the afternoon, then tuck my phone into one of my sneakers and burrow further under the blanket. The pulsing of the shower is like white noise, but it only lasts all of two minutes.

Weston emerges from the bathroom, skin flushed from the heat of the shower, his dark hair damp and wild. He's wearing gray boxers now. As he crosses the small apartment, I steal a peek at his butt. For educational purposes. And it's a nice butt.

He rolls into his bed and buries under his comforter.

"Goodnight, Gracie," he murmurs. "Or maybe good morning."

He faces the wall, his back to me. We are both so quiet, our shallow breathing mixed with the noise of traffic on the street below. At first I think it's the most annoying sound in the world, the screeching of brakes and the whir of engines, but then it becomes comforting. Just like the white noise of the shower, I think it'll be enough to put me to sleep.

Except Weston doesn't go to sleep yet. He tosses and turns a few times, then settles facing me.

"Hi," he says.

"Hi."

In the dim apartment, our eyes lock. I mentally trace lines across his face, painting the curve of his lips, the thickness of his brows, the beauty mark on his cheek. His dark eyes glisten and I wonder if he's examining my features the same way I'm studying his. Eye contact this intense with a stranger shouldn't feel so intimate, yet . . .

"I haven't been sleeping much since Luca left," I whisper, a shiver traveling down my spine. "I don't like sleeping alone."

"Then come here."

Weston shifts back to the other side of his bed and lifts the comforter. He waits patiently, but it doesn't take me long to make the decision. I unfurl myself from the blanket and close the tiny distance between the couch and the bed. Not one single breath escapes me as I crawl under the comforter, my back to him.

"Is this better?" Weston asks, his tired voice husky. I nod into the pillow. He shifts closer, pressing his chest to my back. Warmth radiates from him and he tucks his body neatly against the shape of mine. I feel his breath against my hair, and he folds an arm around my stomach. There's an edge to his voice as he whispers, "And this?"

I'm lightheaded. The apartment spins around me, stars appearing in the dark. I didn't realize until now just how much I was craving someone else's touch like this. I've felt so alone since Luca left. Being held safe in someone's arms and sharing the weight of the world with them has been the hardest thing to let go of, and my eyes burn with building emotion. I miss him. So, so much.

I squeeze my eyes shut and reach for Weston's hand that rests on my stomach. We intertwine our fingers, gently at first, then tighter. I suppress the overwhelming urge to cry. Again. There are no words to describe how desperately I needed this – the simplicity of sharing a bed with another being, the warmth of our bodies igniting like a fire, my hand in his.

A pained cry of grief involuntarily escapes my lips. Releasing Weston's hand, I twist around in his arms so that we are face-to-face. Our chests together, his arm still around my waist, our gazes only inches apart.

We share a silent agreement in the way we look at each other.

I need him, and I think he needs me.

So, I make the jump.

I take Weston's face between my hands, and I press my lips to his.

Neither of us moves for an excruciatingly long moment while we register the sensation of our mouths together, new and unfamiliar. Then Weston kisses me deeper. His hand travels from my waist to my jaw, then slides into my hair as his tongue works hungrily with mine. Heartache fuels our desperation. I push myself harder against him and feel how ready for me he is.

Our movements grow erratic. Weston rolls onto his back, taking me with him. I straddle his hips, flattening my body against his chest, and kissing him fiercely. My skin tingles with a million goosebumps and my heart thumps agonizingly in my chest.

I've never kissed, never touched, never felt anyone but Luca. He was my first *everything*. It's all so foreign to me, the scent of a new man's skin, the different contours of another body, the way a new pair of lips fit uniquely with mine. It's terrifying, but I need this. I need intimacy.

Weston runs his hands under my sweatshirt, his fingertips blazing over my ribcage. My skin is so sensitive that a shiver soars down my spine in response. He hooks his arms around my body and brings us upright, still holding me in his lap. He is so hard beneath me. I press my hand over his boxers, feeling him bulging as he pushes into my palm.

He takes hold of my neck and angles my chin up as his lips trail from the corner of my mouth along my jaw. I rock my hips back and forth on his lap, a heat rising between my legs, full of anticipation. Weston grunts and grabs my sweatshirt, hastily pulling it off. As he toys with the clasp of my bra, he kisses my breasts and I wind my hands into his hair, pulling on the ends a little too hard as I suppress a moan. *Fuck*. This feels dangerously amazing.

"If you're tired, we don't have to," I murmur, my head back, eyes rolling. My bra is on the floor now.

"Do I feel tired now?" Weston hisses. He clasps my hand and moves it back to his boxers. His muscular arms take hold of me again and maneuver us with ease, flipping me onto my back.

It's unbearable now, just how badly I'm craving him inside of me. I am nothing but a shell right now, so empty and hollow, and I know I'll be a little more whole again if I can just *feel* him.

Weston kisses his way from my chest down to my stomach, then wrangles off my yoga pants. He glances up at me with an arched brow and a smirk to match when he realizes I'm not wearing any underwear, and I bite down hard on my bottom lip as he cups a hand between my legs to feel just how wet for him I am. This urge to be close to him has me feeling insatiable.

Removing his boxers and stretching over me to pull open the top drawer of the bedside table, he scrambles for a condom. My stomach knots with nerves as I watch him tear open the wrapper with his teeth, then slide the condom on and reposition himself. He curls one hand beneath my thigh. Our eyes meet and apprehension fills the space between us. A moment of questioning. Second-guessing.

"Are you sure about this, Gracie?"

"I'm not sure about anything these days, but yes," I whisper. "Please."

Weston grips my thigh tighter, and I clench my teeth as he enters me slowly, carefully, and then fully. We gasp in synchronization. There are a few seconds of stillness as I adjust to him inside of me and as he embraces the feel of me. My hands move to my face, my eyes shut.

"Don't hide," Weston says. He reaches for my hands and pulls them away, the magnetic force of his gaze drawing me back to him. Somehow, he seems so recognizable to me. "It's okay. We're okay."

He keeps one hand interlocked with mine and his thrusts are cautious and tender to begin with, but then he picks up the pace when he feels how well my body responds to him. I throw my head back into the pillow and arch my back, moaning with pleasure as he reaches the depths of my core. His free hand is between my thighs, touching me in all the right places. As the intensity builds, I claw at the bedsheets and my body writhes. Weston's breaths are heavy now and it feels incredible knowing I'm desired this way, a man wanting me so bad he's left breathless.

Weston slows, leaning forward and burying his face into my neck. The heat of his breath fills my ear, driving me insane. I drag my nails down his back and buck my hips in sync with his. The way he groans against the soft skin of my neck is enough to throw me over the edge. Being with someone new is so exhilarating, I don't know how long I can last. The pleasure mounts to a heavenly pain and I know I'm close.

"I think I might—" I gasp, but Weston fucks the words straight out of me.

He thrusts faster again, harder than before, drawing sounds out of me I had no idea I was capable of. Beads of sweat roll down his face, his chest, making his skin hot and damp. That heavenly pain intensifies, so unbearable yet so, *so* good. I squirm, my thighs trembling as I squeeze them together, trying to push Weston away yet praying he doesn't dare stop. I can't take a second more.

"*Weston,*" I hiss, but my voice hits an octave, my gasp tearing from my throat.

Tingles of muscular spasms shoot through me, my body contracting and then releasing with insurmountable satisfaction.

A groan tears from Weston. He tenses inside of me, pulsing with waves of pleasure, and drops his head back into the crook of my neck as he too reaches his peak. He exhales a deep breath against my ear, and I slide my fingers through his hair, holding him against me. Our chests rise and fall as we fight to catch our breaths.

"Now I really do need to sleep," he murmurs. He rolls away from me, running a hand back through his damp hair as he sits on the edge of the bed. My vision feels starry, like the beginning of a migraine, yet I admire the definition in his back, the lines etched around his shoulder blades.

And then he glances back at me, and I feel myself crumble into a thousand pieces. He's not Luca. And when I realize that, I realize that all I want is Luca.

"Gracie?" Weston says, his expression warping with concern.

My lower lip quivers as my emotions explode into overdrive. I grab the comforter and pull it over my body, shielding myself from Weston and turning my back to him so he can't see the first of a flood of tears brimming in my eyes. This is humiliating.

"Fuck, Gracie." Weston snuggles in behind me, the comforter separating us as he offers me a tender hug. "I'm sorry. We shouldn't have—"

"No. It's not you," I interject, pressing my face into the pillow to catch some of my tears. "I'm such a mess right now. It just feels so new to me that I'm here . . . with you . . . and not Luca."

"I know," he says with an understanding sigh, and I wonder if he feels the same way. I'm not Charlotte. I'm new to him, too. "I'm sorry."

"Stop saying sorry. I'm the one crying in your bed."

"Don't worry about it. You already ugly sobbed in the Uber, remember?" he reminds me, and it lifts all of the weight from the situation. I manage a small laugh and I dab my eyes dry with the sheets.

"I needed that," I admit after the moment of silence passes.

"I needed that too," Weston says.

Our breathing has calmed now. He remains pressed against my back, still on the other side of the comforter, but an arm wrapped around my body securely. We don't say another word as he drifts off to sleep first, but only because we have no idea *what* to say. Quite frankly, I've had no fucking clue what I've been doing since Luca left.

WESTON

One Sunday each month, Dad has us kids over to his place for the most insane homemade burgers. It's been our routine ever since he retired and moved out of the Bay Area three years ago. If we didn't always have the next date in the diary for getting together, then time would run away from us too easily. We haven't had a full house in a while. Often I'm the only one who can make it, but my older brother and his family are making the three-hour drive today to join us in Bodega Bay.

It's always so peaceful here, and although I didn't like the idea of Dad moving, I know a place like Bodega Bay is exactly where he needs to be to enjoy his retirement. It's a tiny village on the coast, home to less than a thousand residents, and has a golf course, marina, and great hiking trails. He spends a lot of his days fishing down by the harbor. He's only an hour and a half north of San Francisco, but still. The thought of not being able to reach him quickly in case of an emergency leaves me unsettled.

It's hot out today, so Dad has the grill up and running on the driveway. The front of his home overlooks the bay and has the most stunning view. Grass stretching down to the beach, the beach disappearing into the calm waters of the bay. Tranquility, that's what Dad came here for.

"Lily just texted. They're five minutes away," I tell Dad, as I put my phone away and relax further into the camping chair, stretching my legs out in front of me.

Dad springs into action. He can never sit still, and he's just dying to get his tongs out and start grilling those burgers. He's still young, not yet sixty, and he's as fit as a fiddle. Yet I worry about him all the damn time.

"Do you need help with anything, Dad?"

"Nope. You just relax," he says, dismissing me with a lazy wave as he heads inside the house. The fold-up table in the middle of the drive has a spread of salad bowls, burger buns, *so many toppings,* an ice cooler full of beer, and a pile of disposable plates and forks. Everything was already set up before I got here, so now I feel useless.

I take a swig of my cold beer and look out over the bay. It's clear blue skies and the sunlight glistens over the water. Normally Charlotte would be here with me, but I told Dad she couldn't make it due to work commitments.

I need to tell him the truth, that we broke up and there's no salvaging the relationship, but I'm embarrassed to admit it. He'll be disappointed: he often dropped subtle hints to me about proposing. I disregarded the idea every single time.

Dad emerges from the front door with a tray of fresh beef patties, which are always seasoned to perfection. He's wearing his chef's apron now too, the one my sister got him for Thanksgiving one year, personalized to say, "*Mark owns the grill.*"

"I think I hear them," he says, pausing to listen.

And I hear it too, the growing purr of a car engine approaching in the distance. The BMW SUV rolls down the street a few moments later, parking up at the foot of the driveway behind my beat-up Honda, which is overdue its oil change. I really, really need a bigger apartment and a new set of wheels. Keaton has things together way more than I do.

"Hey, hey!" Keaton says cheerfully as he steps out of the car. They couldn't make last month's get-together, so it's been a while since I last saw my brother and he's grown a god-awful mustache in that time.

"What is *that?*" I point my bottle of beer at his face.

"You don't like it?"

"You look like Dad," I say. But Keaton has always looked more like Dad, regardless. They share the same soft, rounded features, whereas Peyton and I took after our mom and share her sharper, bold features.

"Which means he looks handsome as hell!" Dad chimes in, stroking the wisps of hair above his upper lip. He walks down the drive with open arms to hug Keaton and pat his back hard, the way only fathers do.

Keaton's wife, Lily, hops out of the car and helps their daughter, Sophia, out of the backseat. Lily's blouse stretches tight over her rounded stomach. Their baby boy is due to make his arrival next month, and I can't *wait* to have a nephew. No offense to Sophia, but I'm clueless when it comes to roleplaying with her dolls. I still give it my best shot.

"Lily, you look great!" I say as I pull myself out of the camping chair and join them. Dad takes Sophia up into his arms and twirls her around, her childish giggles pumping serotonin into the air.

"Aw, thanks, Weston, but my feet are starting to swell and, trust me, it's not a good look. Hence these," she says, lifting her foot to show off her Crocs. She quickly scans the driveway and asks, "Where's Charlotte?"

"She couldn't make it," I say. The lie leaves a bitter taste in my mouth. I hastily turn to Dad and pluck Sophia out of his grasp, lifting her high into the air above my head. She gets bigger every time I see her, and I still remember how fragile she seemed when I first held her as a newborn three years ago. Now I toss her around like she's unbreakable. "Hey, cutie!"

"Uncle Wes," she says, and I glower playfully at her.

"*Weston,*" I correct. I fucking hate having my name shortened to Wes. It makes me sound a hundred years old.

"Weston," Sophia repeats, and I lower her down to my chest so I can hug her.

"Can I start grilling the burgers now?" Dad asks, clasping his hands together with impatience, and we all give him the thumbs-up to get started.

I set Sophia down and Lily takes her inside the house to retrieve some toys to play with in the yard. Meanwhile Dad tosses burger patties onto the grill, and Keaton cracks open an ice-cold beer.

"It's good to see you," he says, tapping his beer against mine. "How's the field training going?"

Fucking terrible, I think. *I hate it. And I'm useless. And I never wanted to be a cop to begin with.*

"Good," I lie. I settle back into my chair and chug my beer to fill the silence. "Life on base still treating you well?"

Keaton drags another chair next to mine and collapses into it, but his eyes remain set on the front door of the house as Lily and Sophia reappear with a toy box. "Never better," he says, then sighs heavily. "But I'm dreading the day I get deployed again. Things are different now. I don't know if I can leave them."

Keaton works in cyber within the Air Force, and he and Lily live and work on base at Beale. He hasn't been overseas in years, not since before Sophia was born, and works a comfortable schedule. Any day, however, he could be sent out to only God knows where. There's more to lose now, what with a wife and daughter and a son on the way.

"Yeah. Have you heard from Peyton lately?" I muse, picking at the label of my beer bottle. "I wonder how she's doing."

"Nah. I think she called Dad a few weeks ago, though. She's fine, but homesick," Keaton says, and we pause for a moment to let ourselves process our worry.

It's inevitable, worrying about Peyton. To Keaton, she's his little sister. To me, she's my big sister. That makes us both protective, yet we are rendered useless when she's stationed thousands of miles away in Kuwait. But she's also the most badass person I know, and I have no doubt in her ability to take care of herself out there. It's in our blood to put ourselves in physically demanding careers, after all.

I blame Dad. Before he retired, he was the deputy chief of field operations at San Francisco PD. He lived and breathed work. A great cop. Always balanced and fair, always fearless. Even got shot in the arm once when I was a little kid, and he couldn't *wait* to get the go-ahead from his doctor to get back to working the beat. Although he never explicitly said it, there was a certain pressure for us kids to be just as resilient.

Keaton, being the eldest, was of course the first to prove his worth. He applied for the Air Force straight out of high school, was deployed several times to

Japan, then worked his way into cyber. Peyton had to do one better. She enlisted in the army, knocked her aptitude test out of the park, and bagged herself her dream career as an explosive ordnance disposal specialist. It doesn't get more dangerous than that, so she trumps both Keaton and me when it comes to being the toughest sibling.

It was my turn after that, but I didn't have the balls to go into the armed forces. I wasn't really sure *what* I wanted, so I was the first to go to college. I majored in criminal justice, much to Dad's approval. And although Keaton and Peyton had both stepped things up another level when it came to protecting and serving, neither of them followed in *his* footsteps, and I knew that would make him the happiest of all. So, I decided to be the one to do it, to be a run-of-the-mill city cop.

I can never tell him now that I hate it.

"Did Peyton call you, Dad?" I call across the drive.

"Yes, and she's fine," Dad reassures me, waving his set of tongs dismissively over his shoulder. "And don't ask when she'll be coming home, because she still doesn't know."

My chest deflates. Peyton's been deployed for almost a year now, and I'm really starting to miss her. I can talk to Dad and Keaton about most things, but the best advice always comes from my sister. There's no bullshit with Peyton; she tells me things straight. If she was here now, I'd have some clue how to get myself out of this mess.

I should probably start with telling the truth about Charlotte.

"There's something I need to tell you guys," I announce, clearing my throat. Dad turns from the grill, Keaton eyes me sideways, and Lily glances up from helping Sophia set up her dolls on the drive. I don't drag out the suspense. I just say it. "Charlotte and I broke up."

"What! How'd that happen?" Keaton asks, scratching his temple with apparent confusion. "I thought you guys would be engaged soon. You've been together for years."

I press my beer to my lips, but realize it's empty. Avoiding eye contact with everyone, I get up and cross to the table to grab myself another. "I can't give her what she wants," I admit in a low voice. I hate that I fucked things up, and I don't want Dad and Keaton to think less of me for it. "I haven't been putting her first, and she says it's too late for me to fix that."

The grilling tongs hang limp in Dad's hand as he stares, visibly shocked. So was I when Charlotte first broke the news to me. I took it for granted that she'd be mine forever, and I think Dad believed one day she'd be his other daughter-in-law. "I'm sorry to hear that, Weston. I'll miss her coming around," he says. "Are you alright?"

I shrug, attempting nonchalance, but the lump that rises in my throat betrays me. "It's an adjustment. I'm mostly just pissed at myself."

As I sit back down, Keaton leans over to clasp my shoulder in sympathy. "Hey, you're still young. I didn't meet Lily until I was twenty-four!"

"That's true," Lily says. "You have so much time to meet someone else, Weston. Just give yourself time to get over her first."

I stare straight down the rim of my beer bottle, and I think of Gracie. I'm not sure jumping into bed with a new girl so soon was the right thing to do, but it made so much sense to me in the moment. I'm *not* over Charlotte, and Gracie definitely isn't over her ex either, so neither of us were thinking clearly. There was just this overwhelming desire for intimacy that we both needed. I don't know how I feel about it now, about what happened.

It's been a week, and I've had no contact with Gracie since she woke in my bed and ran out the door. There are a lot of emotions to work through, so maybe we can't be friends now, not after what happened, but I'd still like to be. We can be vulnerable around each other, and I really need that right now. Gracie may not be Charlotte, but being with her, feeling that closeness . . . It felt so natural and right. Gracie doesn't feel like a stranger to me, but maybe I've ruined things now. I hope she doesn't regret what happened, because we were there for each other in a moment where we really needed one another, and that is not a bad thing. It doesn't even have to turn into a big deal. We can forget about it and move forward, because I still want to be there for her through this tough time in her life. I want to help her learn to put herself first, and I want to prove I can be caring and selfless.

I just hope she still wants the same.

GRACIE

My heart sinks as I scroll through the latest comments. Our followers know something's up. Mine and Luca's social media accounts have been inactive for three weeks now, which is completely out of character for us. We usually post a new YouTube video every Tuesday. New Instagram posts daily. The radio silence has our most dedicated followers theorizing about the cause of our disappearance. Maybe someone close to us has died and we're grieving, or one of us has become sick, or perhaps our apartment has been burgled and all our equipment has been stolen. However, the majority of our followers believe Luca and I have broken up. They're right, of course, but we can't let them know that.

I usually edit videos in the office in our apartment, but I've been taking every opportunity available to avoid sitting at home on my own, so I've grabbed our MacBook

Air, walked the half hour downtown to Union Square, and found myself a nice corner in one of the many Starbucks stores around here. I'm on my second iced white mocha, and I have yet to even add our intro clip to the start of the video.

I have no idea how I'm supposed to pass off old footage as recent, and I hate that Luca is making me be the one to trawl through old clips of us together when the pain of our breakup is still so raw. I've found some unused photos we took down on Pier 39 at Fisherman's Wharf in the spring. We're at the end of the pier, standing by the wooden railings with Alcatraz Island in the distance behind us. I pick out a photo of Luca and I gazing at each other, my hand playfully grabbing his chin and his hands on my waist. It was an unusually warm day back then, luckily, so we weren't wearing jackets. It could totally pass as a photo taken now in the summer. I edit the coloring, then post it to our Instagram account with the caption: *life is better with you*, followed by a string of cutesy emojis that makes me scowl at my phone.

These photos are meant to be candid, but they aren't. Our entire Instagram feed is carefully manufactured to be as aesthetically pleasing as possible, and behind every photo is a plan. Maddie is great with the camera when it comes to snapping the perfect angles, so often the three of us would go out exclusively to take photos. Other times we'd set up the camera on a tripod with a timer.

Our relationship was genuine, but the *way* we portrayed it to others was slightly exaggerated.

As I watch the likes and the comments roll in on the new post, I feel like a complete fraud.

How long can I keep this up for? It may be our income source, but we can't lie forever. The video footage and photos will run out eventually, and with no new material available to use, we'll have to come clean.

But for now, it's Tuesday. And that means a new video is required imminently.

I grit my teeth, listen to The 1975 at full volume through my earphones, and start pulling together footage. My editing is sloppy, lazy, because my heart isn't in it. The cuts aren't seamless, I don't bother adding background music during a sped-up section, and there isn't exactly a concept to the video. It's just a mundane vlog of Luca and me running errands, and then I throw in a clip from a totally different year of me jumping out from around a blind corner and scaring the crap out of him.

My music abruptly stops as my left AirPod is pulled from my ear.

"Hey!" I say, my head snapping up from the laptop screen. "Oh."

It's Weston. He towers over me, my AirPod pinched between his thumb and index finger. No uniform this time, so he isn't patrolling Starbucks for criminals. Just a pair of jeans and a plain T-shirt, his sleeve of tattoos on full display. He's holding a Zara shopping bag.

"Hey," he says. "What a coincidence to bump into you here."

The smirk he's fighting tells me this is anything *but* a coincidence, so I raise an eyebrow suspiciously. "There are five Starbucks within a five-block radius, and you just so happened to pick the one I'm in. How did you know I was here, Weston?"

His smirk breaks free and he hands me back my AirPod, then holds up the Zara bag. "I was re-buying one of my favorite jackets because the original is at Charlotte's place, so I'll likely never get it back," he explains, "and a friend of yours served me at the register. Madison Pullman."

"How do you know Maddie's full name?" I ask, then mentally face-palm myself as I realize the answer. "Oh. You checked her ID that night of the noise complaint. Okay, whatever. So what? She sent you here?"

"I asked how things were with you."

"Yeah?"

"And she told me to come here and ask you myself." He presses his hands to the top of the empty chair next to me and leans forward as he quietens his voice. "So? How are things with you?"

My pulse picks up and I am unbearably aware of it thumping beneath every inch of my skin. It's so hard to look him directly in the eye after what happened the last time we were together. I know how his body feels against mine, his hot breath against my ear. How do

I look at this stranger knowing exactly how he groans in bed?

"I'm . . ."

"Do you mind if I sit with you for a while? Or are you busy?" He gestures to the laptop, but what he doesn't know is that I'm grateful for the interruption. Then he points to my empty cups. "And can I grab you another coffee? What are you drinking?"

I'm already rattling with caffeine as it is, but one more wouldn't hurt. It keeps me functioning when all I want to do every day is sleep away the hurt. "I'd take another, if you don't mind. An iced white mocha with caramel drizzle and vanilla sweet cream cold foam."

Weston narrows his gaze inquisitively, and I go on the defensive.

"I know, I know . . . A total sugar bomb, but I have yet to get a single cavity."

"No, it's not that." He pauses for a beat as his eyes lower to the floor, and when he looks back up again, there's a hint of longing behind them. "That's Charlotte's drink too."

"Oh." I chew on my lip. I didn't mean to remind him of her. "Sorry."

He waves away my apology and rearranges his mouth into a smile. "I'll be back in a sec."

Weston leaves his shopping bag under the table and grabs my empty cups to discard them on his way up to the register. As he waits in line, I watch his every movement.

He tilts his head back to scan the menu boards, stands with his hands in his pockets, and talks kindly with the barista as he places our order. He lingers by the bottom of the bar and transfers that same smile across the room to me as our drinks are made. He's a cop, his arm is covered in tattoos, and yet there's something sweet and vulnerable about him. Maybe that's just because I know he's going through a hard time right now. Maybe if I didn't have that knowledge, I wouldn't see beyond the hardened exterior.

"One sugar bomb," Weston says as he sets my drink down in front of me. He settles into the chair next to me with his own coffee, a hot one that I imagine is basic, like straight-up filter coffee and creamer. "So, how are things?" he asks again.

"Still weird," I answer. "My head is . . . a mess. You?"

"Still weird. My head is a mess," he copies, and I roll my eyes at him as I take a sip of my coffee to fill the silence. He points to my laptop. "Wild guess: are you working on content right now?"

My screen has faded to black due to inactivity, so I brush my thumb over the touchpad to bring it back to life. I turn the laptop toward Weston and reveal the video I've been editing. "You caught me. I'm a fraud, I know."

"How long do you think you can keep it up? Pretending you're still with him?"

"Not very long at all," I answer, closing the laptop screen. I push it away and sink back into my chair. My head constantly spins with all of the questions I don't have answers for, all of the what-ifs. I wish I could shut it all off. "There's not enough old footage to last for more than a month or two, so I guess I'll have to delete all of our accounts soon, once we come clean."

"And then what? You have to get a real job?"

I glare at him. If only he knew how hard I worked as a teenager to learn how to edit. "Content creation *is* a real job."

"Okay then, another job."

"We're both taking a gap year before we start our careers. It's always been the plan, and even if the income dries up, we were smart. We have savings. Investments. We were supposed to go traveling over the winter, but I guess that plan is out."

Weston cocks his head to one side, listening intently as though he actually cares about the sad state of affairs my life has become. "Why can't you still go?"

"I'm not traveling to the other side of the world on my own, Weston," I state, crossing my arms. Me? Traveling alone? I can't even sleep in my own goddamn apartment by myself!

"Lots of people solo travel," he says.

"Not me. Did you forget the part where I've never been independent? Like, ever? I've always had my parents or Luca around me. This is the first time I've ever been alone, and if you think I'm capable of traveling all by myself just three months from now, then . . ."

"Then what?" he challenges with a smirk. "Then I'm being way too optimistic that you'll learn how to be selfish within the next three months? Fine. Call me optimistic, because I'm going to teach you how to be selfish. Just like you asked."

My brows draw together. I'm surprised Weston even remembers our conversation in the diner over a week ago. When I think of that morning, I think only of his touch and nothing before it. "I was hungover that morning," I say dismissively. "I didn't know what I was talking about."

The atmosphere around us changes. The air grows heavier as tension draws close.

We're both thinking of *that* morning now, and all of the things we haven't addressed.

Weston dips his gaze and traces a circle around the lid of his cup. He parts his lips, but I can't bear to hear what he has to say.

"Don't," I cut in, my voice almost a whisper. "Don't say anything about it. Please."

His lifts his chin, soft eyes finding mine. "Can I ask one thing?" He waits for me to stop him, to hold my hand up and beg him not to talk about us sleeping together, but my lack of response *is* a response. I wait for him to ask: "Do you regret it?"

And it's not a question I haven't asked myself already. A whirlwind of emotions has followed in the week since I fled from Weston's apartment and I've tried to decipher exactly what it is that I've been feeling since. I know only one thing for certain: it isn't regret.

"No," I answer, and I put on a brave front and force myself to look him in the eye. "In the moment it's exactly what I wanted, but I just . . ."

"Feel guilty?" Weston finishes.

"*Yes*." I audibly release the breath I'm holding and shake out the tension in my shoulders. "Guilty, like I cheated on Luca."

"I feel the exact same way."

There is comfort in this knowledge, even though logically, we *know* neither of us cheated. Our relationships are over. We are both single, but of course there are still complex emotions involved. My feelings for Luca will linger forever, I think. And Weston clearly still has love for Charlotte.

"We can't let that happen again," I say quietly, and Weston nods in agreement.

"You may not have meant what you said in the diner," he says, "but I did. That thing about us being friends . . . I still think we could be. We *should* be."

He props his elbows on the table and interlocks his hands together, then rests his chin against them. Patiently, he gives me time to consider the idea of us being more than just two strangers with our heartache in common. There's a flash of hope in his gentle gaze.

"*Just* friends," I agree, and then I surprise myself by adding: "Definitely no benefits, because we aren't emotionally strong enough for that, clearly." I couldn't bear the thought of us discussing the fact we had sex; now I'm poking jokes at it. It's peculiar, how easily I sink into being comfortable around him. It's almost reminiscent of how I felt when I was fifteen around Luca at the beginning. Natural. No pressure. Some people you just click with more easily than others.

Weston rolls his eyes and drops his locked hands from his chin. He points to my closed laptop again. "Do you have your own accounts?"

"No."

He doesn't even grimace. It's like he knew what the answer would be. Is it so obvious to everyone around me that I'm codependent? "Step one of being selfish," he says, reaching across the table for my phone and handing it to me. "Get your own damn Instagram, Gracie."

"But—"

"But nothing," he interjects. "Do it. Right now."

"*You* don't even have Instagram," I remind him. He didn't even know what an influencer *was* when I first told him, because he claims he doesn't use social media. In our generation, that is absolutely bizarre to me.

"Then I'll make one too." Weston swigs his coffee and pulls out his phone. The sound of steaming milk and the idle musings of other customers serve as background noise. After a few moments, Weston turns his phone screen toward me, and I see the Instagram app is currently downloading. "Happy?"

"I'll be your first follower," I tell him with a smile.

"And I'll be yours."

I open up Instagram on my own phone and my heart plummets into my stomach when I see all the new notifications on that photo I uploaded of Luca and me. Quickly, I navigate to settings and start a new account, but I need a username. My full name is already taken by some other Gracie Taylor, so I add some underscores and some numbers. It's not aesthetically pleasing, but it's mine.

I study Weston over my phone. "Done."

"There's a lot of Weston Reeds in the world; every username is taken," he mutters, and I laugh because there are also a lot of Gracie Taylors. "Okay. Done."

We show each other our phone screens in unison. Two entirely blank Instagram profiles. Weston has also been forced to add a string of symbols to his username, and I search it and follow him. He follows me back.

"Do you think maybe I could . . ." Weston sheepishly holds out his phone again. "Can I get your number too?"

I take his phone and add my number to his contacts, and, as I pass him back the device, I hand over my own with it. "Do you think maybe I could get *your* number too? Since we're now friends."

A smile tugs at the corner of his mouth. He puts his number in my phone, and then we both take another sip of our coffees, unsure what comes next in this conversation. I ought to finish editing this video and get it uploaded to the channel, but I don't want to send Weston

away. It was sweet he came to check on me. I find it difficult to believe that he was selfish when it came to putting
Charlotte first.

He sets his coffee down with a small thud. "What are
you doing tonight?"

"Crying alone in my apartment, probably."

Sternly, he looks at me from beneath his eyelashes. I
should be past the crying stage, I know, but it's relentless. "Would you like to go for dinner with me?" he
asks. "I'm not back on shift until Thursday, and I know
I'll end up at the bar with Adam throwing back tequila
shots tonight if I don't make other plans."

"Did you ever cook for Charlotte?" I ask, and Weston
blinks with surprise at what is seemingly a random question. But I'm going somewhere with this, if his answer
is no.

"No."

"Why not? Can't you cook?"

Weston's gaze continues to narrow with confusion. "I
can cook to an acceptable degree. I just didn't think to
cook for her, I guess. We always went out."

"I'll have dinner with you tonight," I say, a smug smile
forming across my face, "but you have to cook. That's
what it means to put in effort. You're now in training, so
that when you meet the next love of your life, you'll be
the *best* boyfriend."

"Hmm." Weston's expression turns playful and I
know instantly by the spark in his gaze that he's totally

on board with taking my advice. "My place around seven?"

"I don't do any pork dishes, and I like white wine."

"Got it." He scoots back his chair and stands, head tilted as he finishes his coffee. "Don't be late, Gracie Taylor."

Something flutters in my stomach as he turns and walks away without another word, leaving me with only anticipation for our dinner tonight. He'll teach me how to be happy on my own, and I'll teach him how to make a woman feel special. Two friends helping each other heal their broken hearts, that's all.

WESTON

"Have candles lit before she arrives," says Brooks.

"I don't have any."

"You didn't buy some?"

"Why the fuck would I buy candles?"

Brooks' sigh rattles across the line. "You really are bad at this stuff."

My phone is pressed between my ear and my shoulder, my hands busy peeling potatoes. I glance at the wall clock, and I still have twenty minutes until it turns seven. To account for the possibility of Gracie showing up late, I've made the choice *not* to have dinner ready upon her arrival. I'll cook the steaks once she's here.

"Remind me once more how I do the sauce," I ask Brooks.

"Pull the steaks out of the pan, toss in the shallots, brown them, then add the wine. Reduce it, lower the heat, whip in cold butter. Add your parsley, then serve over your steaks," he instructs, then pauses. "You did buy parsley, didn't you? Because I feel like you're the type to think it doesn't matter, but it does, Weston. The parsley *matters*."

I roll my eyes and toss the last peeled potato into the pot. "Yes, I bought the parsley."

"And, for the love of God, don't you dare offer her a beer with dinner. You bought wine, right? And you do have wine glasses to serve it in, don't you?"

"Obviously." I move down the counter and tear open the pack of asparagus, spreading them out on a chopping board. "Thanks, by the way. This is so much better than the chicken parm I was thinking of making."

"No problem," Brooks says. "I hope it goes well, even though it's not a real date, so you say." His words are teasing, and I know I should have kept my mouth shut about my situation with Gracie, but I really needed his advice tonight. He's the only one of my friends with a long-term girlfriend who is madly in love with him, so he clearly does things right. Cooking romantic dinners is easy for him. He does this shit all the time.

"It's *not* a real date," I say, trimming the ends off the asparagus. I grab my phone from between my ear and my shoulder and put it on speaker instead, setting it down on the counter. "Gracie is putting me through my paces so I know exactly where I fucked up with Charlotte. That's it."

"Hmm," he says, unconvinced. "Does Adam know?"

"No way. If he finds out I've seen Gracie a few times since that night at the club, I'll never hear the end of it. I haven't even told Cameron, so don't you dare say anything."

It's not that I'm embarrassed about being friends with Gracie. I just don't want the guys – Adam, especially – getting on my case about it. They'll assume I'm into her, that we're sleeping together, that I'm on the rebound. And okay, fine. Maybe I did sleep with Gracie already, but it was under unique circumstances, and it won't happen again. They will never know about it.

"I won't say anything," Brooks promises, and I swallow hard with relief. "But, at the end of the day, you're still cooking a steak dinner for a girl who's single. Have fun. And for God's sake, throw some bleach down your toilet if you haven't already."

I laugh as he hangs up the call. My apartment can be messy, but it's definitely not filthy. I do clean, though admittedly I've been slacking lately, for obvious reasons. Having Gracie over tonight was the nudge I needed to deep clean. After I left her at Starbucks earlier, I called Brooks for advice on what the hell to cook, and then headed straight to the grocery store. I bought two bottles of white wine, one bottle of red for the sauce I plan to make, two filet mignon steaks, asparagus, potatoes, shallots. Oh, and parsley. Then I floored it home and went ham with whatever cleaning supplies I had around. The bathroom is scrubbed spotless, there are fresh sheets on my bed, every crevice of floorspace is vacuumed. I even plumped the damn couch cushions.

I've showered, worked some gel into my hair, sprayed maybe a little too much cologne. I'm wearing the brand-new polo shirt my dad gifted me for my birthday a few months back, and I feel pretty good. I've made an effort.

I finish up my prep work, put the potatoes on to boil, pace my apartment in circles, then pop the tray of asparagus into the oven. Seven o'clock draws closer, and I become antsy. I attempt to relax on the couch, but I can't sit still long enough to last more than a minute before I'm back on my feet again, checking the potatoes and peeking into the oven.

There's a knock on my door. Although I'm expecting it, I still jolt.

On my way to the door, I glance back at the table set-up I've got going on in the middle of my apartment. I do own a table and two chairs, but they're permanently folded away in the storage closet because of the severe lack of room in this damn place. Tonight, the table has made an appearance. I even bought placemats at the grocery store. Though Brooks is probably right – I should have definitely bought candles too. It's very clear the table lacks a centerpiece, and it seems kind of pathetic now that I'm looking at it. It's also a punch in the gut when it occurs to me that I never once pulled out the table for Charlotte. Whenever we ate here, we sat on the couch with our plates on our laps. Fuck. I'm the worst.

I shake away the guilt and open the door.

"Hi," says Gracie.

Even in the harsh lighting of the hallway, Gracie looks nice. Her hair seems more blond than auburn without bright light to pull out the red tones, and it sits a little too perfectly against her shoulders in curls. She's wearing makeup, but not too much, just enough to accentuate her eyes. My gaze travels down her body, drawn to her waist highlighted by the red sundress she wears. There's a denim jacket over her shoulders to keep her warm from the San Francisco breeze.

My chest tightens. It should be Charlotte standing at my door, because she's the only woman I want to cook dinner for. The disappointment seeps through me so intensely it becomes obvious on my expression. Gracie's smile gradually fades.

"Are you okay?"

"You're not her," I say, then shake my head as though to retract the words. I pinch the bridge of my nose, squeeze my eyes shut, and take a deep breath. "Sorry. That was rude. Of course, I'm happy for you to be here, it's just . . ."

"I know," says Gracie, and her voice is soft and understanding. "Can I come in?"

Still kicking myself, I step to the side and gesture for her to enter my apartment. Tonight isn't about Charlotte. My *life* can't be about Charlotte. I ruined that, and there's no repairing it. I have to move on and learn how to be better for someone else.

"You put up a table," Gracie notes, and I force Charlotte's adorable gap-toothed smile out of my mind as I close my apartment door and focus on what's right in front of me, and that's Gracie.

The table looks even *more* pathetic now. "Yeah. There's not much room in here, so I hope you don't mind being wedged between my couch and my bed while we eat."

"That's okay. What's on the menu?"

"Steak in a red wine butter sauce with mashed potatoes and roasted asparagus," I say with flair, and Gracie nods keenly with approval. "I should start frying the steaks. How do you like yours cooked?"

"Medium."

I cross to my cramped kitchen and make another check of the potatoes and asparagus. They're almost ready, so I *really* ought to get these steaks cooking. I pull them out of the refrigerator, already seasoned with salt and pepper, and throw a pan on the stovetop to get it up to heat. Gracie wanders my apartment, removes her jacket from over her shoulders, and leaves it on the couch, then joins me in the kitchen. She leans back against the counter, watching.

"No pressure," I joke, melting butter in the pan and placing in the filet mignon steaks. I have my chopped shallots and bottle of red wine at the ready, and I keep an eye on my watch as the steaks sizzle. "Would you like something to drink?"

"Only if it's that," Gracie says, nodding to the two bottles of white wine at the other end of my countertop.

I grab a bottle, pop open the cork, and pour out two glasses. I hand one to Gracie and stand in front of her, swirling my wine around my glass. She doesn't take a sip of hers yet, either. We are both waiting for something.

"Should we toast?" I ask.

"Probably."

I think for a second, allowing my gaze to naturally find hers. There's still fragility behind her eyes, a pale blue that seems to be missing its sparkle. "A toast to us," I say, holding up my glass, "for being sad motherfuckers yet somehow surviving, and in the hope that soon we might feel okay again."

Gracie smiles, but it's so painfully sad I almost regret saying anything at all. "Yes," she agrees, and taps her glass against mine. We both take a sip while maintaining eye contact. "Mmm. You picked well."

"I'm glad you approve," I say, then set my glass down as I turn back to the stove.

I pull the pot of potatoes off the heat, drain the water, then start mashing them. I add butter, milk, salt and pepper. I make these potatoes the fluffiest, butteriest mashed potatoes Gracie will ever taste. In between, I flip the steaks over, and remove the asparagus from the oven.

"You seem like you know what you're doing," Gracie comments from behind me.

I laugh as I plate up the mashed potatoes and asparagus, replaying Brooks' instructions in my head. "Not really. I had a friend of mine help me out, and I'm trying real hard right now not to screw it up." I grab the steaks and add them to the plates, then get to work on the most crucial part: the sauce. Gracie moves to my side so she can watch up close. I feign confidence as I add shallots to the pan, pour in the red wine, then add butter. Once ready, I pour the sauce over the steaks.

"This looks great, Weston," Gracie says, licking her lips.

It's always so jarring, hearing her say my name, and I have no idea why. It's like it's too personal. "Take a seat," I tell her.

Gracie and her wine move to the table. I follow, setting both plates on the cheap placemats I bought. It's too quiet in my apartment, so I turn on my speaker on the window ledge and connect my Spotify. Music warms the atmosphere. I sit down to join Gracie.

"I'm sorry there aren't any candles," I say, and she laughs.

"Everything is fine as it is," she reassures me, then takes the first bite of her steak. She relaxes back in her chair and closes her eyes as she chews, almost like it's heavenly. "That is . . . so good. See?" Her eyelids flutter back open. "You *can* do this kind of stuff."

Thank God the meal gets her approval. I test it for myself, and I must admit: I am a pretty good cook, after all. I owe Brooks a beer for this recipe.

"I know *how* to be romantic," I muse, thoughtfully drinking my wine. "You cook dinners like this. You surprise her with flowers. You walk her to her door. You make plans ahead of time and just tell her what time to be ready for."

Gracie watches me intently as I talk. Maybe my self-reflection is interesting. "But you didn't do any of those things for Charlotte?"

I give her a minute shake of my head. "I forgot the romance shouldn't stop once I get the girl. Once we got together, once she was mine . . . I didn't realize I had to keep putting in any effort." I screw my face up at my plate, losing my focus as the self-loathing hits me in waves. Analyzing my fuckups out loud only makes them seem so much worse. I got things so wrong. Easy, simple, obvious things. And I don't know what that says about me as a person, to be someone who struggles to do the easy things in life, like giving the woman you love the bare minimum.

"It's not all about the romantic gestures, you know," Gracie says softly, delicately, because clearly she's afraid of hurting my feelings. "We love those things, of course, but that's not what we want the most. We want someone who senses when we're upset and immediately takes us into their arms and checks in on us. Someone who fills us with reassurance when we're doubting our own ambitions. Someone who supports and encourages our goals. Someone who's always on our side, even when they think we're wrong. It's about feeling safe, because you know that no matter what, they won't ever let anything bad happen." She takes her lower lip between her teeth and sucks in a breath, fighting back welling tears. She's not talking about "someone"; she's talking about Luca and all of the things he once did for her. "So, flowers may be nice," she says with a closed smile, "but I'll take a good old bear hug any day of the week instead."

I think of the hug we shared the first night we met. She was upset then, drunk and emotional, and I felt the exact same way she did. That's how I knew she needed a hug in that moment, because *I* needed one.

I set down my silverware against my plate and stand from my chair. I reach for Gracie's hand and tug her to her feet. With great confusion and some degree of resistance, she stands.

"What are you doing?"

I recall her saying those exact words when I hugged her the first time, too.

"*Someone who senses when you're upset and takes you into their arms.*" I repeat her own words back to her, and then tuck her perfectly against my chest. My arms are wrapped securely around her shoulders, my hand on the back of her head, holding her close. It's the first time I've touched her since we slept together, and only now do I realize how much I've been craving the feel of her again. "You're upset thinking about Luca, so I'm giving you a hug. That's what I'm doing."

Gracie relaxes against my body. She snuggles in closer, her face pressed into my shirt. "I'm always upset about Luca," she mumbles. She folds her arms around my back and holds me just as tight while the music continues to play quietly around us. As she wiggles out of my embrace, she looks at me from beneath those long eyelashes and says, "You give really nice hugs, Weston."

I don't often get compliments, but that becomes my favorite.

"I'll grab more wine," I say, excusing myself to take the open bottle from the kitchen. I return and top up both our glasses, then sit down to finish our meal. I forget that when I first opened the door, I wanted to see Charlotte. Now I feel more than okay with having Gracie sit opposite me instead. "Does this feel weird to you? Eating dinner with someone that isn't Luca?"

Gracie swallows her last mouthful of mashed potatoes. "Surprisingly, no. I feel comfortable with you."

I smirk. The joke practically writes itself. "Maybe because we skipped ten steps ahead the other morning. You can't get more comfortable with someone than what we did together."

Gracie turns deadpan. "Thanks. I need more of this now." She grabs the bottle of wine and tops her glass to the brim, then glowers playfully at me as she precariously moves the glass to her lips.

I don't even fight my laugh. Once it settles into a smile, I tell her, "I'm glad you feel comfortable around me."

Gracie blushes a tiny, tiny bit.

"Let me wash up these dishes real quick," I say, taking her plate and stacking it on mine.

"I'll dry."

There's a certain politeness to this girl that is incredibly attractive. A sweet sort of honesty that's a characteristic I recognized in Charlotte, too. Maybe I'm just drawn to the women I feel inclined to protect, not because I believe they *need* looking after, but because I don't want them to ever lose their gentle nature.

I fill the sink with soapy water and Gracie stands by my side, armed with a dishtowel.

"When's your next shift tackling the bad guys of San Francisco?" she asks.

I glance at her out of the corner of my eye and laugh. "Thursday. I'm back on day shifts, so all clear by seven. Much better."

"The other cop who was with you when you answered the noise complaint against us . . . Is that your partner? He's kinda grumpy."

"Bill?" I dunk a pot into the sink, halfheartedly washing it. The other half of my attention is on Gracie. "He's my field training officer, so I've got another ten weeks of having him ride my ass before I get stationed permanently. I'd rather go through the academy again than sit in a squad car with Bill while he flies off the handle because I forgot a radio code."

Gracie dries off some silverware. "Was it fun? The *academy?*" She says the word with flair, like the police academy is something cool and magical.

"No."

"It wasn't?"

"I hated it," I admit, then pause for a second to debate just how honest to be with my answer. I could spin her some lies that make me sound much tougher than I am, but what's the point? She'll learn eventually that I fucking hate being a cop, and I haven't even finished my field training yet. "It was nine months of hell. The physical training was exhausting, and I refuse to do a single burpee ever again in my life. I got pepper sprayed in the eyes and thought I'd gone blind. I got tased and nearly broke my ankle when I fell. The role-playing was embarrassing. The firearm training was fun, though, and I'm a pro at administering first aid now. But I especially hated the active shooter response training."

"Why?"

I turn to Gracie, my lips pressed firmly together. "Why do you think?"

What I don't tell her is that I didn't just hate the active shooter response training because it's something every cop hopes they never encounter during their career, but because I realized that day that if I was ever faced with an active shooter, I wouldn't have the balls to run toward them. I wouldn't have the guts to enter a building. I wouldn't protect anyone but myself.

That was the moment I realized I'd made a mistake. I wasn't cut out to be a cop, and I didn't deserve to be wearing the uniform and badge. In hindsight, I should have quit the academy that day, but I thought of Dad and how proud he was of me for being the only kid of his to follow directly in his footsteps.

When I first told him I was applying for SFPD, he flew out of his armchair and hugged me so damn tight it almost hurt. He triple-checked my application on my behalf before I sent it. I sailed through the written exam, the physical test and the interview, and with every step forward my bond with Dad grew that little bit stronger. We shared something he didn't have with Keaton and Peyton, and that was invaluable to me. Ahead of the basic training academy, Dad spent hours preparing me. He talked me through all of the scenarios I'd have to role-play in front of the other recruits, had me perfect my report-writing, and brought me down to the shooting range every weekend. I was confident I'd always be one step ahead of the program with having a retired deputy helping me out. But the academy kicked my ass harder than I ever imagined.

I couldn't bring myself to disappoint my father. The humiliation of quitting, of visiting him in Bodega Bay and admitting that I couldn't do it, that I wasn't as strong a man as he is . . . I couldn't face the shame of it. So, like a fraud, I scraped by, graduated the academy, and was sworn in as an SFPD officer. Now the field training is even worse. With every call to action, I pray it won't be something that scares me to death.

Gracie stops drying the plate in her hands and tilts her head, her expression as solemn as mine. "Do you actually want to be a cop?"

"Will you think I'm pathetic if I say no?"

She shakes her head.

"Then no, I don't wanna be a cop." I sigh and turn back to the sink, draining the water and drying off my hands. I hate admitting it. I *want* to want to be a cop. I want to be fearless like my sister, intelligent like my brother, tough like my father, and caring like my mother. The four qualities a cop needs, and four qualities I lack. I'm like the runt of the family.

"I need another drink," I say, grabbing the second bottle of wine.

We sit down together on my couch, but the TV remains off. Our drinks are full once again and I've lost count of how many glasses we've both had. Maybe it's the wine that's made me so honest tonight.

I rest my arm over the back of the couch and relax into the cushions. "So? What about you?"

"What about me?" Gracie asks. She's on the other end of the couch with an awful lot of space between us.

"You told me you're taking a gap year," I say, recalling our conversation at Starbucks this morning. "What about after that? What's your degree?"

Gracie's gaze briefly dips to her lap. When she looks back up, there's a shy smile playing on her lips. "Child and adolescent development," she says. "Next year I'll go back to school to get my teaching credential."

"You want to be a teacher?" I mirror her smile, because I'm not the slightest bit surprised by her career choice. Sweet, sensitive, smart women like Gracie are made for nurturing roles like teaching, and as I look back across the couch at her, I can imagine it. Gracie's petite figure at the front of a classroom, stretching on her tiptoes to point at the screen, her coppery bangs falling across her eyes. "But what about your whole influencer thing?"

Gracie shrugs and angles a little more toward me. "Our content is totally kid-friendly. Luca and I always made sure of that, and we agreed that when the time came, we'd take down all of our accounts if it became an issue. As *you* would say, our 'real' jobs would become the priority."

I roll my eyes, then guess, "High school teaching?"

"Elementary," Gracie corrects, and grief stings me.

My smile tightens and I look away from her, subconsciously tracing a pattern on one of the couch cushions with my index finger. "My mom taught elementary too, but she also did kindergarten for a while."

"No way," Gracie says. The note of excitement in her voice only intensifies the ache in my chest. "Does she still teach or is she retired?"

I swallow the lump in my throat and the words are like sandpaper as I tell her, "My mom passed a few years ago."

"Oh, Weston," Gracie breathes, and she sets her wine down on the coffee table and scoots closer to me. Her hand finds its way to my knee. "I'm so sorry to hear that."

I force a laugh and shake away the single tear that forms. "Fuck, this wine is doing strange things to me. It's just been a while since I said that out loud, that's all."

Gracie presses her lips together in sympathy. "You don't need to justify yourself. Do you want to talk about her?"

I meet her eyes this time, so close to me now and soft-ened with care. I'm hyper-aware of her hand on my leg, and, beneath my jeans, goosebumps form. That's why I start talking – to keep my mind busy. "Well, she passed when I was eighteen. Breast cancer. She was diagnosed at such a late stage, we barely had any time with her at all before she was gone. It was tough. She worked at the same school her entire career, so there's a nice memorial for her there now. Every class she ever taught adored her. And as you can imagine, being a teacher also made her a great mom. She always understood us. Always knew the fine balance between offering guidance and sitting back to allow us to learn from our own mistakes. She was . . . great. Really fucking great."

Gracie smiles, and it eases the pressure in my chest. "She sounds lovely."

"She was. But obviously I didn't realize that until she was gone," I agree, my gaze absentmindedly drifting across my apartment. I grit my teeth as my focus blurs. "A bad habit of mine . . . Only realizing how special people are when it's already too late."

When Mom passed, my relationship with Charlotte was only months old. There'd been no roadblocks yet, only the good times, and suddenly I was in pieces. It would have been easier for her to walk away then, but she stayed. She stayed and put me back together. Our bond strengthened beyond measure, and not long after, I told her I loved her.

I blink, tearing my attention from the wall and back to Gracie's hand on my knee. The heat of her touch blazes its way up my thigh. The way I talk with Gracie reminds me of how I used to talk with Charlotte in the beginning. Honest and vulnerable, open and raw. I'm not the most talkative guy to begin with, but somehow I can talk to Gracie.

And the only other girl I ever felt this comfortable around, I fell in love with.

I clear my throat. Gently, I place my hand over Gracie's. Intertwine my fingers with hers. Feel the warmth of her skin. She glances up, her lips parted with surprise. She doesn't pull her hand out from beneath mine.

Just as I open my mouth to speak, something vibrates. Gracie jolts and her hand disappears as she reaches for her jacket next to her and pulls her buzzing phone from the pocket. She stares at the screen and her face pales like she's seen a ghost.

"It's Luca," she says. Her voice shakes with his name. Hesitantly, she presses the phone to her ear as she gets up and crosses to the kitchen. "Luca?"

I crane my neck to watch her, not bothering to disguise the fact I'm listening. My apartment is too small to allow for privacy. She paces nervously as she listens to Luca on the other end of the line.

"Okay. Okay. I'll be right there," she says. She ends the call and hastily cuts back over to the couch, grabbing her jacket while still tapping away at her phone screen. "I'm so sorry, Weston, but I have to go. Thank you for dinner."

I stand up with concern. "Is everything okay?"

"Luca's wasted and he's outside our apartment door, but he's lost his keys. I need to let him in. I've ordered an Uber." She runs a hand through her hair, flustered, as she pulls her jacket over her shoulders and heads for my door. I wasn't ready for her to leave yet.

"You know you don't have to run after him anymore," I remind her.

As Gracie reaches for the door, she casts a hard look back at me. "I love him, Weston. Wouldn't you drop everything to help Charlotte if she needed you?"

I don't answer, because she's right. If Charlotte called, I'd run out of here too. I can't judge her for doing the exact same thing I would. "Okay. You have my number now, so can you let me know when you get home safe?"

Gracie nods and slips through the door into the dim, yellow light of the hallway. By the time it occurs to me to walk her outside to wait for her Uber, she's already long gone. I rub my hand down my face with a groan, then grab the remaining wine from the kitchen and return to the couch. I drink straight from the bottle this time.

GRACIE

I lost count of how many glasses of wine I drank tonight, but I estimate a lot, given by how queasy I feel the entire ride back home. It's not far between Weston's apartment and mine. Ten minutes max, yet it feels like forever when I know Luca is waiting for me.

As I jump out of the Uber, I suck in a breath of fresh air and rush inside my building, take the elevator to the fourth floor, then break out into a pathetic sort of jog down the hall. My shoulders sink with relief and I slow to a walk when I lay my eyes on him.

Luca's sat on the floor outside our apartment, his back against the door and his knees pulled up to his chest. He lifts his head and grins. "I am so glad to see you, though I can't see much of anything right now. You're kinda blurry, Gracie."

I scoff and offer him my hand. He takes it, and I forget that only fifteen minutes prior, it was Weston's hand I felt instead. "Why are you so drunk? It's only Tuesday," I say, hauling him up from the floor.

"So? It's summer. Every night can be a party." Luca wiggles his eyebrows at me and that little smirk of his that I love so much sends my stomach somersaulting. His hair is ruffled, his shirt creased and only half tucked into his pants. "I took too many shots. Regretting that now."

"How did you get here?"

"I walked."

I eye him sideways with disapproval as I stick my keys in the lock. Such an idiot, walking home when he's drunk and alone. "*Why* did you come here? You're staying at your cousin's place."

"Force of habit," he answers with a sheepish grin. "Can I stay? I don't want to sleep on Paul's couch again tonight. He's still at the bar, anyway."

This is why he left me. To be wild and free, to get drunk on a random Tuesday night. *This* is what he chose over me, yet I still let him walk through the door.

I flick on some lights, toss my jacket onto the couch, kick off my sneakers. Luca wanders the apartment in fascination as though he's never seen it before, let alone *lived* here. He grabs a fistful of the curtains and then trails his fingers along the kitchen countertops. The last time he was here, I told him he was never coming back. I have the backbone of a worm.

Leaning back against the breakfast bar, I cross my arms and watch him scornfully. Maybe it's the wine that makes me brazen enough to ask, "So? Did you kiss anyone tonight?"

Luca turns his head. "What?"

"You want to be single. You want to be free to do whatever you want without consequences. So, I'm asking you: Did you kiss anyone tonight?" I glare at him as my stomach churns, and as much as I want to make him squirm, I also can't bear to hear the answer. The thought of Luca even *flirting* with another woman turns my blood cold.

But . . . I slept with Weston. So, I really don't have a leg to stand on right now. Luca would lose it if he knew. He was always the seething, jealous type, but it was rarely an issue. There was never anything to be jealous of. I only had eyes for him.

"Ignore me," I mumble, shaking my head. "It doesn't matter. I don't want to know."

In the silence of our apartment that was once so filled with laughter, Luca closes the distance between us. He moves in, bending to make us eye-level, and touches the ends of my hair. He twists the curl around his fingers and breathes a sigh, the scent of vodka unmistakable. "No one compares to you," he says.

My throat dries, and even my knees wobble. His words may be drunken thoughts, but I cling to them. I grab onto the slightest bit of hope that maybe he's realized the grass isn't greener on the other side of the fence, that he's made a mistake, that he wants to come home. And I should push him away for breaking my heart. I should shove him out of my way for putting me through the pain he has these past three weeks, but when I look into his blue-gray eyes and feel my heart swell with all the love I hold for him, the only thing I want to do is pull him closer and kiss him.

"You're just saying that because you're drunk," I manage to force out. I'm fighting for my life trying to keep my hands to myself when all I want is to sink back into his embrace and remember how it felt when we were together.

Luca smiles and presses his forehead to mine, his hand wrapped into my hair. "No, Gracie. I mean it. *No one* compares."

"You can't . . ." The words get stuck. His mouth is almost brushing mine.

He gazes so intently into my eyes, it's like he's staring into my soul. "I miss you," he whispers, and I squeeze my eyes shut as he presses his lips delicately to mine. He pulls back for a split second, then kisses me again. "I miss you so much."

And just like that, Luca is mine again. I part my lips and deepen the kiss as I cup my hands around his jaw. Our movements are always so perfectly in sync with one another after so many years together. Maybe we're both just predictable at this point, but it's seamless. Both his hands are in my hair and he braces me harder against the wall, pinning his body to mine. I worried I'd never feel his touch again, but he still wants me. My heartbeat rockets with overwhelming relief.

The tender kisses turn fierce and passionate as Luca bites my lower lip, my neck, my earlobe. His hand drops from my hair and travels down the curves of my body before disappearing under my dress. He skims his fingertips up the soft skin of my thigh, so light and teasing it sets my body on fire, and then he slides his hand into my panties.

Luca takes my chin in his free hand, angling my face toward his and forcing me to meet his eyes as he pleasures me. "You missed me too, didn't you?"

"Mm-hmm," I breathe, burying my face into the crook of his neck and holding on tightly as my legs weaken. All I can do is collapse into him. I forgot just how good his fingers feel.

Luca laughs against my ear. "Stand up, Gracie, and tell me just how much you missed me."

I try to regain some strength in my legs to stabilize myself. Luca knows exactly where and how to touch me, with the right amount of pressure and just the right speed. An art he's perfected.

Drawing my head back, I lock my eyes on his and slide my hand over the nape of his neck, guiding his lips back to mine. "I've missed everything about you," I whisper. As I kiss him, I moan softly into his mouth.

Luca slips his hands beneath my thighs and lifts me off my feet. His slim figure is deceiving – he was on the wrestling team all through high school, and his strength catches even me off-guard sometimes. He carries me across the apartment as I kiss him wildly, desperately, and then lowers me onto the couch. I reach out and flatten my palm over the bulge in his jeans, feeling how hard he is. I undo the button and hook my index finger over the waistband of his boxers.

"I want you so bad," I murmur.

Luca grasps my wrist to restrain my hand. He brings his face near and, with his opposite hand, tucks my hair behind my ear. His thumb brushes softly against my cheek. "Then what do you say?"

God, I miss how dominant he is in bed. I'd let Luca do anything, I'm that in love with him. I gaze sweetly into his eyes and plead, "Please, Luca."

I don't know how he does it so swiftly, but suddenly I'm flipped over on the couch, flat on my stomach. We don't even undress. Luca frees himself, his jeans around his ankles, and hikes my dress up around my waist. As he slides off my panties, he leans over me and bites my ear, his breath hot and sensual. I bury my face into a pillow and clench my fists as Luca enters me from behind. I don't know who groans the loudest. All I know is that I love our bodies being entwined as one, because I love this man more than anything else in my life.

"You feel so fucking good," Luca hisses as he fucks me slow and hard.

He presses both hands into the small of my back, keeping me pinned down. I can't keep my mouth shut. The pillow muffles my moans of pleasure as I bite into the fabric. As Luca changes his rhythm, he grabs a fistful of my hair and pulls hard, lifting my face from the pillow and curving my spine, allowing him even deeper inside of me. It hurts in all the right ways.

"I've missed you so much, baby," he whispers into my ear as he releases my hair and I sink forward again into the cushions. He smacks my ass once, twice, three times. "Missed you so much I can't even last." He leans down against me, his chest pressed to my back, his lips against my temple, and his entire body tenses as he finishes inside of me with a low, drawn-out groan. The sound of Luca getting off will always be my favorite sound in the world.

He exhales heavily and climbs off me. I crane my neck to look back at him, waiting for more, but feel my body deflate as I watch him pull up his jeans. We're *never* done until both of us have gotten off, because Luca has never been a selfish lover – until this exact moment. He wipes a hand over his brow and crosses to the kitchen to fetch himself a glass of water. He's just drunk and caught up in the moment. What's really important, I remind myself, is that he's here. He still wants me, still loves me. Everything is going to be okay. *We* are going to be okay.

"I can stay, right?" Luca asks as he approaches with a glass of water for me too. Before I take it from him, I adjust my dress and panties, sitting upright.

"Of course you can stay," I say with a breath of relief.

He wants to move back in. He knows he's made the biggest mistake of his life, and maybe it took too many vodka sodas for him to realize that, but I don't care *how* he figured it out. All I care about is that he did. I may have told him that if he walked away, I would never let him come back, but I can't stand by that threat. He broke my heart and stomped all over the pieces, but he's the only one who can heal me again.

Luca sits down on the couch next to me. He runs his fingers through his ruffled hair and sips his water, blinking hazily. "God, the room is spinning," he mumbles, then casts me a sideways glance. His eyes are bloodshot, glazed. "Where were you when I called? You taste like wine."

"With the girls," I answer. Zero hesitation. There is no *way* I can admit now that another man was cooking me a steak dinner. It may be perfectly innocent, but Luca won't see it that way. My friendship with Weston has to end now. "C'mon. Let me get you to bed."

I take a swig of the water Luca gave me, then stand from the couch and pull him to his feet. He wraps an arm around my shoulders and plants kisses on my cheek as we head into our bedroom, and I'm overcome with relief that I won't have to sleep on my own again. No more crying myself to sleep. No more reaching out for Luca in the middle of the night and feeling my heart drop when the space next to me is empty. He's right back where he belongs.

"I've missed our bed," Luca says, then face-plants onto the mattress with a happy sigh.

I pull off his jeans, wrangle his shirt over his head, and then tuck him under the comforter. His eyes are closed already. I head into our en-suite bathroom to clean up, and by the time I return, he's snoring softly. A smile spreads across my face as I crawl into the bed next to him. His skin radiates heat and I snuggle into his back, finally feeling okay again for the first time in three weeks.

I only wake because I sense movement. A sliver of sunlight creeps into the room through a gap in the blinds and I squint as my sensitive eyes adjust. Luca stands at the foot of the bed, buttoning up his shirt from last night. It wasn't a dream. He really did come home.

Stretching out my arms, I yawn and pat the empty, warm space next to me. "Come back to bed."

"No. I should get going," Luca says, clearing his throat. His voice is hoarse, dehydrated from the alcohol. He tucks his shirt into his jeans and smooths out his hair.

"What?"

"I should get going," he says again, never meeting my eyes.

And maybe I'm naïve, maybe I'm straight-up blinded, but I reply, "To get your stuff?" Because, in my head, Luca is moving back in. He's only leaving to get all his clothes from his cousin's place. He'll be back in an hour or two, and we'll cook up some brunch together.

Luca scratches the palm of his hand. "No, Gracie."

My stomach drops and I bolt upright. "But last night . . . You said you missed me . . ."

"I do miss you," he says, forcing himself to meet my eyes. The guilt twisting his features tells me everything I need to know. "But last night doesn't change anything. We're still done."

I stare at him, my mouth agape. My heart shatters all over again. I didn't know it was possible for it to break even more. I drop my head into my hands and suck in a deep breath, shaking my head in disbelief. He still doesn't want to be with me. Through my fingers, I mumble, "Then why did you even bother to come here last night?"

"I'm sorry," says Luca. "You know how horny I get when I drink."

I lift my head to look at him. *Rage*. That's all I feel now. Burning, all-consuming rage. "You're a fucking pig, Luca," I spit, throwing back the comforter and jumping out of bed. I jab a finger toward him, seething so intensely I'm trembling. "Get out of *my* apartment."

"Gracie—"

I grab a pillow from the bed and fling it at him. Then a second one. "Get *out!*"

"Okay, okay!" Luca holds up his hands in surrender and heaves a sigh of defeat. As he walks backward out of the room, I stalk him, my finger still pointed. How dare he? I can't even *look* at him. "I'm sorry," he says again once he reaches the door.

"No. You're not. Leave," I order, and I step around him to open the door. Anything to make it easier for him to get the hell out of my face. "I said *leave.*"

Luca lowers his head in shame and steps out into the hall. I promptly slam the door shut behind him, then pace the apartment with my hands on my waist as I breathe deeply to fight off the sudden nausea.

I am the biggest idiot. Luca used me last night, and I love him so much I didn't even see it. It meant everything to me, yet nothing to him. How could he hurt me *again?*

My focus lands on the withering, dying lilies in the vase in the kitchen. My mom had them delivered the day after Luca ended things, with a sweet note attached, promising me that things would be okay. I haven't seen her in a while. And my sister clearly misses me, because she's forever tagging me in hilarious TikTok videos. I should visit. I could use a hug from my mother right about now, but I also can't drive. Luca always drove me whenever I went home to Santa Cruz.

God, I need my license more than ever.

I text my mom and ask if it's okay that I drop by today, and of course, it's more than okay. It would never *not* be. I'm always welcome, no invite necessary. She promises to have burritos ready for lunch. My favorite.

Then I scroll to Weston's number that he added to my contacts yesterday at Starbucks, and I dial it before I can wimp out. It rings only twice before he answers.

"Thanks for letting me know you got home safe last night," he says, his tone laced with sarcasm.

I wince, because I forgot all about him as soon as I laid eyes on Luca. "Oh, shoot. Sorry. I forgot."

Weston sighs softly across the line, like he forgives me. "Was everything okay with Luca?"

"No. It was bad," is all I tell him. I *can't* tell him the rest. I'm so humiliated by how easily fooled I am, so I quickly get to the real reason I called. "I know you aren't back to work until tomorrow, but do you already have plans today?"

"I was probably going to hit the gym then grab a beer with the guys tonight. Why?"

"Um. How would you feel about driving me to Santa Cruz instead?" I ask, then hold my breath and wait. It's almost rude of me to make such a request. Weston owes me no favors.

"What's in Santa Cruz?"

"My mom. I really need a hug from her," I say, then bite down hard on my lower lip as I remember the conversation I had with Weston last night. His mom isn't here anymore, but I don't mean to be insensitive. I quickly lighten my tone and add, "There'll be some burritos in it for you. And I'll pay for your gas."

"Why can't you drive yourself there?"

I catch myself blushing and I'm relieved he isn't here to witness it. How many twenty-two-year-olds can't drive? Not many, I bet. "I never got my permit. Luca always drove me anywhere I needed to go that the BART can't reach. But I'm going to take my test soon, I swear."

Weston scoffs. "I'll drive you to Santa Cruz," he says, "but there's one condition."

"Which is?"

"When we get back, I'm taking you to the DMV office to get your damn permit."

My laugh eases the pain in my chest. Only a little, but enough.

WESTON

Cameron calls me a slacker for blowing off the gym with him. Adam calls me a boring lame-ass fucker for being undecided on whether or not to hit the bar with him tonight. When they both ask what I'm up to instead, I lie. I tell them I'm visiting my brother at the Beale Air Force Base, two hours north. But really I'm in the parking garage of Gracie's building.

I drum my fingers anxiously against my steering wheel after shooting her a text to let her know I'm here. It's over an hour's drive to Santa Cruz, and although I feel comfortable around Gracie, we haven't been stuck in a car together yet. When we get to Santa Cruz, I have no idea what to expect. Do I drop her off and leave? Does she want me to meet her parents?

Movement catches my eye. Gracie crosses the garage toward me and gives a little wave, her smile sheepish. I grin back and quit my nervous fiddling. She's so fucking cute and she really doesn't mean to be. Her hair is pulled back into a ponytail, her bangs framing her face, and huge hoop earrings dangle from her ears. They swing as she walks.

As she opens the car door, I try to muster up a witty greeting, but ultimately go with a pathetic, "Hi."

"You cleaned your car!" Gracie says cheerfully as she settles into my passenger seat. A floral, fruity scent follows her into the vehicle. She gestures to the floor space and the empty cupholders, then beams at me. "Did you do that for me?"

"I didn't realize Charlotte probably hated being driven around in this trash pile until you got in here the other week and pointed out the mess," I admit. "So, I made the effort to clear it out for you."

"See? You're starting to get it!"

"I'm trying. So, Santa Cruz?"

"Please," she says.

I pull out of the parking garage. Gracie's apartment building is perfectly located for access to the freeway, so I floor it up the entrance ramp and head south. The sun blazes through clear blue skies for once. Perfect road trip weather. I nudge up the AC and start my music, keeping the volume low. I glance sideways at Gracie. She stares silently down at the camera she twists around in her hands.

"Why do you have that?"

Gracie sighs, but doesn't lift her head to look at me. "I thought I could vlog today. I've already filmed a couple of things here and there. I'm just pretending Luca is out of town, which isn't *too* unusual. We did sometimes make our own vlogs without the other." She sticks the camera into the storage compartment of the door. "Obviously I won't film *you*."

"Obviously."

She looks at me now and succumbs to my smirk. Her laughter is like a breath of air. Light, fragile, barely noticeable. But it's there. "You know, I'm really going to miss all of this when we eventually shut down all our accounts. The filming. The editing. Sharing my life."

"Can't you start from scratch? A new theme? Gracie Taylor and Gracie Taylor *only*."

Gracie bites her lip and quietly says, "But I'm boring without Luca."

"I don't think you're boring," I say. It probably doesn't mean much coming from me, but it's the truth. This girl has me driving to Santa Cruz on a second's notice, after all. She's anything but boring.

My focus is on the road ahead as I switch lanes, but I feel Gracie's eyes fixed on me. "Thank you, Weston," she says with weight, and I become painfully aware of my pulse.

I don't like the way my body tenses every time she says my name. I don't like the way it makes me feel, because it makes me feel *something*.

"So last night with Luca . . ." I say, clearing my throat. "Are you okay?"

Gracie sits up a little, her demeanor shifting to the defensive. "What do you mean?"

"You said things were bad," I remind her, recalling our fleeting phone conversation earlier this morning. I raise an eyebrow at her reaction and shoot her a look full of concern. "How bad? Because your face right now tells me that it was *really* bad."

Gracie shakes her head, relaxing her tight expression. "We had an argument. I kicked him out."

"Probably not a great idea to let your wasted ex back into your apartment in the first place."

"I realized that a little too late," she mumbles, right before she goes awfully quiet. She stares down at her sneakers, her hands together in her lap, and I know there's more she isn't telling me. She's lost inside of her own head.

The silence stretches and stretches as I drive. I glance repeatedly between the road and Gracie. I watch the downturn of her mouth, her soft blinks, the way she twists her fingers together. I glance over at her one time too many before I finally build the courage to think, *Fuck it.*

I reach over the center console and take one of her hands in mine. Her skin is warm and, softly, she squeezes my hand back. We leave them fused together in her lap, and I don't say anything at all. Neither does she. We don't need to.

We head south out of San Francisco and it's a route I'm all too familiar with. I took this freeway all the time to visit Charlotte in San Jose, but that's not where I'm headed today. It's not where I'll be heading ever again, but in this exact moment, I feel okay with that. I wasn't ready for Charlotte yet, and I don't think that makes me a bad person. I still have so much time to figure things out.

Gracie angles further toward me. With her free hand, she touches my arm, tracing the linework of my tattoos as I drive. Her touch is so feathery and comforting, the hairs on my arm stand upright. She starts at the back of my hand, tracing every detail of the wolf I have tattooed there, then works her way slowly up the rest of my arm. She doesn't miss a single spot.

And when I can't take it anymore, I throw her a teasing smile and give her a sidelong look. "Yes, Gracie?"

"Sorry," she says, blushing. Her hand pauses just above my elbow. "I never really looked at your tattoos properly before. What are these for?"

I glance down. She strokes the pair of dog tags I have inked there, one filled with the US flag, the other reading Peyton's date of birth.

"My sister. She's in the army," I say.

Gracie's fingers slide over my skin. "And the Air Force wings?"

"My brother."

"This one is obvious, except it's not." She taps the SFPD police badge that's on the back of my bicep, gesturing to the date of birth incorporated into the tattoo that is clearly too long ago to be mine.

"For my dad. He was a deputy chief before he retired."

Gracie says, "Ahh." Maybe it makes sense to her now, why I chose the career I did. Her hand travels further up my bicep, stopping on the tattoo that disappears beneath the sleeve of my T-shirt. She pulls my sleeve back to see the full picture. It's a pair of hands cupped together, holding flowers. "And this?"

I swallow hard. "My mom."

Gracie meets my gaze, intense and focused. She says, "Because teachers are nurturing." It's not a question. She knows exactly what that tattoo represents, and my smile tells her she's right. "Your theme is family."

"Yes," I say, and I feel a little fuzzy inside.

She runs her hand back down my arm, over all of the other tattoos that relate to my grandparents, my aunts and uncles, my cousins, my niece. "I love that. What's this one for, though?" She's down to the back of my hand again, to the wolf.

I shrug as I fight my grin. "Oh, that one? I only got that because it looks sick."

Gracie laughs now and relaxes back into her seat. Our hands are still tightly locked, and they remain like that all the way to Santa Cruz. She even catches my eye every once in a while, and my pulse quickens each and every time.

GRACIE

Weston isn't massively familiar with Santa Cruz, so I guide him down the freeway to the correct exit and along the streets I rode my bike down when I was a kid. My childhood home is still the same house my mother lives in now, tucked down a quiet residential street in the Eastside. As much as I'll always consider Santa Cruz home, I'll never move back. I'm a San Francisco gal at heart.

"This one," I say, pointing through the windshield to the house I grew up in. Weston pulls into the drive behind my sister's turquoise Mini Cooper. It puts me to shame that my baby sister has her license before I do.

"Are you originally from here?" Weston asks, killing his engine.

"Yep. Grew up on this street," I tell him, then step out of the car into the warm sunshine and stretch out my legs.

My house hasn't changed at all since I was a child, though I notice the elderly couple who've always lived next door have started renovations since the last time I visited. Cars line the road, parked beneath the shade of towering trees, and a woman walks past with her Chihuahua. It's always been a quiet, laid-back street. Safe.

"So is Luca," I add as Weston joins me outside his car. "We went to high school together."

Weston stuffs his hands into the front pockets of his jeans and doesn't follow me up the drive to the porch. When I glance back at him, he asks, "Are you sure you want me to be here? I can go check out the beach or something. Pick you up again in a few hours when you're ready?"

I tilt my head to the side. "Weston, I'd like you to come inside with me," I tell him with sincerity. "I want to introduce you to my mom. She loves when I bring friends to visit. But if *you* don't feel comfortable . . ."

He walks over to the porch and scoops up this morning's newspaper from the step, furrowing his eyebrows playfully at me. "Let's see if these burritos are really as mind-blowing as you've hyped them up to be."

"They are," I quip, and push open the front door. "Mom?"

The house smells of beef and spices, and Weston sniffs appreciatively. I cross the living room toward the kitchen in search of my mother, who I'm bound to find huddled over the stove, but the thundering of footsteps down the stairs stops me in my tracks.

"Finally!" Verity says. She leaps from the stairs straight into my arms, knocking me off-balance. She may be four years younger than me, but strangers always mistake her as the older sister. She's a whole five inches taller than me. It's not fair.

"Hey, hey. Come here," I say, readjusting us both so that I can hug her properly. I press my face into her shoulder and she squeezes me way too hard. It's not our usual hug. It's longer, tighter, full of love. It's the first time I've seen her since the breakup.

Verity, without unfolding her arms from around me, leans back to eyeball Weston behind me. "Umm. Hi."

"This is a friend of mine. His name's Weston," I say, and Weston smiles politely. "And this is my sister, Verity."

Verity shoots me a funny, unconvinced look. We're both naturally blond, but ever since I started adding copper highlights a few years ago, we aren't that alike anymore. "Since when do you have guy friends?"

"Since Luca isn't around to get jealous anymore," I reply with an edge to my voice. I unwrap myself from Verity and ignore Weston's gaze trained intently on me.

"Well. Hi, Weston," Verity says. "I'm a hugger. Sorry."

She pulls Weston into a hug, and he awkwardly embraces her while I mouth an apology.

"Gracie!" I hear my mom sing. She appears from the kitchen, arms extended and her smile so wide it stretches all the way to her eyes. The sight of her immediately sends me bubbling into tears.

"Mom," I say, my voice cracking. I meet her halfway and collapse into the safety of her arms, hugging her the way I used to when I was a kid and the world seemed so scary. It doesn't matter how bad things get when your mother is there to reassure you that everything will be just fine.

"Oh, darling. It's okay. It's okay," she whispers soothingly, stroking my hair and holding me protectively. Verity and I will always be her little girls, no matter how old we are. When we're hurt, she's hurt. "You're going to come out of this stronger than you were before."

It's hard for Mom too. Luca was like a son to her, part of the family. We often excitedly discussed my wedding plans. We checked out potential venues, browsed for my dream dress, even wrote drafts of the guest list. It was only a matter of waiting for Luca to propose.

But he didn't, and now I have to rebuild my entire life.

"Look, Mom. Gracie brought a new *friend*," Verity remarks.

Mom and I separate. I wipe away a tear and fire Verity a disapproving glare for her sarcasm.

"Mom, this is Weston. And we *are* just friends," I say.

Mom's eyebrows shoot up in surprise. The only friends I ever bring down here are Elena and Maddie.

Weston is obviously a very new addition to my life, and it probably doesn't help that he's a *guy*. It's not great timing, him walking into my life immediately after my breakup with Luca. Admittedly, I can see why Verity is skeptical.

"Well, hi, Weston. I'm Erica," Mom says, a little uncertainly. She offers her hand for Weston to shake, and he does so firmly while handing her the newspaper from the porch. "I hope you're hungry, because it's burritos for lunch."

"Gracie's been raving about your burritos the entire drive," he says, and Mom grins proudly. She's a great cook, and if anyone ever said otherwise, her feelings would absolutely be hurt.

Samuel pokes his head around the kitchen doorframe, a dishtowel over his shoulder. Before he can get a word out, Weston steps forward to shake his hand. "And you must be Gracie's father. Nice to meet you."

Verity snickers, and I try not to join in with her because poor Weston is trying his best to be polite in a house full of strangers and I can't blame him for a simple mistake. "Weston, this is Samuel. My mom's husband," I tell him, gently placing my hand on his bicep. "*Not* my dad."

"Oh. I'm sorry," Weston apologizes, and his cheeks flare red.

"All good," Samuel says. He bypasses Weston to give me a comforting squeeze.

I realize it's difficult for anyone to know what to say about Luca. Any reassurances aren't helpful. It's the kind of pain you just have to suck up and deal will. Eventually, it'll just become part of me. And, for now, the hugs are nice.

"Come through, guys, come through!" Mom says excitedly, steering us all into the kitchen. The table is only set for four, and as she pulls out another placemat from a drawer, I realize in hindsight I should have probably forewarned her that I was bringing Weston. But Mom always cooks enough to feed everyone seconds, so there's plenty of food to go around. "Take a seat!"

"Here," I tell Weston, pointing him to the spare seat next to mine. I may have moved out four years ago, but I still have my reserved seat at the table. Weston sits down next to me and arches a brow when he spots me pulling out my camera. "I'm filming today, by the way," I announce to the table.

And, usually, this isn't a big deal. My mom and Verity are used to appearing in my videos every now and again. Samuel is a bit shyer, so tends to dip out of the frame. It's perfectly normal for me to have a camera in my hand at all times. Today, however, I am met with perplexed looks. They're wondering how on earth I can film content without Luca when our entire brand is about *us* as a couple.

"That video you uploaded yesterday is so obviously fake," Verity says, clicking her tongue in disapproval.

"And yet you're still filming new stuff? Without Luca? Your viewers aren't stupid, Gracie. They're going to put two and two together."

I flippantly wave her away and hold up my camera, the lens facing me. She's right, of course, but I plough on with forced naïveté regardless. "It's been a while since you guys last saw Verity, but here she is!" I tell the lens. I lean toward Verity, positioning her in the frame with me. She waves, then pulls away again because it's painfully clear she doesn't want to partake in my false narrative. "Mom's made burritos and Luca *loves* my mom's cooking, but I'll just have to eat double on his behalf. Seriously guysss, just *look* at this." I flip the camera around to show off Mom's homemade guacamole as she sets the dish down on the table.

A little puff of laughter escapes from Weston. I instantly quit recording and glower at him. His mouth is pressed tightly together, fighting back his amusement.

"*Weston!* Now I have to do that again!"

Verity narrows her eyes in scrutiny, like she hasn't quite figured Weston out yet. She's not buying this whole friends thing, but it's the truth. We *are* friends. "You've never seen her vlog before, have you?"

"First time," Weston admits, then pouts his lips at me and mouths, "*Sorry.*"

"You'll get used to it," Samuel says, and he helps Mom carry over the remaining food. Warm tortillas, perfectly cooked minced beef, rice and beans, salsa, cheese, veggies . . . My mouth waters as I film a clip of all of the food.

Mom passes out cans of soda around the table and sits down to join us all.

"So, you haven't been friends for that long," Verity presses, her chin resting in her palm. I fix her with a death stare as I sprinkle jalapeños into the burrito I'm assembling. "How do you know each other?"

"Yes, Gracie," Mom says with a suggestive nod toward Weston. "How *do* you know each other?"

"My friends took me out for my birthday, and Weston got into a fist fight inside our booth and ruined the entire night. We all got kicked out," I say truthfully. I look at him and smirk. "Deny that. I dare you."

Samuel laughs, whereas Mom looks thoroughly alarmed.

Weston scratches at his temple with a sheepish grin. "Well, that *is* true . . ." he says. "But I'm a decent guy, I swear. That was a one-off. I'm normally a great follower of the rules . . . I'm a cop. I answered a noise complaint made against Gracie and her friends, actually." He flashes me a teasing wink. Payback.

"Gracie!" Mom exclaims.

"Too much wine," I murmur, then elbow Weston in the ribs.

He laughs and says, "We let them off with a warning."

As we all put together our burritos and tuck in, Samuel picks Weston's brains about life working the beat, Mom asks me careful, safe questions that skirt around the subject of Luca, and Verity relentlessly fires me skeptical glances. Having Weston sit with us for dinner isn't as awkward as it could have been. He fits right in.

As always, Verity and I take care of the clean-up afterward. I wash the dishes, she dries them. She purses her lips at me as I rinse off a plate.

"What?"

She glances back at the dining table where Mom and Samuel chat with Weston, then huddles in closer to me. Her expression is strangely solemn as she quietly asks, "Did Luca end things because you met someone else? You can tell me the truth, Gracie."

I recoil from her in shock. How can she make such an accusation? Quite frankly, I'm hurt Verity can even *consider* the idea of me stepping out on Luca. I loved him with every fiber of my being. I am absolutely broken without him. "Of course not, Ver. How can you even ask me that?"

Verity's gaze moves slowly to Weston, and she says, "You look at him the way you always looked at Luca. It's something in your eyes. Like, they just look *soft*. I don't know. I thought maybe . . ."

"You thought wrong," I cut in, angrily scrubbing a bowl. I slam it down on the drying rack and turn back to her. "You really think if Luca had left me because I'd met someone else that I'd then bring that man *home* with me to parade in front of Mom? We're friends. His girlfriend left him too, so we're helping each other through a tough time. That's *it*."

Verity holds up the dishtowel in apology. "Okay! I didn't think he was your type, anyway."

I scoff and finish washing the remaining dishes. Weston would never have been my type before, but the tattoos have grown on me. Even the stubble he sports on his days off is kind of attractive. And I was always a blonds-only kind of girl, but now I'm not so sure.

I glance over my shoulder, and Weston's eyes find mine.

He's not a bad guy. I don't even think he's selfish, honestly. It's clear he's not quite sure what he wants out of life yet, and losing Charlotte is the nudge he probably needed to think hard and long about what he does want. I don't think it's a case of getting his priorities straight – he needs to figure out what his priorities even *are*. Right now, he doesn't seem to have any.

"You're doing it *again*," Verity hisses, and whips the dishtowel against my leg.

I shove her away and say, "You're so annoying," even though I love her to death. Verity and I have always been close as sisters. Best friends more than anything. I'll miss her when she heads off to college in September.

"Gracie," says Mom, waving me back over to the dining table. "Weston tells me you've abandoned your travel plans! Why? Don't you have your flights booked?"

I sigh and press my hands to the back of her chair. "We hadn't booked anything yet. And there's no *way* I'm going on my own. Maddie can't afford to travel for six months, and Elena can't think of anything worse than eating cuisine that isn't McDonald's. And surely you wouldn't want me traveling alone?"

"Lots of people travel alone," Mom says, and Weston nods as though to say, "I told you so."

"I don't really know *what* I'm supposed to do now," I mumble, and Mom reaches back over her shoulder to squeeze my hand comfortingly. I kiss the crown of her head. "Don't people always say that after a breakup you need to focus on yourself? Self-care and self-improvement and all that. Weston's taking me to the DMV later. I'm going to get my permit and I'm going to buy a car. That's a good start, right?"

Maybe *I* need to set some priorities for myself, too. This is going to be one long year if I don't find a productive way to fill my time. If only the application deadline hadn't already passed, I'd scrap the gap year entirely and start my teaching credential program this fall instead. But it's too late for that now. So, I'll learn how to drive, I'll become more consistent with the gym, I'll teach myself new recipes, I'll maybe switch out the copper highlights in my hair for something new. That's all I *can* do. Learn how to be happy and content alone.

Mom and Samuel agree that *finally* getting my driver's license is a sensible first step, and after several minutes of them throwing more ideas at me, I excuse myself and Weston from the kitchen. My head feels like it weighs a thousand tons, and I just need a moment of silence. Weston follows me upstairs to my childhood bedroom. It's always kept just the way I left it four years ago. My pictures hang on the walls, the bedspread remains unchanged, there's even some old sweaters still hanging in the closet. It may be used as the spare room for Verity's friends when they stay over, but it's all still mine.

I fall back onto the bed and spread my arms out wide with a hopeless sigh. "I miss being a kid," I say. "Life was never complicated back then, was it? No broken hearts."

Weston studies my room, and I prop myself up on my elbows to watch him as he narrows his eyes carefully at each of the framed photographs on my walls. They're collecting dust. He straightens the frame of a picture of Luca and me at our high school prom, his tie matching the blue of my dress.

"You haven't changed," Weston says.

"Great. Thanks," I reply with sarcasm, and he laughs.

"It's a good thing. Are you keeping these up?"

I frown as my eyes dart from photo to photo. They don't *all* include Luca. There are photos with my middle school best friends, photos with Mom and Verity, photos with my grandparents. Those photos are definitely staying up, but the Luca ones have *got* to go. "Wanna help me purge this room of all things Luca Hartmann?"

Weston grins a little too wide. "You really have to ask?"

I leap from the bed and tear the prom photo straight off the wall. I hand it to Weston, then grab another picture for myself – one of Luca looking goofy with a mouth full of food. We take the photographs from the frames, then move on to the next ones, gradually removing every memory of Luca from the wall of my childhood bedroom.

Once we've purged half of my old photos, I pull open the bottom drawer of the dresser. The only thing inside is an old jewelry box. It's exactly what I'm looking for. It doesn't contain jewelry, though, it contains memories. All of the little, insignificant things I held on to when I was a teenager and falling in love with Luca, because I knew one day they would mean something. The movie tickets for our first date, the tacky keyring Luca won out of a coin pusher at the arcade, the receipt for the first meal we went out for together that *wasn't* fast food. I knew they would be sentimental to me one day, because I always knew Luca was the one.

I sit on the edge of my bed as I rummage through the box and Weston sits silently by my side, not daring to point out how embarrassing it is that I kept all of this stuff. At the bottom of the box, I find a photograph face-down. I flip it over, expecting to see Luca, but my lips part in surprise.

It's an old, old, *old* photo of my father holding Verity and me as kids, one of us on either hip. I have no idea how that got in here. I got rid of every memory of my dad years ago when he left.

Weston edges in a little closer to check out the photo. "Your dad?" he guesses.

"More like my sperm donor," I correct, rolling my eyes bitterly. I enclose my fist around the photograph, crumpling it with disregard. Verity wouldn't want me to keep it, either. "Haven't spoken to my dad in . . . Hmm. Four years, I think. He's not a part of my life anymore."

"Why?"

"He chose not to be." I shrug as though I'm indifferent to it now, but God, it still hurts. It always will. "My mom left him, which is whatever. They weren't happy together, so it was kind of a relief when they finally called it quits. Dad was going to get his own place nearby and I was okay with the idea of maintaining separate relationships with both him and Mom, but then he just . . . left. Didn't even tell us where he moved to, and even now I still have no idea where he is. I think he just wanted a fresh start, and Verity and I were collateral damage."

I clench my jaw. It angers me, the pain Dad caused. I will never forgive him, and I will never ever, ever let him step one foot back into my life. There's no redemption for a man who doesn't put his children first.

Those first few months, I was lost in disbelief. It was impossible to contact him and I realize now it's probably because he changed his number. He didn't *want* to be found. So many nights I lay in this very room and cried myself to sleep, wondering why I wasn't enough. How could my dad raise us our entire lives and then throw us out of the picture so easily, like we were disposable? He used to tell us all the time how proud of us he was. Always reassured us when we turned to him with any worries. We may be adults now, but we still need our father. How can he just not care? Often, I wonder if he ever watches mine and Luca's videos to catch a glimpse into my life. Sometimes I *want* him to watch our videos so he can see that I'm doing just fine without him. Except it still haunts me sometimes, knowing my father is alive and well, but isn't around by choice. The hardest thing of all, though, is knowing I won't have a father to walk me down the aisle one day. There'll be no Father of the Bride speech at my wedding, but I guess that's another dream of mine that went up in flames?

"Gracie? Hey." Weston's hand brushes mine as he uncurls my fingers from around the scrunched photograph. He moves the photo aside and turns his body toward me, his forehead creased with concern. "It's his loss. Don't you dare cry over him."

"I'm not . . ." I sniff, shaking my head. There *are* tears welling in my eyes, but they aren't for my dad. I raise my chin to look at Weston, and his caring expression sets me off entirely. A sob escapes my throat. "Luca was there through all of it, and he promised me my father would be the first and only man to ever break my heart."

Pathetically, I wipe away my tears as they fall, and I scoff derisively. "Now look. He's a liar."

I grab the box of keepsakes and throw it across the room. The contents scatter across the floor and I double over, pressing my hands to my face to smother my pained cries. Weston immediately shifts closer and pulls me protectively into his chest. He's so used to my ugly sobs by now that I don't even make the effort to sound graceful as I smear damp tears into his shirt.

"I slept with him last night," I whisper, and I feel the weight lift from my chest as I admit it. It's a secret I've been holding back all day in fear of judgment. If I told Elena and Maddie, they wouldn't understand how I was so easily fooled, but they've never been in love. Weston has. "I thought he missed me. I thought he'd realized he'd made a mistake. I thought . . ."

"Shh," Weston says, his hand placed softly on the back of my neck. Part of me expects him to push me away a little, but he only holds me tighter. "It's okay, Gracie. You love him."

"I'm so *stupid*. I feel like the biggest idiot in the world," I groan, leaning my head against his shoulder. "I woke up so happy this morning only for Luca to break my heart all over again. Am I really this naïve to believe he could change his mind? And am I stupid for being willing to take him back if he did?"

I angle my face to meet Weston's eyes as he looks back down at me. The space between us is so tiny it's almost nonexistent. I wonder what he thinks of me now, so hopelessly in love with a man who clearly doesn't think I'm worth staying for. Luca's exactly like my father, leaving me behind to get more out of life. Why am I the one who always gets sacrificed, rather than having sacrifices made *for* me?

"Why am I never enough, Weston?"

Weston flinches as though my words have physically hurt him. His gaze softens as it dips to my mouth, then travels delicately back to my eyes. "You'll be everything to the right person." My head still resting on his shoulder, he softly skims his thumb beneath my lower lash line to catch another tear that falls. "I think," he murmurs, "you need to fall out of love with Luca and fall in love with Gracie instead."

I close my eyes, focusing on the sensation of his skin brushing my cheek. I snuggle in a little closer. There's something about Weston that makes me feel safe, and it's not because he's a police officer. My eyes ping back open and I say, "Do you have any idea how difficult that is?"

A smile pulls at the corner of his mouth. "Something tells me it's not that hard."

My heart skips a beat. How does he always know the right things to say? I'm starting to think he doesn't need me to show him how to treat a woman right. He treats me . . . perfectly. Somehow Weston might just be about the most important person in my life right now. He's the one who's caught most of my tears, after all. Maybe it was fate that he ruined my birthday celebrations. Maybe we were *meant* to pick up the pieces of each other.

Our eye contact intensifies and my breath catches in my throat, my body still. Weston moves his thumb down to my chin and tilts my face up, then carefully touches his lips to mine. The kiss is tender and cautious, like he's terrified I'm going to push him away. But I could never push Weston away.

I press my lips harder against his, an unmistakable signal that I want this too. I slide my fingers through his hair as the kiss builds with enthusiasm, growing deeper. His lips are so soft and gentle, yet fierce and passionate. I swing my body over onto his lap, bringing our chests close, and his warm hands slide over the soft skin of my waist beneath my sweatshirt. A nervous chill surges down my spine. I want his hands to travel further, to explore more.

"Just friends, huh?"

The sound of another voice startles both Weston and me. Our mouths break apart and we turn abruptly toward the door where Verity leans against the frame, arms folded and brows raised.

"Verity." I gulp, then realize Weston's hands are still on my waist. I shuffle off his lap and stand upright, tugging at the hem of my sweater. I don't even know what to say. This bond I have with Weston . . . I'm still trying to make sense of it myself. But figuring it out under my mother's roof is not the time nor the place.

Verity smirks and gives Weston a clipped nod. "You okay there?"

I exchange a glance with Weston. He's still sitting at the end of my bed, but he now has one leg crossed over the other and his hands are purposely interlocked over his lap. He grimaces and says, "Yup."

This normally wouldn't be mortifying. I've lost count of how many times Verity caught Luca and me up to no good when we were teenagers and I still lived here at home, but we always laughed it off. This, however . . . It feels like I've been caught red-handed doing something I absolutely shouldn't have. It's not even been a month yet since Luca left, and here I am, kissing another man on my childhood bed. It's not because I'm over Luca. I don't know if I'll *ever* get over Luca, but Weston . . . Why am I being pulled so strongly toward him?

"So?" Verity prompts, tapping her foot. "Are you going to tell me what's going on?"

"I don't know, Ver," I say, flustered. My cheeks feel hot and my heart pounds at a million miles an hour. "Genuinely. I don't know. We *are* friends . . ."

"With benefits," she finishes.

"No," Weston says.

Verity narrows her eyes and studies both of us one at a time. With a sigh, she holds up her hands and says, "Whatever. Not my business. Mom wants you back downstairs."

190

It's very clear Weston needs a couple minutes before we can make our way back downstairs to see my *mother*, so Verity heads off without us. We wait until we hear her footsteps fade, and then we both exhale loudly.

"She already thinks I cheated on Luca with you," I murmur. I gather up the contents of the old jewelry box from the floor and add it all to the small trash pile that's accumulated on the dresser. "And what she just saw? That probably doesn't make her believe otherwise."

Weston's eyes widen. "Why the hell would she think that?"

I only shrug, because I don't dare tell him exactly what Verity said, that whole thing about me apparently looking at Weston the same way I look at Luca. I'm not sure if I do or if I don't. What I do know for sure is that when I look at Weston, I feel at ease. I have a soft spot for him.

"I'll clean this up later," I say, nodding to the trash pile. "Are you ready to go back downstairs?"

Weston laughs and uncrosses his legs. "I think so."

"And thank you."

"For what?"

As he stands, I smile at him. It's sincere, meaningful. "For always saying the right things."

"It's something I'm working on," he says lightly, and we share a small laugh together as we make our way downstairs, praying that Verity quits with the skeptical looks.

WESTON

"Hey, you'd be slamming tequila too if you had your arm snaked down someone's toilet all afternoon," Adam mutters, pointing his shot glass at me before he drinks it. He's still in his work pants, his shirt greasy. It's perfectly normal for Adam to hit the bar straight from work. "And my right hand hasn't been the same since I hit that incredibly solid bone structure of yours."

Adam *is* hilarious, even though I hate to admit it. "Yeah, yeah," I say. "It's a shame I didn't leave any lasting damage. A permanently bruised eye might have looked quite badass next to that nose of yours."

Cameron chuckles as Adam flips me the middle finger. It's been a few weeks since our fight at the club, and although this is the first time I've seen him since, there's zero animosity there. It's easy to clash with Adam, but equally easy to forgive him. I'm glad I decided to meet him and Cameron for a beer tonight. It's been a while, and it's nice to be back in our favorite bar together. There's a good crowd here and the atmosphere is relaxed. The only thing missing is Brooks, but it's not often he joins us anyway.

"Right, when are you getting your ass back into the gym?" Cameron asks, eyeing me over the rim of his beer bottle. "Because those arms of yours are losing definition. You're going to lose your street cred on the force if you have scrawny arms, you know."

Adam looks me up and down. "Yeah, he's right. Did they stop providing donuts at work?"

"Give me a break," I say. "It's been a rough couple weeks. I'll hit the gym again soon."

"And I'm going to make you suffer," warns Cameron with a gleeful smirk. As a personal trainer, he thrives off of making his clients' legs tremble when he forces them into the hack squat machine. He isn't joking – he *will* make me suffer when I have my next session with him.

"Hey, are you still training that hot housewife?" Adam asks Cameron.

As they chat, I swig my beer and absentmindedly scroll through my phone. I click on the Instagram app by accident, immediately swipe back out of it, then pause. There was something on my usually blank home page. I open the app again, and I grin way too hard at my screen. Gracie is the only person I follow, and she's finally posted her first photo to this new account of hers. It's a picture of her and her sister that I took of them earlier today in Santa Cruz, their arms around each other's shoulders and smiling happily. The caption reads: *cute genes*.

"Hey." Cameron clinks his beer on the table in front of me to break my focus. When I glance up, he and Adam both stare at me. "What are you smiling at?"

"Nothing," I say, but before I can lock my phone and put it away, Adam launches himself across the table and snatches it straight out of my hand. "Hey! C'mon, man. Don't be a dick."

Adam is, of course, a dick. He studies my screen and arches one single brow. "Since when do you have Instagram? And Gracie Taylor? Isn't that Elena's friend?"

"Elena?" Cameron looks at Adam, perplexed. "That girl you brought home with us the night you fought with Weston? You actually remember this one's name?"

Adam screws up his face in sarcasm and says, "Haha. Original. But let's focus on Weston." He turns my phone around, showing off Gracie's photo to Cameron and me. "Why are you grinning like a weirdo at a photo of some chick you said you weren't interested in? Did you take my advice on board? Are you banging her? If so, put it here." He holds up his palm for me to high-five, but he's met with a steely glare instead.

I rip my phone out of his hand and shove it into my pocket. Adam makes it so easy to want to punch the living daylights out of him, but I keep my temper in check this time. "I've been seeing her, okay? But it's not like that. We're friends. She's a nice girl."

Cameron rolls his eyes. "*Friends*."

And maybe I can't argue with him, because I'm not sure if I even believe it myself anymore. I press my beer to my lips and think of that kiss with Gracie earlier. I wanted to kiss her *so* bad. As I held her in my arms, it felt right. An urge I couldn't fight, and I could see it in the shine of her blue eyes that it felt right for her, too. Fuck, I hate it when she cries. It brings out this intense protectiveness in me that I've only ever felt with my mom, my sister, and Charlotte.

When I drove Gracie back to San Francisco to hit up the DMV office, she was adorably giddy and a little nervous. She filled out the application, passed her vision test, got her photo taken, and even took the knowledge test right there and then after skimming through the California Driver's Handbook on her phone during the journey home from Santa Cruz. When she pranced out with her shiny new provisional license, her grin seemed permanently etched onto her cheeks.

"I'm your friend and you don't smile at photos of me the way you just smiled at that photo of her," Adam says to me, his voice relentlessly mocking.

"That's because she's cute and you ain't," Cameron says, and I nod in agreement.

"I'll grab another round," I tell them, and polish off the remainder of my beer as I stand from the table.

It's the perfect excuse to end the conversation, because Adam will never turn down another drink.

I head up to the bar, but it's still pretty packed. I squeeze into a gap in the crowd and wait patiently with my elbows resting on the bar top and my credit card in my hand. Honestly, I don't mind the wait. The barman is already working at speed to get everyone served, so I watch the baseball game on the flatscreen above.

"Tell me about it. I shouldn't have gone back there last night, but c'mon. You'd do the same, right? You're drunk and there's no decent women at Alchemist, but it's alright because you've got a girl at home who's still in love with you. I was being resourceful, and exes smash all the time. It's not a big deal."

My ears prick up. I keep my eyes set on the TV, but I'm now fully tuned in to the conversation next to me. It sounds awfully familiar, and my pulse quickens with adrenaline. There's no way there are really guys out here talking about their exes so disrespectfully. Charlotte may have left me, but I could never, ever say a single bad word about her. How, when I love her?

"I could have her back like this," the guy continues, snapping his fingers together, "so she's still an option. And, honestly, I'll probably go back to her eventually once I get bored."

Now I turn my head to look, and my intuition was right. It *is* fucking Luca. I remember his face from that morning in his and Gracie's apartment when I went

196

over there in search of my phone. I'm getting better at memorizing the faces of strangers and storing that mental image of them. It comes in handy at work, and it's coming in handy now.

Luca's not the biggest guy in the world, but he projects confidence and, right now, straight-up arrogance. He's definitely had more than a couple beers tonight and he moves his hands drunkenly as he talks to his buddy. They howl with laughter, and my blood boils. I am fucking seething.

I stare straight ahead, taking deep breaths. The barman catches up to me now, and I'm on autopilot as I order three more beers. My vision blurs with anger as he returns with the beers and I hand over my card.

How could Gracie ever love this guy? Seriously. They dated for *seven* years, and this is how he talks about her? How the hell was she convinced their life was perfect, that *he* was perfect? He's a complete douchebag.

I take back my card and sign off the receipt, then grab hold of the beers. Luca is still running his mouth, and when he snickers with laughter as though Gracie's feelings mean absolutely nothing to him, I can't take it anymore. It's really not my place to say anything, but I can't just walk away and forget about it. I eyeball the half-full glass on the bar top in front of him, and I think of how easy it would be to tip it over. A simple accident. Happens all the time when the bar's this crowded. It's also really fucking immature of me, but my intrusive thoughts win, because that's exactly what I do. As I turn away from the bar, I nudge my elbow hard into the glass. It tips over with a *clink* and the liquid splashes over Luca's shirt.

"Hey! Watch it!" he snaps, jumping back from the bar. His jaw tightens with irritation as he looks down at his shirt, patting pathetically at the fabric with some napkins.

I shrug nonchalantly. "Sorry, bud."

"Yeah, you should be," he mutters, and his friend next to him shakes his head threateningly as he takes a step closer to me.

What they don't know, however, is that if they dared to get up in my face, there are two other guys across this bar who'd fly over here in a nanosecond. Cameron is all muscle, and Adam loves a brawl. I know who'd win, and it wouldn't be Luca. That's why I only laugh.

"Where'd you think you're going? You owe me a drink," Luca says, blocking my path and holding his hand in front of my chest. "I'll take a vodka soda. Actually, make it two."

I glance down at his hand and say, "Nah." Rolling my eyes, I step forward to move around him, but his footsteps follow mine and he blocks me more aggressively this time. I sigh like I'm bored, but really my adrenaline is pumping.

Luca narrows his eyes and looks me up and down with intent. "What's your problem?"

And I shouldn't say it. I *shouldn't*. I've been in one fight too many as it is, and it's really not a great look for an off-duty cop to keep finding myself in hostile altercations. But I think of all the tears Gracie has shed over this piece of shit, and how he couldn't care less. So, I say it: "You, asshole. You're my problem."

"What the fuck?" Luca opens his mouth in surprise and exchanges a confused look with his buddy, then turns back to me. "Do I know you?"

And now that I've already let my temper slip, I don't hold back. I'm too damn heated. "What – you don't remember me? What if I said you had a nice apartment? Do you remember me now?"

Luca's features gradually harden as realization dawns on him. I was the guy he caught with Gracie that morning in their apartment. And although there was a genuine, innocent reason for me being there, I like the idea of making Luca question otherwise. "That was you, huh? You know Gracie?"

"Sure do. You really believe she just found my phone at the club?" I scoff and say, "I left it in your apartment the night before." And I know I'm insinuating that I hooked up with Gracie the night of her birthday after we left the club together, and I know it's not the truth, but I want Luca to feel hurt. I want him to panic at the thought of Gracie moving on without him. I want him to realize that maybe she won't be his backup plan, after all. I won't *let* her wait for this guy.

Luca lunges forward, his hand curled into a fist, but his buddy immediately grabs his shoulder and yanks him back. "Go ahead; be the rebound," Luca hisses. "I don't give a shit. At the end of the day, she'll always come back to me." His lips curl into a cruel smirk. "That's if I even still want her."

Would it really be so bad if I *did* hit him? I release a shaky, furious breath. I edge in real close and bring my jaw up to his. "I think, Luca," I growl, "you should shut your fucking mouth. She loves you, even now, and the best thing you can do is stay out of her life. I'd never hurt that girl the way you have."

I barge my shoulder against his and finally walk away. I'm so blinded by rage I can barely find my way back to my table. The beers shake in my hands, my heart thuds inside my chest, and my skin feels like it's on fire. I cast a glance over my shoulder to make sure Luca isn't following after me, and I'm relieved to see he's stayed put at the bar. He throws his hands around angrily as his friend calms him down. If we were outside, just the two of us, I'm sure things would have taken a different turn. I'd love to have that motherfucker sprawled out on the concrete, but I also would rather keep the job I hate so much. I don't fancy having my sergeant pull me out of a jail cell.

"What was that?" Cameron asks when I reach them.

I dump the beers on the table and collapse into my chair. I wipe away the sweat from my forehead and focus on my breathing for a moment. I'm so amped up, I almost feel nauseous. I grab my beer and swig half of it at once, quenching my thirst. "Gracie's ex," I finally reply.

"*Friends*," Adam says again with a laugh. "Yeah, right. You're really getting into a tussle at the bar with some guy over a girl you're only *friends* with? You're not a good liar, Weston."

I slam my bottle against the table. I'm ready to obliterate everything and anything within a twenty-foot radius. "Look, she's a really sweet girl. She wants to be a teacher just like my mom. She's keeping my head above water right now. I care about her, okay? And that guy . . . He's a piece of shit. She deserves better."

"And you're better, are you?" Adam jokes.

Cameron gives him a pointed look and a quick shake of his head, telling Adam to cut it out. Cameron can always read my expression well enough to know that I'm no longer in the headspace to brush off Adam's jibes. If Adam says the wrong thing like he did that night at the club, it won't be Luca I'll be fighting tonight, it'll be him again.

"Weston, take a minute to calm down," Cameron says. His frown is concerned as he studies Luca over at the bar. "Do you want to head somewhere else once we finish these beers? I need to head outside for a smoke, anyway. Adam?"

"Sure. Whatever." Adam leans back in his chair and watches the baseball game on a nearby TV screen, silently enjoying his beer, unaware of the holes I'm burning in his skull with the force of my glare.

I grab my beer and push away from the table, storming through the bar toward the exit. I desperately need fresh air, and I sense Cameron following behind me. We break outside and I furiously pace the sidewalk while sipping my beer.

"You good?" Cameron asks. He leans against the wall and lights up a cigarette, scrunching his eyes at me as he takes a long drag. The plume of smoke fills the air around us.

"Why are we still friends with him?" I ask. It's a genuine question, because I have no idea *why* we keep Adam around. "I know, I know. He's good fun, usually, but he's never *serious*, and this blasé attitude of his is getting so fucking old."

Cameron shrugs. "Teenager trapped in a grown man's body, our Adam." He smokes while I drink, and after a few moments of silence, he lifts a brow and says, "So . . . Gracie."

I eye him sideways with a heavy look. "Spit it out."

"Why didn't you tell me about her? We talk about everything, you and me," Cameron says, and there's a genuine flicker of betrayal in his eyes. "Is she really just a friend, Weston?"

"I'm trying to figure that out," I admit. "I thought we *were* just going to be friends, but that line is starting to blur."

"And that's a bad thing?"

I set my empty beer down on the sidewalk and lean back against the wall by Cameron's side. It's clear to him from my tense demeanor that I *do* think it's a bad thing. "Probably?" I say, then push my hand back through my hair with a groan. "We both only *just* got out of long-term relationships. I still have love for Charlotte, and Gracie still has love for that loser inside the bar. What if we *are* just rebounding?"

Cameron exhales another puff of smoke into the air. "Do you really think that's what's happening?"

I think about this for a second. Rebounds are supposed to be casual, fun, temporary. I don't want Gracie to be temporary, even just as friends. I'd very much like her to stick around in my life, because I like who I am when I'm with her. She may still have deeply embedded feelings for Luca, but that doesn't mean there can't be a small flame burning for me. I could be wrong about that, sure . . . but I could also be right.

"I can't explain it," I say, swallowing hard, "but I definitely feel something for her."

Cameron snaps his head to look at me and, when I turn to meet his gaze, I realize he's smiling wide. "Good for you, man. Seriously. You're allowed to meet someone else, so quit feeling guilty about it. You don't owe Charlotte anything."

I press my lips into a bold line. That's easier said than done. Of course, I'm allowed to meet someone new eventually, but after three weeks . . . What does that say about me? Can I really be in love with someone yet build a bond with someone else so soon after they leave? Maybe I'm overthinking this. It's not like I'm falling for Gracie. I just like being the shoulder she feels she can cry on.

The door of the bar swings open and Adam clumsily steps outside, shrugging on his jacket. "Right, where are we going next then? Sambuca shots are on me."

GRACIE

I stare at the text from Luca for an awfully long time.

It reads: *Meet me for coffee? Pier 39 at three? I need to talk to you.*

There's been an anxious tremor in my hands since I first read his message. What could Luca possibly want? Why does he need to talk to me? Dread fills me, because I don't know if I can so much as look him in the eye after what happened the other night, let alone hold a conversation with him. What is there to say? Perhaps he wants to apologize, but that's my naïveté taking over once again.

I don't want to hear what Luca has to say. Weston told me I don't have to run after him anymore, so I try something I've never done before – I put myself first and I text back: *No thanks*. Besides, I'm taking my first lesson with an instructor from a nearby driving school this afternoon, so I don't have time to meet him even if I wanted to.

My phone immediately starts ringing in my hand as Luca's name flashes across my screen, and I toss it away from me in a panic. I let it ring until the call gets sent to voicemail, but then a few seconds later, it rings again. I stare at my phone on the couch, my heart racing. Luca won't stop calling until I answer.

I grab my phone and press it to my ear. "*What?*" My irritation is clear.

"Why won't you meet me?" Luca asks abruptly, though he doesn't deserve a reason. He played with my feelings, and that's *not* okay when he's already broken me enough as it is.

"Why do you think?"

Luca has the nerve to release an aggrieved sigh, and I almost hang up on him for it. "Fine, I'll talk to you right now, then," he says. "That guy who was in our apartment a few weeks ago when I came to get my stuff. Who the fuck is he, Gracie?"

I'm so taken aback by the question, I can't even say anything at first. I had no idea what Luca wanted to talk to me about, but I never guessed for a second that it would be about Weston. It was weeks ago now that he caught Weston in the apartment retrieving his phone, and although he questioned it briefly at the time, he let it go. It's never been mentioned again until now.

"Why are you bringing this up again?" I finally reply, forcing the words out. There's a lump in my throat, because Weston isn't *just* some guy who once came to collect a lost phone. A lot of things have happened since then. "I already told you. I found his phone at the club on my birthday and he came by in the morning to pick it up."

"Liar," Luca spits.

"Excuse me?" I blink, astonished. I absolutely am a liar, but how the hell does Luca know that?

"You're a liar," Luca repeats coldly. "I had a nice talk with him at the bar last night."

I hate the way my stomach drops. I only lied about Weston at first because I was worried Luca would flip if he knew another guy had been in the apartment the night before, especially after I'd been at the club. Even though nothing happened between Weston and me, it didn't look good. It made more sense to just pretend I'd found Weston's phone at the club.

That was before. Now I'm lying about Weston because there's actually something to lie about.

"You spoke to Weston?" I squeak.

"So that's his name, huh? Weston," says Luca. "I didn't have much of a choice. He knocked over my drink."

After Weston brought me home from the DMV office, he did say something about catching up with his friends at the bar for a couple beers. Out of all the bars in downtown San Francisco, what are the odds of Luca hitting up the same one?

"I'm sure it was an accident," I mumble pathetically. I'm so scared of what's going to come out of Luca's mouth next. What happened between him and Weston last night?

"No, Gracie. It wasn't," Luca says. "He knocked over my drink and then made it perfectly clear that there's something going on between the two of you. You're a hypocrite, you know that? You don't want me to explore other options, yet you're clearly wasting no time when it comes to doing the same for yourself."

My jaw slackens and I grip my phone hard with exasperation. I am *not* doing the same thing as Luca. Weston is . . . accidental. And maybe Weston isn't even anything at all.

"I am *not* exploring other options, Luca," I manage to say with a surprising amount of conviction despite how stunned I am. "*You* were everything I wanted, but you walked away and now I'm trying my fucking best to survive without you, okay?"

Luca snorts. "And this is surviving, is it?"

I pull my phone away from my ear and stare at Luca's name on my screen in disbelief that this is really Luca, *my* Luca, that I'm talking to. When did he become so callous with me? A month ago, this man would have gone to the ends of the earth for me. I know breakups are ugly, but I honestly believed Luca and I would remain civil. Now it's like he doesn't care about me at all, and after seven years together, I deserve so much more respect than what he's currently giving me.

I press my phone back to my ear, and my anger sears through me, all hot and fierce. "Maybe I *should* explore my other options," I muse, my tone taunting and unfamiliar. It's so not like me. I would never purposely hurt the people I care about, but right now . . . Oh, I am seeing red. "With the way you're acting this week, Luca, I think it's highly likely there *is* someone out there who's better for me than you are."

"Do whatever you want, Gracie. I honestly don't care," he says, and his words are so believable it's like a punch in the gut. "Just don't act righteous about it when you're the one who's sleeping with someone else already."

If only Luca was standing in front of me now, he would see all the color drain from my face. For the longest of moments, I even forget how to breathe. "Weston told you?" I whisper.

"So, it's true?"

"Luca . . ."

"No," he says harshly. "I don't want to hear it, Gracie. Just pass on the message that next time he tries to screw with me, he won't like what happens."

Luca hangs up the call before I can get another word in, but I can't speak anyway. I am shocked to my core and grappling with my confusion. Is Weston out of his fucking mind? He has been so, so sweet to me that I can't fathom what could have possibly possessed him to tell my *ex* that we slept together. And in the middle of a bar! I never wanted Luca to ever find out about that.

Full of nervous energy, I pace my apartment in circles. I'm not an angry person. I'm naturally calm, patient, understanding ... but recently I am seriously being tested. Now I'm furious at Weston too.

I scroll through my contacts until I find his name, and just as I'm about to call him and find out for myself exactly what he was playing at last night, I remember he's back at work today. He's on the day shift, and I'm almost positive he said he gets off at seven. He works in this neighborhood, and I know he's based out of the station on Fillmore Street.

I set down my phone. I'm not going to call Weston. I'm going to ambush him.

There's a McDonald's directly opposite the Northern District Police Station. I sit at a table by the window, eating chicken nuggets and fries and washing them down with a strawberry milkshake while I wait for seven to roll around. So far, my plan to get back on track with eating healthy meals has been going well, but tonight I was in no mood to cook. The poor veggies in my refrigerator are probably rotting away right this second, but sometimes all you need is fast food. Plus, I walked a mile to get here, so I deserve this milkshake. *And* I survived my first driving lesson.

When it turns exactly seven o'clock, I head outside into the golden, warm (but, of course, breezy) evening.

I pass the front doors of the station and head around the corner to the parking lot at the rear. There are a lot of police cruisers parked up, obviously, but also regular cars. There are trespassing signs, so I don't enter the lot, however much I'd like to find Weston's car and camp out next to it. I stand firm on the sidewalk between the back doors and the parking lot, and I wait. I'm not sure which direction he'll appear from.

Finally, at fifteen minutes past seven, the doors push open and Weston is the officer who emerges from the station. He's still in his uniform, minus his duty belt, and his jaw is clean-shaven. He only takes one step out the door before he jolts with surprise.

"Gracie?" His expression lights up as a smile spreads across his face. "What are you doing here?"

As he walks toward me, that smile of his falters. My stance is tense and closed-off, my arms folded across my chest. I don't greet him. I jump straight into what I've been waiting hours to ask.

"What exactly did you say to Luca last night at the bar?"

Weston places his hands on his hips and cocks his head to the side, regarding me carefully. I don't let the uniform intimidate me.

"Last night. The bar. You. Luca," I say, keeping my voice strong. "I want to know *exactly* what happened."

"How long have you been waiting out here?" Weston asks. His features are so relaxed, I swear it's almost like he finds this amusing. "Did you seriously wait out here for me to get off work just to ask me what happened with Luca?"

"*Yes*, Weston." My words are laced with frustration now, and I uncross my arms and march toward him. I point an accusing finger at his chest. "You antagonized him, didn't you? You spilled a drink on him."

Weston lowers his smoldering gaze to my finger, then lifts it back to meet my eyes. "Come with me to my car," he says, gently grasping my wrist. We cross through the parking lot, past the police vehicles, and come to a halt next to his Honda. He's the one who crosses his arms now, as he leans back on the hood of the car. "Yes."

"What?"

"Yes, I provoked him."

My glower strengthens. "You *admit* it?"

Weston laughs and draws his brows together. The evening sun shines gold in his eyes, lighting the darkness and turning them a softer, warmer brown. "What? You expected me to deny it? Yes, I spilled his drink on him. How do you know? Did you talk to him?"

I swallow hard as I stare back at Weston. My chest feels squeezed tight and I wiggle my fingers in an attempt to release some energy from my body, but God, I feel kind of . . . sick. There's something so mesmerizing about the glow of sunshine against Weston's arm of tattoos and the navy blue of his uniform as he sits on the edge of a dusty old car. So effortlessly attractive . . .

"He called me earlier," I choke out. My chest is so restricted, I can hardly catch my breath. Even my brain feels foggy as I attempt to recall my conversation with Luca this afternoon. "He was pissed, because somehow he's gotten the idea that you and I are . . . a thing."

Weston pushes off from the car and steps forward in front of me, and I realize now exactly why my stomach is starting to hurt. It's *butterflies*. "You want to know exactly what happened?"

"Yes."

"Okay, here's what happened," he says, holding my gaze. "I was minding my own business at the bar, and I overhear some douchebag next to me bragging about keeping his ex on the backburner as his backup plan. I turn around and yep, you guessed it, Gracie. It was Luca."

My blood runs cold. "He said . . . He said that?"

"In similar words." Weston grimaces. "I know I shouldn't have gotten involved, but I couldn't stand there and listen to him talk about you like that. He laughed at how easily he could get you back if he wanted. He *laughed*, Gracie."

I release a slow, controlled breath as I absorb Weston's words. Running my hand back through my hair, I collapse against the car door and blink fast. Luca spoke so cruelly on the phone earlier, it should be no surprise that he would talk *about* me just as ruthlessly, but it stings deep. The pain of him leaving is still so raw, and the wound stretches further, deeper now. Is that really how Luca feels? That I'm some pathetic loser putting my life on hold and waiting patiently to welcome him home from this little bachelor's adventure of his? It makes sense now, his outrage over Weston being in my life. Luca says he wants me to take the time to find myself too, to explore a life without him, but it's apparent that he wants me to always choose him. He wants the decision over our future, ultimately, to be his.

"I'm sorry to be the one to tell you," Weston apologizes after allowing me a minute of silence to process it. There's genuine regret in his gaze, and he shrugs, abashed. "My blood was boiling and I couldn't just walk away. So, I tipped over his drink."

"And?"

"And called him an asshole."

"And?"

"And told him to stay out of your life."

"*And?*" I prompt again, harder this time.

A flicker of confusion races across Weston's expression. "And . . . I don't know? That was it. I walked away before I could knock his lights out." He smiles wryly, only to be met with my reproachful look.

"You're not telling me the most important part."

Weston's confusion transforms into exasperation. "What, Gracie?"

I glance around us, ensuring there's no one else in the parking lot, then straighten up from the car. Lowering my voice, I hiss, "You told Luca we slept together. Why? What would possess you to tell him that?"

"I didn't," Weston argues, but then his shoulders sink and he sheepishly scratches his temple. "Well, I told him I'd left my phone in your apartment the night before he saw us together, which is true, because I did . . . I was only *insinuating* that we slept together because I wanted his heart to stop, I wanted him to suffer, just for a second."

"Wait. You *didn't* tell him about that morning at your place?"

Weston shakes his head, seemingly appalled that I could believe he would tell Luca that in the first place. "Of course not. I'd never do that."

I stare wide-eyed at the cracks in the concrete below my feet. Luca only *suspected* that I'd slept with Weston, and what did I do? I only went ahead and confirmed it! Weston didn't tell him. *I did.*

"*Weston!*" I groan, throwing my head back to the sky. "I thought you'd already told him, so I didn't deny it."

"Hey, relax." Weston steps in front of me and places both hands beneath my jaw, gently lowering my head down. Our eyes lock and my stomach lurches. He keeps his hands on my face as he smiles reassuringly. "So what if he knows? What's he going to do about it, anyway, huh?"

I fight really, really hard to keep my gaze from fixating on his mouth. "He wanted me to pass on the message for you to stay away from him, otherwise you won't like what happens."

Weston's smirk teeters on the edge of mischievous. "He threatened me? A cop? Real smart." He rolls his eyes, and then his features soften. With his hands still cupping my jaw, he brushes my cheeks with his thumbs, and I feel my knees buckle. "Please never go back to him," he murmurs, quietly desperate. "Please, Gracie. I mean it. He doesn't deserve you."

The butterflies erupt. There are thousands of them now, fluttering in my stomach, my chest, my lungs. Every inch of my body aches from their presence.

I reach up and wrap my hand around Weston's wrist, pressing my face harder into his hands, embracing how protective they feel. "Falling out of love with Luca is going better than expected," I tell him, and there's an unmistakable sparkle in his brown eyes as he kisses my forehead.

"Good," he whispers, and I kind of want to die.

Maybe I do look at him the way I used to look at Luca, because I'm starting to realize now that Weston also makes me *feel* everything Luca once made me feel too.

He makes me feel lovely.

And that's terrifying, because a month ago, I never would have thought it possible to feel that way again.

I bite my lower lip, fighting my blushing smile. Being this close to Weston is unbearable. The goosebumps, the knot in my stomach, the racing of my heart. I pull away from him and step back. My cheeks feel so hot, I wonder if they're noticeably red.

"That was all I really came here to say . . . I'm sorry for cornering you outside your station like this," I apologize, my smile timid. I was going to give Weston hell for daring to talk to Luca at the bar, but how can I be mad at him *now*? He was defending me, and that's awfully charming.

Weston fishes his car keys out of his pocket. "Do you need a ride home?"

"No thanks. I'll walk," I say, and I put my words into motion and head for the parking lot exit. I don't mind walking home. It's a nice evening, sure, but I'm mostly nervous about what might happen if I get into the car with Weston. I can't handle these heart palpitations. As I walk away from him, I call over my shoulder, "I'm trying to be independent, remember?"

Weston's laugh travels over to me, and he shouts back, "I may be off-duty, Gracie, but you can always call me whenever you need me. I'll come running."

WESTON

The night shifts always go one way or the other. Either we respond to call after call with zero down time, or we wait it out in the patrol car and twiddle our thumbs. Tonight is one of those slower shifts. It's been thirty minutes since we attended to a domestic dispute. We've completed the incident report, we're up to date on all other paperwork, and now we're aimlessly patrolling in the cruiser. It's only 1 a.m., so there's still another six hours to fill before we clock off. We've grabbed some coffee to keep us going through the slog.

"How's your navigation skills coming along?" Bill asks, breaking the silence. He always drives, though it's probably about time he let me take a shot behind the wheel. "You should have every street memorized by now. And not just this district, but the entire city. You don't know where you'll end up being stationed, so you better know them all. Do you?"

I glance over at him, relieved that it's too dark in this car for him to see the way I roll my eyes. Bill may be my field training officer and it's his job to put me through my paces, but he's so goddamn insufferable. I can't wait to be fully certified just so I don't have to deal with these patronizing tests.

"Bill, you *know* I've lived here my entire life," I remind him. "I know San Francisco like the back of my hand."

"Hmm."

We continue further down the road in silence. I keep my eyes peeled for any suspicious behavior, but the streets are dead at this time. This may be boring, but honestly, I don't miss the panic that floods through me every time dispatch radios us. I sip my coffee in peace.

Bill turns down a narrow side street. Out of nowhere, he slams hard on the brakes and my coffee splashes onto my lap. I stare wildly at him.

"Gunfire. I've just been shot. Our GPS is down. Where are we?" he asks, an eyebrow arched challengingly and his tone sharp.

God, I hate when he pulls stuff like this on me. I dump my coffee cup into the cupholder and squint through the windshield at the dark street outside. I know *where* we are, as in which neighborhood, but this literal street? No idea.

"Uhhh . . ." I mumble.

Bill glares at me. "Figure it out before I bleed to death, Reed."

Angrily, I kick open the car door and step out into the cool night air. With my belt fully loaded, my equipment bounces against my hips as I jog all the way to the corner of the block. I scan the buildings for any hint of a street name, but there aren't any, and I'm even more pissed when I reach the end of the block and there isn't even a fucking street sign there. I glance back at the cruiser, its headlights blinding me. If I walk back there with still no idea of where we are, Bill will lose it. I pick up the pace and run to the next cross section, and thank fuck. There's a sign.

I run all the way back to the cruiser and throw open the door, sticking my head inside. "Pixley," I say, breathing heavily. "We're on Pixley Street."

"Too late. I've bled out and died by the time you've put in the call for help," Bill says nonchalantly. He looks away and shakes his head.

I slide back into the passenger seat and slam the door behind me. Every single shift I am reminded of how badly I do this job, only confirming yet again that I've made a terrible, terrible decision. "Realistically though, what are the odds of the GPS shutting down?"

"That's not the point. You're supposed to know this stuff. Your father knew every single street in this city. Even every dead-end alley," says Bill.

The muscle in my jaw twitches. *This* is why Bill gets on my nerves so much. He's close to retirement, and once upon a time he worked alongside my dad. Bill holds a lot of respect for him, and I think that's why he rides my ass so hard. He pushes me because he expects better. My dad worked his way up the ladder, after all. A great officer. In Bill's mind, why should I be anything less?

"Yeah? Well, I'm not my father," I mutter, grabbing some napkins to dab at the spilled coffee on my pants. I'm too tired for this.

Bill opens his mouth to say something, but instantly clamps it shut again when the static of our vehicle's radio erupts into life. Dispatch requests our immediate response, but Bill has thrown me off my game and my head is so scrambled that I don't even remember what the dispatch code means.

"Buckle up," Bill orders, and he lights up the street with our blues, reds and whites.

The one good thing about working nights is the lack of traffic. It's easy to maneuver diligently around vehicles at this time and I have to hand it to Bill, he is a great driver. I pull up the dispatch notes on the computer and my adrenaline starts pumping. We're assisting a medical emergency – someone has fallen from a hotel roof.

The hotel is only a few minutes away, so we reach the scene in no time at all. The ambulance has made it here before us, and two medics burst from inside and race toward the person sprawled out on the sidewalk. Passersby watch on in horror.

Bill radios dispatch to inform them of our arrival on the scene, then kills the engine.

I peer through my window at the hotel building. It's seven stories, and the roof has barbed wire around the edge. "How did they fall from the roof? There doesn't even look to be a terrace up there."

Bill pauses with one foot out the door. He throws me a puzzled look, but within a split second, it changes to sympathy. He's been on the force for decades and there's not a single thing he hasn't seen in his career, but me? There are a lot of things I'm only encountering for the first time. He says flatly, "They didn't fall, Weston."

My stomach drops as Bill gets out the car. *Fuck*. This is something I haven't dealt with yet during the first eight weeks of my field training, but I have to face it like I face everything else – by pulling myself together as best I can and keeping my composure even when I'm terrified.

Sucking in a breath, I leave the safety of the cruiser. Morbidly curious hotel guests rush outside to spectate, and Bill stretches his arms wide, creating a physical barrier as he instructs the public to stay back.

Every step forward feels weighted. The medics tear open their supplies as they kneel by the person on the concrete, and I edge closer and closer until I realize it's not really a person anymore, but a severely mangled body. Dead on arrival.

222

"Reed, cordon off fifty feet in every direction," Bill calls over to me, but I'm so paralyzed with terror, his command doesn't even register.

It's a man. I think. Their skull is split open, brain matter seeping onto the concrete, their face barely even human anymore. Two limbs are definitely broken. There's so much blood, I don't know how it'll ever be washed out of the ground. It's the gnarliest thing I have ever seen in my life. I can't even fathom that it's real.

"A cordon, Reed!" Bill shouts again.

No. I'm gonna hurl. I seal my mouth shut, but I still gag. I press my hand over my mouth and back away from the body. There's so much frantic commotion around me, but I can't focus on a single thing except the grotesque image that's now permanently seared into my mind. I *know* I need to do my job, but I simply . . . can't.

"*Weston!*" Bill snaps with exasperation.

I look at him. Shake my head slowly. Swallow the trauma.

He runs over and grasps my shoulder, pushing me away from the scene. I expect him to yell at me to get my shit together, to grab the tape from the trunk and set up the damn cordon, but all he says is, "Breathe."

I can't. I'm hyperventilating now; my breathing so erratic, I feel pain in my chest. Dad always warned me that there would be days where you come home and bawl your eyes out because you see unspeakable, unimaginable things in this job, but then you bury that scene in the back of your mind, brush yourself off, and then show up to your next shift as a more resilient officer than you were the day before. Right now, I can't imagine ever showing up to work again.

"Sit in the car, Weston," Bill orders, and it's the gentlest command he has ever given me. It's the tone of voice I only ever hear him use when dealing with kids.

"But . . ."

"*Sit in the car*," he repeats, pulling open the passenger door of the cruiser. My body is so numb, he even has to guide me into the seat. "Your shift is over."

Bill shuts the door on me. He retrieves the tape from the trunk and I watch him through the windshield, pale and expressionless, as he does the job I couldn't. He cordons off the scene and deals with the prying public while the medics work.

And as I sit in the cruiser, trembling and panting, I bury my face into my hands and weep.

Bill drives me back to the station in silence. It's just after two. Our sergeant is busy filing reports when we find him. Bill tells him I'm not mentally capable of completing my shift. My sergeant dismisses me for the night. Tells me to go home and get some sleep. Says he'll check in on how I'm feeling ahead of tomorrow's shift. Bill tucks my duty belt into my locker, grabs my belongings, then walks me back out into the parking lot.

"Are you good to drive?" he asks.

I nod. My body feels numb with shock, the same way it did the day I learned my mom had died. I'm fighting back tears with everything in me, and I know if I even so much as part my lips to say a single word, I'll break down. So, I remain speechless.

Bill hands me my keys. Opens my car door and sets my phone and wallet down on my passenger seat. He watches me with great concern as I slide behind the wheel.

"Call the station if you need me," he says, and then steps back from the car. "I mean it, Weston. Take care of yourself tonight."

I pull my door shut, click on my seatbelt, turn on the engine. I shouldn't be driving right now when I'm this emotional, but I'm on autopilot. Before I know it, I've pulled out of the lot and left Bill behind in my rearview. Every minute that passes, I blink and wonder how I even drove this far without being aware of it. It scares me a little, being so out of it like this.

I don't want to go home. I don't want to be alone.

I think of Charlotte and how badly I wish she was still a part of my life. I need her more than ever right now. But she's gone, and I have no one to offload this weight onto.

Except I do.

I have Gracie.

And I think I need her more than I ever needed Charlotte.

I take a sharp turn. Gracie's apartment complex is just around the corner, and I don't care that it's the middle of the night. If I go home alone, I won't sleep. When Mom died, I paced my dorm in San Diego for hours every single night for weeks. I didn't sleep again until I'd processed and dealt with the grief.

I park my car in the garage, then take the elevator to the fourth floor. There's no guessing which apartment is hers anymore, and the closer I get to her, the more desperate I am to collapse into her arms. I run down the lobby to the corner apartment and pound on the door.

"Gracie?" I call weakly through the door. "Gracie, it's me. It's Weston."

I press my forehead to the door, panting heavily as I choke up with tears again. What the fuck is wrong with me? All the other rookies seem to take traumatic scenes in their stride, or at least hold it together long enough to finish their shift. Maybe I'm not emotionally detached enough. I *knew* I couldn't do this job. I knew it all along. I'm pathetic.

The sound of the chain lock sliding open jolts me back a step. The door cracks open and Gracie peers through the gap, eyes squinting into the sudden brightness of the hallway. I've woken her, of course. When she realizes it's only me, she opens the door wider. She's wearing gym shorts and a tank top, her hair pulled back.

Her voice is raspy as she quietly asks, "Weston? What are you doing here?"

"Gracie," I whisper, but I can't hold myself up for a second longer.

I fall straight into her arms.

She's much smaller than me, but she bears my weight. Instinctively, she wraps her arms around me and holds me close as I bury my face into the crook of her neck and cry against the softness of her skin. She smells like flowers in the spring, and fuck, I need her.

"Oh, Weston," Gracie breathes. "What's happened? What's wrong?"

Together we move further into the apartment and Gracie nudges the door shut with her foot. I cling to her like my life depends on it, my chest heaving.

"I can't do this," I choke out between sobs. "I can't handle this fucking job, Gracie."

"Hey, hey. You're okay," she says soothingly as she weaves her fingers through my hair. "You're shaking."

I slide my hand around the nape of her neck, my other on the small of her back. She may be small and dainty, but she feels so secure. My cries are so full of sorrow, they echo throughout the darkness of the apartment.

"Someone jumped," are the only two words I can manage. A pained groan escapes me, leaving its trace on Gracie's skin where my tears are embedded.

Gracie squeezes me so tight, it almost hurts more than this ache in my chest. I try to press closer to her, but I'm as near as I can get and, somehow, it's still not enough. There's not a single light on, but she pulls me across the apartment with her, guiding me carefully around the furniture. She strokes my hair in comforting gestures the entire time, her touch perfectly reassuring. The only thing I want more than to never let go of her is for her to never let go of me.

We move into another room and the backs of my legs hit the edge of a bed.

"You're staying with me tonight," she whispers, and I nod against her shoulder.

Gracie pushes me back until I'm seated on the bed, but it takes every ounce of strength within me to break apart from her. As she stands in front of me, I reach out for both her hands and try to focus on her silhouette in the dark. I blink hard and slow, fighting off the burn in my eyes. She's here. With me. And as long as I'm not alone, I might just be okay.

Gracie steps forward into the small space between my legs. She presses the palm of her hand to my forehead, moving it slowly down the side of my face and cupping my jaw. I close my eyes and concentrate on the softness of her skin and nothing else. Only Gracie and her warmth.

"I'm sorry you had to see whatever it was you saw tonight," she says, and I press my jaw harder into her palm. "But you're safe here. It's only me."

"Only you," I whisper. But Gracie is never just *only*.

She drops her hand to my shirt and slowly undoes every button in the dark. Takes off my bulletproof vest. My undershirt. She kneels to the floor and unties the laces of my boots. She pulls them off, then sits up a little and reaches for my belt. The click of the buckle reverberates around the room.

As she rises from the floor, she grasps my wrist. "Can you stand up for me, Weston?"

I try. Still trembling, I push off the bed and straighten up in front of her. My breath hitches as she slips off my belt. When she reaches for the zipper of my pants, I grab her hand. The only thing I hear is the sound of her soft, calculated breathing.

"Gracie."

"Weston."

I find her face in the dark and brush my thumb over her parted lips. I'm not thinking about that awful scene anymore. I'm thinking about her, about Gracie. I picture the sunshine highlighting the copper in her blond hair and turning it auburn; the splash of freckles across her nose and cheeks; the sundress she wore the night I cooked her dinner.

"You are the only thing I see right now," I whisper.

"But it's dark."

"I know."

And I don't think about it this time. I don't question it or doubt myself, because this time . . . This time I know kissing her is right.

My lips find Gracie's and I kiss her tenderly with purpose, with meaning. She immediately presses closer, hard up against my bare chest and her hand disappearing into my hair. The tension throughout my body instantly dissipates and I allow myself to sink into the feeling of her, to lose myself in it. My hands slip underneath her tank top and I clasp her waist, noticing the way she shivers at my touch.

"Is this okay?" I ask, my mouth traveling along the edge of her jaw.

"Kiss me harder, Weston." She guides my lips back to hers and kisses me deeply, passionately, her mouth working against mine in unimaginable ways. She takes my lower lip between her teeth, so seductively I'm nearly bursting out of my pants. "Focus on me."

I rake her tank top up over her head and toss it across the bedroom, kissing her with a crazed hunger as I grab her breast. This girl makes me feel things that I still don't understand, but I do know one thing for sure: I'm so fucking glad she hopped into my Uber a month ago. I slip my hand into her shorts and she's so wet already. She gasps as I touch her, her nails digging ever so slightly into my back. When she lets out a tiny whimper of pleasure, I groan with her. It feels so good making *her* feel good.

So much for never letting this happen again.

Gracie reaches for my zipper again. I step out of my pants, my boxers, and now I'm the one who's succumbing to her touch. Breathlessly, I take her face in both hands and kiss her hard. I want to feel her again so badly. It's not even desire anymore. It's a *need*.

Gracie presses her hands on my chest and pushes me down onto the edge of the bed. She slips off her shorts and takes me by surprise when she slides onto my lap, straddling me. I grab her hips, trying to meet her gaze in the dark. I may not see the blue in her eyes right now, but I see the sparkle.

She trails a kiss down my temple and grabs hold of my shoulders, then slowly lowers herself down onto me. A groan rumbles in my throat at the same time as she releases a breath. *Fuck*. I throw my head back as I grip her hips even tighter. She feels *so* fucking good. I can't even move. All I can do is feel her. Admire her. Adore her.

"Gracie . . ." I moan through gritted teeth. I press my forehead to hers, reaching for the hairband of her pony-tail and pulling it loose. Her hair falls over her shoulders and I immediately wind my fingers through it. "You feel incredible."

A tiny little sigh of satisfaction emits from her. She folds her hands around the back of my neck and rocks her hips back and forth, slowly at first, and then gradually faster. I grab hold of her ass, letting my hands follow the movements of her body.

"Fuck, Gracie, you do that so good."

Gracie switches up her rhythm, rotating her hips in a circle now. I'd be convinced she was a pro dancer if I didn't know otherwise. The way she moves, so confidently and so sure of herself . . . It's intoxicating. It's an entirely new side to her that I haven't discovered yet.

"Do you like that, Weston?" she whispers.

"I like *you*," I say, and I cover every inch of her neck with kisses.

She tilts her head forward, drawing our gazes level. God, how I wish I could see her in the light. "Do you?"

"Of course."

And it's so sexy, the way she grabs my jaw with such dominance and angles my face upward, crashing her lips to mine. I can't get enough of her. How did she dissolve that pain in my chest so easily?

"You're going to have to stop, Gracie," I groan, squeezing my eyes shut as I fight to suppress the mounting pleasure. It's usually easy to distract my mind with algebra equations when I'm trying to hold out, but Gracie is the only thought occupying my mind and that's getting me there even quicker. "I'm going to—"

"Then do," she cuts in. "Do it for me."

Every muscle in my body tenses. Pressure builds deep within my core and I know I'm a goner. I'm past the point of no return. All I can do now is hang on.

"But what about you?" I ask, my breathing ragged.

Gracie rolls her hips faster. Presses deeper. "This isn't about me."

Oh, fuck.

I find that soft nook between her neck and shoulder blade again and smother my face into it. My heartbeat is through the roof as my body convulses. Gracie knots her fingers through my hair and slows down her movements just as warm, throbbing waves of pleasure pump through me. The final contraction passes and the euphoria of the release is over too soon. Both Gracie and I become still, and even now, she strokes my hair. It's so goddamn soothing.

I have no words. She is mesmerizing. "Wow."

"I'll be right back," she whispers, planting a kiss on the corner of my mouth. She pushes off my lap and darts to the bathroom to clean up.

I fall back onto the bed, blowing out a breath. Tonight feels like a blur, but this moment? Crystal clear. My head feels less fuzzy now, my body feels more stable. I'm okay. *I'm okay.*

Gracie returns from the bathroom. She gathers her clothes from the floor, considers putting them back on for a second, but ultimately tosses them away again. She crawls onto the bed next to me and rests her head on my chest. I wrap my arm around her, and she hooks one leg over mine. The skin-to-skin contact is so intimate, but I could hold her like this all night. Intimacy with Gracie doesn't make me nervous, it makes me feel shielded.

"I needed that," I tell her. "I needed *you.*"

"I'm glad you came to me," she whispers, skimming her fingertips down my arm. I wonder if even in the dark, she realizes she's tracing my tattoos. "You can trust me, Weston, because I . . . I care about you. A lot. More than I thought I could."

"Do you?"

I sense her smile against me. "Of course."

GRACIE

I almost don't want to wake him. He's an adorable sleeper. He sleeps on his stomach, face buried into the pillow, his breathing slow.

"Weston," I say quietly, but he's in too deep a slumber to register the sound of my voice. He didn't even stir when I pulled open the curtains half an hour ago and let blinding sunlight into the room. I sit on the edge of the bed and touch his shoulder. His skin is warm, clammy. "Weston," I repeat, louder.

Weston flinches. He lifts his head from the pillow, eyes half closed with sensitivity, and takes in his surroundings. I think it takes him by surprise, the sight of an apartment that isn't his own, because he instantly flips over and bolts upright. His hair is tousled in a thousand directions, but I don't know if that's from sleeping or the way I raked my fingers through it last night. He rubs a hand down his face.

"Hey. I made you some breakfast," I say with a smile. I hold out the plate of poached eggs on sourdough toast I've just cooked up for him. "No avocado, because I remember you once said you don't like it."

Weston blinks away the tiredness in his eyes as he adjusts to the sunlight. It's after ten, but he *was* on the night shift, so his body clock is probably screwed. "This looks great, Gracie," he says, taking the plate from me. I pass him a fork and knife. "Thanks. Seriously. Thank you."

Suddenly, I'm hyperaware of my pulse. I can feel it throbbing in my wrist. Pounding in my neck. Weston's morning voice . . . It's so low, so husky. *So hot.*

"How are you feeling this morning?" I ask, clearing my throat.

I'm kind of nervous. I've been awake for a few hours while I left Weston to sleep, so I've had plenty of time to gather my thoughts. When Weston knocked on my door in the middle of the night, he was completely broken. He was shattered, distraught. He could barely stand upright. Seeing him so destroyed like that even hurt *me*. All I could do was hold him with every ounce of strength I had in me while he cried on my shoulder. And of all the doors he could have knocked on, I'm so glad he knocked on mine.

Over the past few weeks, I've developed a soft spot for Weston. I ignored it at first. Denied it. But last night, I realized *just* how much I cared for him when I held him in my arms and wished I could take that pain away from him. I felt, as insane as it seems, that he was mine to take care of.

"Better," Weston replies. "I don't know what came over me. I've seen some awful things already, but this one really got to me. It was . . . Gracie, it was the worst thing I've ever seen in my life. I got dismissed from my shift, but I couldn't bring myself to go home. I'm sorry for waking you. Can you please forget you heard me cry like that? Because I'm mortified about that now."

He blushes as he says this, but I reach out to touch his forearm with a sense of reassurance. I haven't forgotten that he's still naked beneath my comforter.

"Don't be embarrassed. What you do can't be easy," I say. "Do you have to go back today?"

Weston takes a bite of toast, but he chews lethargically. "Yeah. Back tonight, but we're encouraged to talk about this stuff, so I'll check in with Bill and our sergeant when I get to the station. I'm praying for a shift full of noise complaints. Can you and your friends play your music too loud again?" He manages to crack the smallest of smiles, and I laugh.

"Sorry. I'm a law-abiding citizen." I lean forward and peck a kiss on his cheek, then hop off the bed. I point to the dresser where his uniform sits in a neatly folded pile. "Your clothes are there, but there's still some things of Luca's here that you're more than welcome to steal."

Weston cocks his head and says, "I'm also a law-abiding citizen."

I scoff dramatically. "*Fine.*" I grab Weston's uniform and set it down on the bed beside him, running my fingers over the fabric. "So, I have plans today. Independent woman kind of plans. Gracie-being-brave kind of plans." I lift my gaze to meet his, and I get those butterflies again. The ones that hurt. "I'm renting a bike and I'm cycling across the Golden Gate Bridge, because I've never done it before even though I've always wanted to. Luca said it was lame and refused to do it with me. So, I'm doing it. By myself."

Weston nods with spirit. "There ya go. I told you: you can do anything you want to do in life, Gracie, even if it means doing it alone."

"*Except* . . ." My cheeks flare red. "I'd now really like you to join me."

"That doesn't make it an independent woman kind of plan anymore."

"So? It counts because I *was* going to do it alone," I argue. "But now I'm extending an invite to you, because I think it would be good for you to keep yourself busy today before you go back to work. Don't you agree?"

Weston doesn't miss a beat. He smiles and says, "I'd love to come with you."

"Really?"

"Yeah. Fuck Luca. It's definitely cool," he says, and swallows another mouthful of breakfast. "But do you mind if I head home first? I'm not biking across that bridge in last night's uniform."

Weston agrees to meet me at the bike rental shop at noon. I hop on a trolley north toward the Marina District, bubbling with excitement. I've wanted to do this for years, but Luca never entertained the idea. I know it's a cliché and touristy, but we are so lucky to live in such a gorgeous city and I'll be damned if I don't experience cycling across the Golden Gate Bridge just *once* in my life. It's a perfect August day, with the sun shining bright and warm, but I'm not an idiot. Crossing that bridge is going to be freezing, so I've pulled on a sweatshirt. I've filled a backpack with bottled water and granola bars, and I've brought my camera. I'm not sure why. I haven't picked it up again since I attempted to vlog the day I went home to Santa Cruz, because the footage was a disaster and I scrapped the entire lot in frustration. Quite frankly, I'm not that interesting on my own without Luca.

I arrive at the rental shop a little early, so I find a sunny spot on the street and relax against the wall, letting the sun kiss my skin even though it'll trigger more of my freckles. While I wait, I check in on mine and Luca's accounts. I've posted *one* carefully manufactured video in a month, and I'm not sure it's fooling anyone. Our viewers are still skeptical about our disappearance from social media.

Although I've posted a couple more photos on Instagram, our most devoted followers keep outsmarting me. It seems the differing lengths of my hair between photos (by a mere inch, I might add) makes it obvious I'm using old pictures. At this point, I've stopped caring about seeming authentic and real. I don't even care if the breakup gets out.

So why the hell am I still holding on to these accounts?

I pull up our YouTube account on my phone. Seven years of memories, over three hundred videos, six hundred thousand subscribers ... I think of the ad revenue. The brand collaborations. It's been fun, that's for sure, and I'm so grateful for the life it's given Luca and me, but I can't be a fraud. I have more integrity than that. There's nothing left of our relationship except this, and it's time to shut it down.

I navigate to the account settings. A small tremor takes over my hands as I find the option to permanently deactivate the account. I give it approximately three seconds of consideration before the intrusive thoughts win. Just a couple of clicks, that's all it takes for six hundred thousand subscribers to evaporate into thin air. A weight lifts from my shoulders and an unexpected joy radiates through me. I can't stop now. I flip over to the Instagram app and delete our account on there too. It's so easy, deleting everything we worked so hard for ... But it was also so easy for Luca to leave.

I exhale a sigh of relief. Shutting down our accounts finally makes it all seem so real to me now. It's like closing the final page of the book. Luca and I are done. It's over. I will never let him walk back into my life, because Weston's right: I *do* deserve more than a man who picks and chooses when he wants me in the picture. I deserve someone who can't bear the thought of ever living life without me.

"Gracie," Weston calls.

I look up from my phone, beaming with a renewed sense of relief. Weston approaches and I can't tell what's more attractive: him this morning, naked in my bed with messy hair, or him right this second, wearing loose-fitting blue jeans that hang low on his hips and a plain white T-shirt that contrasts way too nicely against the black ink on his arm. I doubted I was capable of ever finding another man attractive after being so in love with Luca for seven years. The first time I saw Weston, I didn't even register that he was good-looking. It's taken time for him to come into focus, but now he's in glorified high definition, and it's making me weak.

"Guess what?" I say cheerfully, bouncing forward. "I just deleted everything. Mine and Luca's accounts. All gone!"

Weston reaches for my wrists and holds me steady. "Nice. Did you agree to that with Luca?"

"No."

Weston laughs and says, "You're getting so good at this."

I look down at his hands around my wrists and bite my lip. If I recall, he may have said something very similar last night. I glance up at him flirtatiously beneath my lashes, my gaze easing into a smolder. He sets it up so perfectly, I have to go ahead and say it. "I'm good at a lot of things."

Weston's laugh is gorgeous, but I catch him blushing. I know he remembers how I moved against him last night. "Well, I know for sure you're about to be real good at riding this bike."

Now I'm the one whose laughter echoes down the street.

We head inside the shop together and rent out two bikes for the day. We get kitted out with helmets, u-locks and a map which we instantly discard. We know San Francisco. It's an easy route to the bridge from here, and once Weston and I finish snickering with laughter at each other wearing goofy helmets, we set off.

It's around three miles from the rental shop to the bridge, but we take the Golden Gate Promenade. It's a gorgeous gravel trail along the waterfront, packed with pedestrians and cyclists as the bridge sits in the distance. Even from here, the views are stunning and we have to constantly maneuver around tourists pausing to snap photographs. Alcatraz Island is visible out on the water. I've walked this path many times, yet never followed it all the way to the bridge, and my excitement builds the nearer we get. I take living in the Bay Area for granted a lot of the time.

Weston cycles a little ahead of me and I call out to him, "Do you ever do bike patrols? You'd look pretty good doing this in uniform."

His laughter dances through the breeze and he abruptly turns, circling back and pulling up alongside me. "My quads are burning, I'm not gonna lie. This is yet another reminder that I need to hit the gym soon before my buddy Cameron kills me."

"My legs started to hurt fifteen minutes ago, but I didn't want to admit it," I huff. "Can we stop up there for a photo op?"

We both lack some serious power as we battle our way up a gradual incline. The path is winding as it curves upward toward the bridge, and I honestly fear I'll get to the other side and have no stamina left to make it back again, but there are *kids* doing this. When an elderly gentleman flies past us, I make a mental reminder to sign up to a spin class at the gym.

The path widens to create the perfect viewpoint of the bridge from below and others have seized the opportunity for (1) a great picture of the bridge in its entirety up close and (2) a break from the exertion of this hill. Weston and I pull over, leaning our bikes against a giant rock.

"Snack time," I say enthusiastically, swinging my backpack off my shoulders and rummaging inside. I hand Weston some water and a granola bar and we sit on the edge of the rock together, looking out over the still waters of the bay, the red paint of the bridge vibrant in the sunlight. Honestly, I'm just amazed at how clear the skies are with only a few scattered clouds. This is the perfect spot to take some photographs, and Weston has no idea that I'm about to put him through a photoshoot.

Out of the corner of my sunglasses, I sense a pair of eyes on me. It's a young girl, maybe around fifteen, who's also stopped off for a quick break with her parents. She looks over once, twice, three times, and I know immediately that the gears are turning in her head. I recognize it all too well, the furtive glances while they pluck up the courage to approach. She nudges her mother, nods in my direction, and then shyly proceeds toward me.

"Hi," she says, twisting her fingers together anxiously. "Sorry to bother you, but is your name Gracie?"

Weston leans back on his hands and watches with interest.

"Hi! Yes!" I say cheerfully, my tone pitching higher. I can't help it. It's the same chirpy, bubbly voice I always used when filming videos. Still my own, just emphasized. I push myself off the rock and nudge my sunglasses up into my hair, making a conscious effort to be polite and warm.

"I watch your videos!" the girl says, and she glances back to her mother with excitement.

"Aw, thank you so much!"

I see the way she steals a look at Weston and the confusion that follows. "Is Luca here too? You guys are the best!"

Our viewers are predominately female (well, were), and it was never lost on me that, naturally, Luca tended to be the favorite for obvious reasons. Whenever we bumped into viewers in public, they *melted* when talking to him. Always leaned slightly closer to him than me when we took photos. Maybe if Luca were to continue making content on his own, he'd do just fine, whereas I'm pretty sure I'd have to work harder.

Weston's brows lift with smug curiosity, wondering how exactly I'm going to navigate this conversation. Lie? Come clean? Tell this poor girl that Luca has treated me like a doormat the past month? I avoid his gaze.

"Actually," I say, tightening my smile, "Luca and I broke up. I *just* closed down our accounts, so you're the first person to know. It's better for both of us."

The girl's face falls in horror. "*What?*"

"Yeah. But thank you *so* much for supporting us." I don't let my smile falter, because I'm determined to maintain a positive front. "Who knows, though? Maybe I'll start my own channel!"

"Please do," the girl says, but the joy in her voice has faded. Maybe I should have posted an explanation on our accounts before I removed them. Our followers will have no idea what the hell has happened. "I'll leave you alone now, but do you mind . . . Can we?" She smiles sheepishly as she pulls out her phone.

We take a selfie together, and it's probably my favorite photo I've ever taken with one of our followers. We have the Golden Gate Bridge directly behind us and the sun is shining. The girl thanks me several times and skips off to rejoin her parents.

"Does that happen a lot?" Weston asks, and I turn around to look at him. He's still so unfamiliar with this whole influencer thing that it leaves him fascinated.

"Maybe once a month?" I guess. I tilt my sunglasses back down over my eyes and hold out my hands for him to take. "C'mon. We need nice photos to add to our new Instagrams, because *you* still haven't posted anything yet."

"Call me camera shy."

I wiggle my fingers with urgency, and Weston sighs and places his hands in mine. As I pull him to his feet, he doesn't put up much of a struggle. In fact, he's smiling. Just a tiny bit.

"Stand right . . ." I guide him into position, angling him perfectly in front of the bridge. " . . . Here." I shuffle back a few steps and pull out my phone, adjusting my settings and squatting down low, much to Weston's confusion. He for sure takes photos like a millennial. The old point and snap. *Boring.*

He stands there adorably awkward as though everyone else around us isn't doing the exact same thing. "What do I do?"

"Nothing."

"What?"

"It's a *candid,* Weston. Be candid." I take a couple shots, angling him differently in each one, but he still

246

requires instructions. "Just move loosely. Look off to the side. Touch your sunglasses. Stick a hand in your pocket. Just . . . act natural."

He lifts his sunglasses to glare at me. "Are you done?"

"Oooh. The seductive stare. Nice." I keep snapping photos as he strides toward me, filled with laughter. Is it the sunshine? The fact I erased Luca and mine's social media accounts? Weston? I'm so damn happy today.

"Show me how it's done," Weston says, nudging me forward.

I find a nice spot, flick out my hair, and start alternating between different poses as Weston holds up his phone and tries his best to capture different angles.

"Are you using square mode, though? You *have* to be in square mode so they'll definitely fit on Instagram. And you need to—"

"Gracie – respectfully – shut up."

He takes a few more photos of me before we decide to get moving again. We hop back on our bikes and power our way up the remainder of the hill, finally reaching the south entrance of the bridge. As expected, the breeze is strong and we're biking into a headwind. I'm glad I wore a sweater, because Weston seems a little chilly in his T-shirt. Cars whizz past, and the sidewalk is bustling with other cyclists, pedestrians and too many dogs on retractable leashes. We're thousands of feet above the water, and the views are stunning. We pull over again halfway across.

"Worth the burning quads?" Weston asks.

"Definitely."

We lean against the railing together, our arms touching. Even with the noise of the traffic, it's peaceful looking out over the water. San Francisco rises on the right, the hills of Sausalito on the left. I had dreams of settling down in a lovely, quaint suburb somewhere in the Midwest with Luca in a few years' time once we'd kickstarted our careers, but now ... Now I have no idea what my future has in store for me. I don't know where I'll be five years from now, but I'm learning to be okay with that. I want to live in the moment, and this right here with Weston, looking out over a city I adore, *this* is the moment.

"Thank you."

Weston's voice takes me by surprise. I turn to him and we immediately lock eyes. Something tells me he's been watching me for a while. "For what?"

"For asking me to come out here with you today. For last night," he says softly. He touches my hand on the edge of the railing and suddenly it's like we're the only two people here. "For giving me the chance to prove I *can* treat a girl right ... But maybe you disagree. I don't know. Do I?" He swallows nervously. "Do I treat you right, Gracie?"

"I can't even imagine how you ever got it wrong."

Weston's smile has a hint of sadness. He wraps an arm around me and pulls me in close, and I snuggle up to him, resting my head against his shoulder. I still don't know what we are. I can't tell what's real and what's not anymore, and I'm too scared to hear the answer. That's why I don't ask the question.

I just enjoy the moment.

WESTON

How the fuck I get through my next three shifts, I have no idea. My sergeant has been incredibly understanding with me, pulling me to the side before and after each shift to check in on how I'm feeling. Even Bill has eased off on his strict training regime for the past few days and instead focuses on building up my confidence again. I take charge of each call we get dispatched to. I even get to drive the cruiser. He says, "Good job. You've got this," a lot. But I'm not sure that I do.

When I wake on Monday after coming off my last night shift, I'm relieved to have three days off. The usual feeling of dread that hangs over my head during the lead-up to a shift is kept at bay for now. It allows me to relax, and I stay in bed for way too long, scrolling through my phone.

I've gotten into the habit of checking Gracie's Instagram daily, and she posted another photo last night. Her second one on the account so far. I sent her the photos I took of her by the Golden Gate Bridge and they clearly aren't terrible, because she's posted one of those. In the picture, she's laughing naturally, her coppery hair dancing in the breeze, and the caption reads: *simply happy.*

I love that she's happy.

I stare at the picture much longer than I care to admit, because when my phone rings in my hand, it breaks me out of my trance. My dad's calling.

"Hey, Dad," I answer, sitting up in bed. It's almost three in the afternoon, so I really ought to get up anyway. These night shifts always leave me so scrambled.

"Are you working today, bud?" Dad asks.

"No. Just finished a bunch of nights. What's up?"

"I'm in the city," he says. "Can you meet me? I've got something for you."

Dad's tone is often impassive and it makes me nervous. I never know if he's calling with good news or bad news. I figure his calmness is built into his nature from decades on the force. He keeps himself hard and collected, my dad. That's why I momentarily panic that he's come to San Francisco bearing bad news. Then it crosses my mind that perhaps he's performing a welfare check on me. Bill most likely reached out to Dad and told him about my traumatic shift.

"Sure . . . Where?"

"Well, do you want beer or do you want food?"

"Can't I have both?"

"I'm paying, so no."

"Then beer."

I meet Dad at a bar in Fisherman's Wharf. When he still lived here in the city, it was his favorite bar despite it drawing in nothing but tourists, but that's what he likes. Striking up conversations with the tourists and bombarding them with his local knowledge and offering recommendations. He especially loves helping visitors figure out how to ride the BART system. That's why today I grab us a table way in the back.

We order a couple beers *and* a plate of nachos.

"Don't grumble about the prices when you drink at bars in tourist hotspots," I tell him, pulling the nachos toward me. They're overloaded with melted cheese, pulled pork, jalapeños . . . Mmm. "Remember that big house of yours? Remember the asking price you paid for that? Yeah. Don't you dare whinge about buying your kid some nachos."

Dad grins and plucks a nacho from the plate. "Don't you want to know what I brought for you?"

"Let me guess: advice?"

"Nope," he says. "Turn around."

I crane my neck and find someone standing immediately behind my chair. They lunge forward and grab my shoulders, scaring the fuck out of me, so I don't even realize it's her at first. Why would I even *consider* the possibility of it being her? She's been deployed in Kuwait for the past year. Why would she be here in San Francisco?

Dad chuckles, and I turn around fully in my chair. I stare at her wide-eyed until the shock wears off and my brain recognizes her face again after all this time.

"Peyton?" I splutter, shaking my head in disbelief. "*Peyton!*"

"I'm home!" Peyton cheers, and I fly out of my chair and take my sister in my arms. I lift her off her feet and spin us around in a circle, her joyous laughter filling the bar. "Holy shit. You have no idea how glad I am to see you." I set her back down on her feet, but I keep my hands on her, terrified that if I let go, she'll disappear. "When the hell did you get back? You didn't tell me you were taking leave!"

"I got back to base on Saturday, then flew in yesterday. I wanted it to be a surprise," Peyton says, grinning. She looks so much like our mom. The dark eyebrows, the hollow cheekbones, the angular jaw. She's glowing.

"Nearly gave me a heart attack when she knocked on my door last night," Dad grumbles, but he's beaming.

"I can't believe you're here right now," I say, and I have to hug her again. "I've missed you so much. I'm so damn happy you made it home."

Peyton punches my arm as she pulls away. "What? You didn't think I would? Have a little faith in me, Weston. I take out bombs; they don't take out me."

"You know I don't like those jokes, Peyton," Dad says with a scolding glare, and Peyton apologizes with a quick kiss on his cheek. Although Dad is proud of us kids for pursuing such challenging, high-risk careers, he worries about each of us. Constantly. I know how relieved he must feel to have both Keaton and Peyton back on US soil at the same time. It's been a while.

I pull over a chair for Peyton to join us and ask, "Where were you hiding?"

"In the restroom." She flags down a waitress and orders herself a super-sized cocktail intended for sharing between two. "Don't judge me. I deserve it."

"You do," Dad agrees, and the three of us exchange ecstatic smiles around the table. We can't wrap our heads around the fact that we're sitting here together. If only Keaton was here too, it would be perfect.

"So? How was it?" I urge, taking a sip of my beer and getting comfortable in my chair. Peyton has nearly twelve months' worth of stories to share with us, and I imagine she has some pretty wild tales to tell. We'll probably be here for hours.

"We'll get to that." Peyton hunches forward, crossing her arms on the table. The waitress returns and sets down a giant fishbowl of liquor. Peyton takes a sip through her straw, licks her lips, then sets her reproachful eyes back on me. "Dad says Charlotte dumped you because you treated her like shit."

I fire Dad a look, and he sheepishly shrugs his shoulder. "I didn't say it like *that*."

"Do I need to kick your ass, Weston?" Peyton asks, and I suck in a breath, bracing myself for an earful. I shouldn't have expected anything less from my big sister. She always puts me in my place. "I *loved* Charlotte and I'm a little bit heartbroken that she won't ever be my sister-in-law now. What did you do to that poor girl? I better not have a fuckboy brother, I swear."

"*Peyton*," Dad says, but Peyton's response is to simply chug her cocktail. God, I've missed her.

"I didn't treat her like shit," I say, "but I definitely didn't treat her *right*."

Peyton narrows her eyes fiercely at me, her jaw clenched as she shakes her head with dramatic flair. "I'm so pissed at you. Idiot. Are you okay, though?"

"I wasn't at first. It was a hard lesson to learn, but I'm trying to be better," I admit, staring down the rim of my beer bottle. Should I tell them about Gracie? Is it too soon? Maybe they'll be happy for me. I glance up and nervously tell them, "I've met someone else."

"*Already?*" Peyton gasps. She grinds her teeth even harder. "Did you even love Charlotte? How can you meet someone else this quickly? Charlotte's side of the bed isn't even cold yet."

"Don't be so hard on him," Dad warns Peyton. It's the first I've mentioned anything about Gracie around him too, so although he seems surprised by this news, he's mostly curious. "What do you mean, you've met someone else?"

"I didn't *want* to meet anyone else," I say, but I'm perturbed by Peyton's deadly glowering and my voice is shaky. "I wasn't sure how I'd *ever* want to meet anyone else, but I went out with the guys one weekend and this girl sort of just . . . stumbled into the picture. She's just come out of a long-term relationship too, so we've leaned on one another. That's all it was at first, but now I think I really like her."

"Wow. You're blushing," Peyton points out.

"I'm starting to think I liked it better when you were in Kuwait."

"Nope, you're glad I'm home, because you're desperately in need of my female advice," she says confidently, and finally eases off with the tough, stern act. She takes her fishbowl in her hands and sits back, hugging it to her chest while she drinks. "This new girl. Will I like her? I'm only here for three weeks before I need to head back to Fort Carson, so I'm going to need to meet her sooner rather than later. What does she do? What's her *name?*"

"Gracie Taylor," I say, clearing my throat. A month ago, I never thought I'd be telling Dad and Peyton about the girl from the club whose birthday celebrations I ruined. I've conveniently left that part out. "Just turned twenty-two. She's taking a gap year before she goes back to school to get her teaching credentials."

Dad's brows shoot up and his tone becomes awfully soft. "She's pursuing teaching?"

"Elementary school teaching," I say, and I let the words hang in the air. Dad's expression has saddened, while Peyton manages a smile. All three of us think of Mom.

"Okay, fine. She doesn't sound that bad," Peyton huffs. "But I'm really going to miss Charlotte. Don't screw up again this time."

Dad reaches over to clasp my arm. "You seem happier today than you did when you visited me a couple weeks ago. I hope this works out for you, and I'd like to eventually meet Gracie too, when you're ready."

"Thanks, Dad," I say, and my sigh of relief is audible. Bill obviously hasn't told him what happened at work last week, and I'm not going to bring it up. Dad seems happy for me. I don't want to crush his spirits by telling him I hate life on the force, so I keep my mouth shut for now. I turn to Peyton and say, "Now tell me about the bombs."

Dad tuts.

On my way home from the bar several hours later, I walk past a florist. Vibrant flower arrangements are on display in the window and they serve as a reminder of all of the flowers I never sent Charlotte. And Charlotte deserved all of the flowers in the world. Charlotte *still* deserves flowers.

I head on inside. The store smells earthy and floral and a kind woman immediately comes to my aid, because it's clear by my dumbfounded expression that I'm not the kind of guy who usually sends flowers. There are roses, lilies, orchids, daffodils, tulips . . . I don't know where to start.

"What do you recommend?" I ask the florist.

"Well, what's the occasion?"

"An apology."

We put together a bouquet of white orchids that I request to be delivered to Charlotte's apartment in San Jose tomorrow, and the florist hands me a tiny card to write out a note, if I wish. Or she says I can remain anonymous. The choice is mine. I decide to leave a note with the flowers, and I write: *Charlotte, I want you to one day find the love I couldn't give you. You deserve to be happy. Weston.*

And I learn that flowers are way more expensive than I expect them to be.

I pay up and head for the door, but a box of giant red roses in the corner catches my eye. I don't know a damn thing about flowers, but I do know red roses are the most romantic of the bunch. That's what you're supposed to send on Valentine's Day, after all.

I think of Gracie and the conversation we had the night I cooked her dinner. *It's not all about the romantic gestures*. Key word being *all*. Treating a woman right isn't exclusively about the romantic gestures, but they play a big part.

Gracie is special to me, and I need her to know that.

"Actually," I say, turning back to the desk, "I'd like to send another arrangement. Red roses, please."

GRACIE

There's an inexpensive one-way flight to Thailand the first week of October. I don't know why I'm even bothering to check, but I've fallen down a rabbit hole. I only checked out someone's blog post on their experiences traveling solo as a young woman, and three hours later, I've plotted a route around Southeast Asia and checked out flights. The majority of solo travelers hop from hostel to hostel, but mine and Luca's budget always included luxury hotels, and if I *did* travel on my own, my safety and comfort would become even more of a priority. I can afford it. I can actually afford *months* of traveling in style, but my stomach still knots at the thought of doing it alone. My stomach also knots at the thought of *not* doing it.

What if, thirty years from now, I look back on my life and regret all the experiences I missed out on simply because I was too afraid? That's way more terrifying than the fear of eating dinner by myself on the island of Ko Lanta.

But still.

I can't do it.

I close my laptop and set it to the side just as there's a knock on the door. Elena's coming by soon, so I race to the door and pull it open, already smiling.

"Oh," I say.

It's not Elena. A woman stands outside my door, her head poking around the giant box of red roses in her arms. Her apron bears the logo of a florist downtown.

"Hi! I have a delivery for Gracie Taylor."

"*Oh*," I say again. "That's me."

The woman maneuvers the flowers into my arms and I can barely see around the arrangement. She laughs at the surprise on my face, wishes me a good day, and takes off. I stagger into my apartment, balancing the box of roses precariously in my arms as I carry them to my kitchen. I set them down on the counter and stare silently at them.

They're absolutely gorgeous. Twenty-four vibrant red roses, perfectly handpicked with not one single imperfection. I press my nose to them, inhaling their freshness. There's a tiny envelope tucked into the arrangement, which I gently pull out. As I slip the card out of the envelope, my pulse races.

These roses have to be from him.

I *want* these roses to be from him.

The note reads, in scrawly handwriting: *Flowers or bear hugs? I'll always give you both, Gracie Taylor. Love, Weston.*

My heart swells. Happiness rips through me, shooting outward from my chest all the way to my fingertips, until it feels like I'm close to bursting. There's nowhere else for this joy to go. It hurts, feeling like I'm on the verge of exploding. I love this feeling more than anything else in the world.

I move the roses over to the coffee table where they become the centerpiece, and then I sit down on the couch and gaze fondly at them. My head spins with deep thoughts. Weston has sent me roses. *Red* roses. The most romantic flowers of all. It's a grand gesture, but maybe that's exactly what he's aiming for. A gesture with a meaning so romantically clear-cut, there's no doubt at all where his head is. You never have to question what red roses mean.

I can't sit still. I bounce my legs up and down as a giddy squeak erupts from me.

Weston hasn't sent me expensive roses for the sake of proving that he's capable of being romantic. He's sent roses because this is real. He even said it last week: *I like you.* Somewhere between him cooking me that dinner and now, the lines have become blurred. I may have told Weston I'd show him how to treat the next girl who walks into his life right, but I never for a second thought that girl would ever be me. Maybe it has been fate, after all.

A key jangles into the lock of the apartment door, and I snap my head around in alarm. I'm expecting Elena any minute now, but she doesn't have a key. It can only be Luca.

He shoves open the door and I'm in his immediate line of sight. He storms toward me, a finger pointed angrily. "What the fuck did you do?"

"What?"

"Our accounts," he spits. "Where are they?"

It's sickening, just how quickly I've had to adjust to this new dynamic with Luca. When we were together, our voices were hardly ever raised. Disagreements were settled with understanding and resolution. He always had my back, no matter what, and he would *never* have let anyone speak to me the way he has recently. How unfathomable, that the person who promises to protect you can be the one who ends up hurting you the most . . .

We aren't Gracie and Luca anymore. There's venom woven between the lines of our failed relationship, and I hate that I'm now used to it.

"You can't be that invested in them if it's taken you three days to notice that they're gone," I say nonchalantly.

"Damnit, Gracie!" Luca slams his fist down on the kitchen counter and I flinch. "Why would you delete them? We could have kept making money until the end of the year *at least*. What gave you the right to shut everything down without consulting with me first?"

I stand from the couch and approach him, my hands on my hips. "For starters, I was the one who always handled the admin. Second, I'm the one who did most of the work. Third, our entire brand is now a lie. We're done, so guess what, Luca? That means our brand has to be done too."

"We should have discussed this," he growls, shaking his head furiously at the ceiling, like he can't bear to look at me. "I'm letting you stay here while I slum it on my cousin's couch, and this is how you repay me? By throwing away our income source?"

"You clearly haven't checked our bank account recently," I say. "We're doing just fine."

Luca scoffs, and as he looks back at me with his piercing blue-gray eyes, he notices something over my shoulder. "Now who gave you those?" he sneers. He fixes me with a hardened look as he crosses by me on his way to the coffee table where the box of roses sits. He tears out the small card. "*Love, Weston.* Surprise, surprise."

"Don't touch them," I warn.

Luca mockingly holds up his hands and retreats from the coffee table, advancing back toward me. "I don't care about your flowers. What I do care about, though, are both our names being on this lease. You want to bring a new guy around? Then I suggest you move out and find your own place."

"Who *are* you, Luca?"

It's terrifying that I don't recognize the person standing in front of me despite our being together for seven years. He's callous, bitter, selfish. He's *awful,* and that hurts. It hurts that there's still love for him deeply rooted inside of me. If only hating him could be as easy as loving him . . .

Luca places his hands on the edge of the kitchen counter either side of me, trapping me in place. He shrugs, his eyes fastened on mine, and says, "This is Luca Hartmann without Gracie Taylor."

There's a cough at the door. Elena struts into the apartment and whips off her sunglasses, suspiciously looking us over. "Are you guys fighting or fucking?"

I press my hands to Luca's chest and shove him away from me, immediately dashing to Elena and pulling her into a brief hug. In a hushed voice, I tell her, "Fighting. Thank God you're here."

Elena's demeanor shifts from blasé to poised and ready for war. She steps protectively in front of me and folds her arms, her brunette hair bouncing as she swings to face Luca. "You should get out of here."

"It's my apartment," Luca counters.

"Don't be a dick, Luca," she says with a scathing look. "Just leave."

Luca narrows his eyes at her, a beat of tense silence filling the apartment, and then he reluctantly gives in. As he heads for the door while Elena burns holes in his skull, he says, "We'll finish this conversation later,

Gracie." He swings his keys to the apartment around his index finger as he leaves, and an uneasy feeling settles in the pit of my stomach.

The second Luca is over the threshold, Elena rushes to the door and slides on the chain lock. She even checks out the peephole to confirm his departure while I release a deep breath. Although I held my own while Luca was in front of me, I'm left feeling shaky in the aftermath.

"What was that about?" Elena asks, joining me.

"He finally realized I shut down all our accounts," I say. I fill myself a glass of water and swig half of it, soothing the dry irritation in my throat. Elena and Maddie were thrilled when I told them I'd taken some initiative and deleted all of our social media accounts, but they were, of course, concerned when I admitted not having discussed it with Luca first. "He's not happy about it. He's . . . God, Elena. I don't even know who he is anymore."

"He's an ass, that's what he is," Elena says, and then she gasps. "Oooh. Roses!"

Elena runs to the box of roses, and I hastily set down my water and follow after her, reaching out for the card that Luca left on the coffee table. "Wait!" I plead, but Elena grabs it first.

I cover my eyes with my hand as she reads the note Weston wrote, because I know my weeks of denial and omissions of the truth have finally come to an end. The jig is up. It's time to come clean.

"Weston? *Weston?*" Elena gapes at me wildly. "The guy who got us kicked out of the club? The cop who attended to our noise complaint? You told me you've only seen that guy a couple times, and now he's sending you *roses?* Spill, Gracie. Right now."

I collapse onto the couch with a sheepish groan. It was inevitable that my friends would find out about Weston, but I've been trying to buy myself some time to understand my relationship with him first before confiding in anyone else about it. Admittedly, it'll be nice not to lie to Elena and Maddie about my whereabouts going forward. On Friday, when Weston and I biked across the Golden Gate Bridge, I told them I did it on my own.

Elena taps her foot impatiently, an eyebrow arched.

"Okay, you caught me. I've been seeing Weston." I grab a pillow and hide behind it, shielding myself from the tirade of questions Elena will surely throw at me, but she takes me by surprise when she gushes, "*Awwww!*"

She settles on the couch next to me and yanks the pillow out of my grasp. "Why don't you ever listen to me? I knew you guys would be good for each other!"

I purse my lips and remind her, "You mean you thought we'd be good for each other in the way of rebound sex."

"Well, yes," Elena says, "but if it's become something more than that, then even better! He's hot. And he's a cop. Now I understand why you've been somewhat stable recently . . . Fuck heartbreak. You've got a new man!"

I roll my eyes and grab the pillow back from her, scratching anxiously at the fabric. "I'm handling the breakup better than before, not entirely because of Weston, but because of Luca himself. He's turned into an insufferable jerk. Him and Weston even got into it at a bar the other week. He was talking trash about me and Weston put him in his place."

"Mmm. A man defending your honor. That's sexy." Elena sighs dreamily. "Tell me *everything*."

And it's not a difficult thing to ask of me, because I have so, so much to say about Weston. All good things, of course.

WESTON

Cameron has somehow roped both Brooks and me into a joint training session at the gym. How he pinned Brooks down, I have no idea, but I'm glad he's shown up. The only person slacking with their workout routine more than me is Brooks, so at least there is comfort in unity. Cameron is hell-bent on making us suffer.

"Hold up," Brooks says, heaving himself upright from the bench. Sweat drips from his brow. "Why are you grabbing more plates?"

Cameron slides a weighted plate onto one end of the barbell. "Because it's too easy. You aren't struggling enough. I need you to rep until failure." He adds another plate to the other side.

Brooks exchanges a horrified look with me, and I shake my head sympathetically. "My elbows almost caved in during that set and I momentarily lost my breath," he says. "You don't consider that struggling?"

"Nope."

"I hate this shit," Brooks grumbles, and he lies back down on the bench, praying to God above that Cameron lets us walk out of this gym alive. He grits his teeth with determination while Cameron steps up behind the bench to spot him.

I've already agonized through my bench press, so I'm nursing my noodle arms pathetically while sipping on a protein shake. Cameron isn't having it.

"Didn't I tell you to do lateral raises?"

"You're the worst," I mutter as I slink off to grab some dumbbells.

Although my shoulders burn, my chest aches, and I can no longer feel my arms, this push session isn't actually *that* bad. It's good to be back in the gym after so long and already my head feels clearer, so I promise myself I'll try and fit in workouts on my days off. It'll help my sanity.

When I return with my dumbbells, I find Brooks close to death, the barbell dipping dangerously low to his chest, until Cameron sighs and jumps in to rescue him. It's a good thing Adam has never stepped foot in a gym and never plans to, because he couldn't handle Cameron's militant regime. There'd be a fight in the middle of this weights section.

"I'm done. I'm *done*," Brooks splutters, grabbing his towel and wiping sweat from his face.

Cameron gives me a pointed look and I begin repping out lateral raises to appease him.

"I only came because I wanted to tell you guys something," says Brooks. He remains seated on the bench and interlocks his hands between his knees. "You know Nicole and I just celebrated our third anniversary at the weekend ... Well, I've been thinking about this for a while now, and it's definitely what I want." He looks up from the floor with a smile. "I'm going to ask her to marry me."

I stop cranking out reps.

"Congratulations, man!" Cameron says, clasping Brooks' shoulder.

This is an exciting declaration for Brooks, but it feels like a punch in the gut to me. Charlotte and I were together longer, yet not once did the thought of marrying her *ever* cross my mind. I never envisioned buying a home together, never pictured her in a bridal gown, never thought about kids with her ... I never thought of Charlotte as my future, but was that another selfish mistake of mine, or was she just never *meant* to be my future?

"That's great news," I say, plastering a grin on my face. It *is* great news for Brooks, but it throws up a lot of questions for me. "When are you planning on proposing?"

"This month sometime," says Brooks. "I need to think of something unique and romantic first, but I'm sure she'd say yes even if I got down on one knee with a gummy ring."

"Oh, she absolutely will. Can I be your best man?" Cameron asks.

"After what you just put me through? No chance in hell."

"It's not my problem you haven't hit the gym in over a year. Look at the chick deadlifting three plates over there. She puts you to shame." Cameron nods across the gym and I throw a quick glimpse over my shoulder.

There is, unbelievably, a girl deadlifting six plates in total with ease. I tear my eyes away just as fast, because although I'm checking her out with admiration, no guy ever wants to be *that* guy in the gym. But then I do a double take. I look back a second time. As the girl finishes off her set, the friend by her side does a little applaud. I recognize both of them.

"That's Gracie," I blurt, throwing down the weights in my hands.

Cameron shoves me out of the way for a better look. "*Your* Gracie can deadlift over three hundred pounds?"

"*No*. That's her friend. Maddie."

"Well, introduce us then!" Cameron says, and he breaks into stride.

Brooks laughs and nudges me forward. "Just be thankful for the break."

In their defense, I don't have to worry about Cameron and Brooks acting up. They're both chill guys. If Adam was here, *however*, I'd be much more nervous about officially introducing Gracie to my friends. They were at the club too, but Gracie was only a blip on their radar then. Even mine, admittedly. I didn't pay any attention to her in the club.

"Hey, you," I say, tapping Gracie on the shoulder.

She jumps in fear and spins around, her hand over her heart. Her panic instantly disappears when she realizes it's only me, and her parted lips transform into a grin instead. "Weston!"

"Looks like we decided to make our gym debuts on the same afternoon."

Gracie isn't the only one who's been slacking with working out recently, but breakups do that to you. They throw your life into turmoil, and taking care of your mental health becomes the priority. Gracie has mentioned more than once her plans to hit the gym again, but out of *all* the gyms in San Francisco, what are the chances we already go to the same one? I reckon about the same chances of me being the cop dispatched to check out a noise complaint made against her. Some greater force is adamant on throwing us together, but I'm not complaining.

"Hey, Maddie," I say, and Maddie blows out a breath and waves. She was more than happy to help me out the day she served me at the register in Zara, letting me know where exactly I could find Gracie, so she seems pretty cool.

"Three-fifteen . . . Damn," Cameron says apprecia-tively, counting the plates. "You did that effortlessly."

Maddie blushes. "You were watching?"

"Personal trainer, this hunk. If you lift heavy, he'll notice," I say, gesturing to Cameron. Brooks stands a little awkwardly to the side, and I can't help but laugh. "I just realized all of us have already met. Gracie, Maddie . . . These are my friends. Cameron. Brooks. They were also gatecrashing your booth that night at the club."

"Where's the other guy?" Maddie asks, adjusting her glasses. "The one you punched in the face."

"Adam? Oh, he's a slob. The gym's his worst night-mare."

Maddie exchanges a knowing look with Gracie and they both laugh. Maddie says, "Same for Elena. That explains why they bonded so well." She ducks down and begins dragging a plate off the barbell she has set up on the lifting platform, and Cameron and Brooks instinct-ively assist her.

"I didn't know this was your gym," Gracie says, shuffling up close. "I've been coming here for years, and I don't think I've ever noticed you."

"Neither of us were even capable of noticing anyone else until a month ago," I say, then tilt my head a degree to the side as I study her with a dopey fucking grin.

She's so cute. She's wearing little booty shorts and a sports bra, and I don't even hide the fact that I'm check-ing her out. My gaze travels up and down her body more than once. Her legs are toned in such a defined way that I question how she possibly struggled biking uphill last week. She's wearing a pair of old Nikes and there's a blue scrunchie around her wrist, though her hair is already scraped back into a high ponytail, her bangs framing her face. She's not wearing any makeup, but she doesn't need to. Her skin glows with a layer of perspiration, and I don't know if it's pheromones or what, but the desire to touch her, to kiss her, to feel her, suddenly becomes uncontrollable.

A hue of red tints Gracie's cheeks. "*Weston*," she says shyly, stealing a glance at our friends. The three of them are still unloading the barbell.

"I don't mind coming to the gym if it means I get to look at you," I say, emphasizing the smolder in my eyes as I reach out for her wrist, guiding her in a small circle. She complies, offering me a spin. "Damn."

"Someone's feeling extremely flirty today," she remarks, and the twinkle in her blue eyes is unmistakable.

"You make it easy, Gracie Taylor."

I slide my hand from her wrist down into hers, interlocking our fingers. Everyone who matters to me now knows about Gracie and that's so freeing. I'm not sure exactly what Gracie has been telling her own friends about our situation, but she doesn't try to tear her hand from mine in front of Maddie, and that says a lot.

"The roses," Gracie murmurs, and I shake my head to silence her.

"You've already thanked me a thousand times. Don't you dare do it again," I warn her.

The roses were delivered to her apartment yesterday, and the gesture went down extremely well, much to my relief. After I'd left the florist, I began to overthink it. I worried Gracie would think I was trying too hard, but mostly I was terrified that she would realize I *do* really like her, and that the roses would scare her off if she didn't feel the same. However, she blew up my phone multiple times yesterday, expressing gratitude. A green light.

"Okay . . ." Gracie says. She steals another peek at our friends out of the corner of her eye, then tugs on my hand. "How about I show you how much I appreciate the roses, then?"

Her sultry voice sends that craving for her through the fucking roof. She pulls more firmly on my hand now, leading me across the gym. I'd be an idiot not to follow, so I do, albeit in a daze.

"Where are you two going?" Brooks calls.

"Important business," I say. "You guys keep each other company and we'll be back in a sec."

I don't look back at them long enough to see their expressions change. All I care about is Gracie and where the hell she's taking me. We weave around machines and equipment, all the way to the other side of the gym and through the door to the unisex locker rooms. Still holding my hand, she yanks me with her as she pokes her head down the row of lockers to the left, then the right. There's no one else in here right now.

Gracie steps in front of me, pushes me hard against a set of lockers with a thud, and passionately presses her lips to mine. I'm so into it, I only need a nanosecond to process my surprise before I immediately kiss her back just as fiercely. There's no easing precariously into things, because there's no doubting how desperately we want each other. I tilt her chin up, kissing her deeply, slowly, teasingly.

"You really like the roses, huh?"

"No," Gracie breathes. "I really like you."

Her declaration only adds fuel to the fire. I take her face in my hands and crash my mouth against hers. She's a lot stronger than I give her credit for, because despite being so tiny, she has her entire body weight pressed against me, pinning me to these lockers. She begins pulling at the waistband of my shorts and I tear my lips from hers, still cupping her face in both hands. Our gazes lock.

"Here?" I ask, glancing left and right.

Gracie smirks, grabbing the hem of my tank top. "Are you scared we'll get caught?"

"No, it's just . . . I didn't think you'd be the type . . ."

"Oh my God." Gracie throws her head back and releases the most gorgeous laugh that bounces all the way down the row of lockers. "You totally think I'm vanilla, don't you?"

I stare at her, deadpan. "Your name is Gracie. You aspire to be an elementary teacher. Yeah. I do think you're vanilla."

"Oh, Weston," Gracie says, thoroughly amused as the seductive glint in her eye only intensifies. "I was with Luca for *seven* years. I've tried a thing or two."

"Don't say his name," I growl, grabbing her waist and pushing her backward into a changing cubicle, locking the door. Fervently, I kiss my way up her neck until my mouth reaches her ear. "I'll fuck you so hard you'll forget he ever existed."

Gracie shudders with anticipation. It's my turn to take control now, and I press my chest to hers and hold her against the wall of the cubicle as I slide my hand inside those tiny little shorts of hers. She knots her fingers through my hair, her breathing broken with gasps. She bites down hard on her lip, fighting back her moans of pleasure, but they still fill the cubicle. She's so wet, she soaks her shorts. I help her out of them before freeing myself from own, and then I flip her around. She braces herself with her hands against the wall, bent over with her back perfectly arched. The view alone is enough to make me groan. I grab her hips and slowly guide myself inside of her.

She gasps, and I clasp a hand over her mouth.

"Can you keep quiet for me, Gracie?"

Gracie nods. I wrap my other hand around her ponytail as I thrust steadily, biting my own tongue. I love fucking her so much, but it's dangerous *just* how good she feels. It's impossible to last for long. I fuck her harder, quickening my pace and building up power, her body jerking forward with each thrust. She sinks her teeth into my hand to stifle her whimpering, but the sting of her bite is euphoric, and I throw my head back, eyes rolling in pleasure. I'm going to come soon.

"You're being such a good girl for me," I whisper, breathless.

I pull out just as I'm nearing the edge and turn Gracie back around to face me. She kisses me like she *needs* to kiss me to survive, and I slide my hands beneath her ass and lift her from the ground. She wraps her legs around my waist, her hands on my shoulders and her ecstatic gaze locked on mine as I guide her down onto me. It's so intimate, facing each other like this.

"Are we still just friends?" Gracie whispers, tenderly pushing my hair back.

"No," I say with finality.

I don't know how I find the strength in my arms, but with my hands still on her ass, I bounce her body up and down and she flows with the rhythm. She grinds and rolls against me, and even when we hear the door of the locker room swing open, neither of us stop. We double down on our focus. I fight with everything in me not to let a single sound slip past my mouth, and Gracie digs her nails into my shoulders. It doesn't help contain our chaotic breathing, but I don't care at this point. I'm about to blow.

I lock my arms around Gracie's waist and slow her to a stop. My legs start twitching as an explosive warmth spreads through my body, and I bury my face into that little crook of her neck that I love so much, overcome by the pleasure of my release. I can barely support either of us anymore, so I can't help but stumble back into the wall with her.

There are voices in the locker room now, but it's only some guys having a casual conversation about an upcoming concert. No one has suspected a thing, and Gracie and I grin back at one another with exhilaration. That wasn't quite the workout I'd planned for when I rocked up at the gym today, but it's one way to work up a sweat.

"You go out first," Gracie whispers, and I pass her her shorts from the floor. "I'll clean up and meet you back out on the floor in a second."

I kiss her on the temple as I adjust my own shorts, then unlock the cubicle door and step out into the locker room. I give an obligatory nod of acknowledgement to the guys we overheard chatting and head back onto the gym floor, shaking my hands through my hair in a half-assed attempt to tame it.

Gracie and I have only been gone for a few minutes, and in that time, Cameron, Brooks and Maddie have relocated to a squat rack. Maddie seems thrilled to have some assistance, because Cameron and Brooks are loading up more plates for her. She's enjoying her moment as the main character. Cameron is in a bubble of admiration at watching a woman lift incredible weight, and Brooks is just relieved to have a break from Cameron's grueling workouts.

"You did not," Cameron says as I approach them. He clangs another plate onto the barbell and then shakes his head at me in a stern, fatherly way. "I work here, Weston. C'mon."

"What?" I feign innocence, furrowing my brows in forced confusion.

"You totally just got laid in the locker room!"

"Yup. Look at the smile he's hiding," Brooks chimes in, and then bursts into laughter as he gives me a once over. "You could have looked in a mirror before you came back out here. Your hair wasn't like that five minutes ago."

Maddie places her hands on her hips as she nods to the locker room door. I glance behind me and find Gracie emerging from the locker room, running her fingers through her bangs and setting them neatly back in place, a sheepish smile on her face as she catches all of us watching her.

"Oh yeah," Maddie says, giggling. "They definitely did."

GRACIE

I meet Weston for dinner on Friday evening after his shift. Although he still believes working for the police department is the worst decision he's ever made, he's had a relatively easy ride this past week since he showed up at my door in the middle of the night, traumatized. No other shift has come close to affecting him the way that one did, and I make a point now of checking in with him every time he finishes work in case there's anything he'd like to offload on me. By the sounds of it, today's shift was pretty quiet and mundane.

"But at least Bill is being a bit more chill," Weston says, tossing a French fry into his mouth, and I smile across the booth at him like a giddy teenager nursing a lifelong crush. "How did your driving lesson go today?"

"I parallel parked!" I exclaim, and although parallel parking is a skill the majority of the population has,

Weston still beams with pride. It's only my second lesson, but I already know *how* to drive, so it's all about the fine-tuning. "I'll maybe take one more lesson and then I'll take the test."

"And then you need to buy a car."

"Would you like to come with me to shop for one? I think I'd like a Mercedes. A black one."

Weston rolls his eyes and says, "*Of course* you want a Mercedes. I can't picture you in a Toyota."

But I know how I picture Weston. I picture him with his hand over my mouth in that cramped cubicle in the gym's locker room, and I completely melt every time the image crosses my mind. I worry about my own sanity, because it's almost becoming an obsession. All I think about is him.

He lifts his burger to take a bite, but his phone starts ringing. He answers it immediately and, after only a few seconds on the call, his posture straightens. I sip my soda and watch curiously. The call only lasts thirty seconds before Weston hangs up, looks at me with a dazzling grin, and says, "Keaton's wife just had their baby. James. How do you feel about a road trip to meet my nephew?"

"I'd love to! Congratulations, Uncle Weston."

We polish off the remainder of our food, pay the bill, then hightail it out of the restaurant and into Weston's car. His older brother, Keaton, lives a couple hours north. Halfway into the journey, I question whether it's my place to show up at the hospital with Weston. I've never met any of his family before. He reassures me, more than once, that his family are keen to meet me. His father and sister are also en route to the hospital, and it'll be a late night for Weston and me by the time we get back to San Francisco later. It's already after nine.

"That happened so fast," Weston says, fidgeting with nervous excitement as we pull into the hospital's parking lot. "Keaton didn't even tell any of us she'd gone into labor. Man, I love my niece more than anything, but I can't wait to throw a ball around instead of squeezing tiny dresses onto Barbies." His excitement is adorable. He doesn't know what to do with himself, and as we cross the parking lot hand in hand, he accidentally breaks out into a jog.

"Slow down!" I laugh, struggling to keep up with his long strides.

Even though it's late, the maternity wing of the hospital is still a hive of activity. *Obviously.* The nurses here wear pale pink scrubs and they dart quickly down the halls, off to their next patient. There's a waiting room where visitors wait patiently for good news while loved ones endure labor, but Keaton's baby is already here, so we head off down the hall in search of the room they're in. Weston's dad and sister made it here before us and have given us the number. Weston's so antsy, he ends up completely missing the room.

"It's here," I say, reaching out for his arm and tugging him back.

He laughs nervously, then takes a deep breath before knocking gently on the door and poking his head around it. I follow him inside, hiding slightly behind him. Now that I'm here, I feel even more like I'm overstepping a boundary.

The room is quiet, dark, peaceful. There's only a standing lamp switched on in the corner, but I realize why: Keaton's wife is fast asleep in the bed. I glance around at everyone else. There's an older man with a mustache that must be Weston's father seated in a chair in the corner with a toddler on his lap, a younger guy also with a mustache that must be Keaton, and then the female must obviously be his sister, Peyton. The three of them watch us as we settle into the room, each of their expressions lit with joy. On the other side of the bed, a newborn with a baby blue hat sleeps soundly in the crib.

"Hi," Weston whispers to the room. He embraces his brother first, pulling him in for a hug and patting him on the back. "Congratulations, dude. How's Lily?"

"A rockstar," Keaton replies, his voice equally as hushed. "She just fell asleep."

"Uncle Wes!" the toddler exclaims, leaping across the room and wrapping her arms around Weston's legs. *Uncle Wes.* So cute. He scoops her up into his arms and snuggles with her.

"*Shhh.* Mommy and James are sleeping," Keaton reminds his daughter.

With his niece still in his arms, Weston looks sheepishly around the room and gives me a pointed nod as I hover anxiously by the door. "This is Gracie, by the way," he whispers, and then he gestures to everyone else one by one. "That's my dad, Mark. Keaton. Peyton. And this little superstar is Sophia." He kisses his niece on the forehead and she giggles. It's an age-old fact that seeing a guy be good with children only makes them more attractive, and I can totally vouch for that. Watching Weston cuddle into his niece makes my heart hurt a little, and he hasn't even held the newborn yet. I'm not going to cope when he does.

"It's nice to meet you all," I whisper with a little wave.

Weston looks most like his sister. They both have dark, bold features and the same brown eyes, and I can totally picture her as a badass soldier working overseas. Honestly, the Reed family is kind of intimidating. Weston's dad's a retired cop, his brother is an airman, his sister a soldier . . . It says a lot about their values and discipline, and as I watch them across the dim room, I notice how each of them hold themselves with a definite degree of dignity. Heads held high, shoulders relaxed, stances confident.

"Would you like to hold him, Weston?" Keaton asks, pointing to the crib.

"Please," Weston says. He sets Sophia down and shifts to the crib, gazing inside at the sleeping newborn, as his smile stretches even wider. "I hope he has a strong throwing arm when he's older."

Keaton laughs. He slips his hands into the crib and delicately lifts the baby, placing him securely into Weston's waiting arms. And yup. I can't even deal.

"Hey, little dude," Weston says.

Keaton feels confident enough in Weston's ability to take care of the baby for a few minutes, because he takes Sophia off to grab a juice from a vending machine. Mark and Peyton, after a moment of deliberation, also decide they could do with a snack. They disappear out of the room, leaving Weston and me alone with tiny James and a sleeping Lily.

"Come see him," Weston tells me, his tone cheerful.

He sits down in the empty chair his father has left, the newborn still tucked safely in his arms and fast asleep. Weston can't tear his eyes from him, and I move by his side and place a hand on his shoulder. I love kids. I always have. Kids are so pure and optimistic, always seeing the good in the world. The only thing I love more than kids are babies, so my heart combusts as I lay eyes on James. Plump lips, button nose, tiny fingers. *Ahhh.*

I squeeze Weston's shoulder a little tighter. "Would you like kids someday?"

"I would," he says, but his sigh tells another story. He pokes his finger into James' hand and the baby clenches his dainty fist around it. "But I grew up with a cop as a father, and every time he was out working the beat, I had this all-consuming feeling of dread. Keaton and Peyton didn't worry at all, yet I'd have my face pressed against the window waiting for Dad to get home. Any time he was more than an hour late, Mom would start to pace and make calls. One time he really *didn't* come home, because he'd been shot in the arm and was at the ER. I cried for *hours*. I was super young then, so I thought it meant he was going to die." Weston glances up from the baby, his eyes a deeper shade of brown in the dim lighting of this hospital room. "So yes, I do want kids, Gracie . . . but I worry that one day I won't come home to them."

"Oh, Weston," I breathe. I hate that he already worries about the future like this, and it pulls at my heartstrings so intensely, a physical pain throbs in my chest. I kneel down by his side and place my hand on his knee. "I think you should quit the force. And I know it's not my place to tell you that, but it's clear that's what you want to do, and you just need someone to tell you that it's okay. It's okay to step away from something that isn't for you, Weston. Quit."

"But my dad . . ."

"Would understand," I finish. No father would want their kid to follow in their footsteps if it made them *this* scared, but Weston can't swallow his own pride. He needs some time to figure out what path he wants to pursue instead. He needs a break. "Quit, Weston, and travel with me instead."

The corner of his mouth twitches with a sad smile. We're still talking in hushed voices, and he snuggles

James into his chest a teeny bit more. "I can't travel to the other side of the world for six months, Gracie. That's *your* challenge. I want you to do that alone to prove to yourself that you're capable of anything, even though I think I'd miss you . . . Just a little." He lets go of James' hand and touches my jaw, skimming his thumb over my cheek.

"If I face my fear and go traveling alone," I whisper, pressing my face into his palm and absorbing the warmth of his skin, "would you face yours and quit your job?"

"I can't, Gracie."

The door clicks open, and Mark and Peyton arrive back first with bottled soda and bags of chips. I stand up from the floor and manage a smile as though my mind isn't spinning. I care about Weston so much that when he's hurting, I'm hurting.

"Can I have him?" Mark asks, and Weston transfers the baby from his arms into his father's.

"Hey, Gracie," Peyton whispers, scooting up next to me. "Do you want to go outside for a second so we can talk?"

"Don't grill her," Weston warns, and Peyton scoffs.

Oh no. I don't let my apprehension show, and instead nod politely and follow Peyton out of the room. Weston's already warned me that Peyton is the toughest one to crack, so I have no idea what I'm in for. What if she doesn't like me? Weston is close with his siblings, and I figure their approval matters.

Peyton and I find some empty seats just down the hall, and she opens up her bag of chips and offers me one. An icebreaker.

"That's okay," I say. "Weston and I were out for dinner when he got the call, so we're both well-fed. Congratulations, by the way! You must be so happy you aren't missing this."

"I won't lie and say I didn't plan my leave around their due date," Peyton admits, tossing another chip into her mouth. She's around the same height as me, but her petite frame is clearly misleading. She must be one tough woman if she survived basic training for the army. I'd tap out after one push-up, that's for sure. "I think Weston needed me home too. I'm the one who keeps him right. Can I ask how you guys met? He was vague about it."

So, this is, indeed, an interrogation. I'm not sure how much Peyton knows, but I definitely don't want to get off on the wrong foot with her by lying. My laugh is nervous. "My boyfriend of seven years left me the week of my birthday, and I was a wreck. My friends dragged me out to a club to cheer me up. I think Weston's friends had the same agenda for him, because he was in the club that night too."

Peyton frowns. "So, you met in a nightclub?"

"No, we met in the Uber afterward," I say, then realize how that sounds. A blazing heat spreads across my face. "Wait, no. Let me go back a step. Weston and his friend got into a bit of a tussle, and *all* of us got kicked out of the club."

"Was it Adam, by any chance?"

"Yes."

"Of course," Peyton says, rolling her eyes. She nibbles the edge of another chip as she listens. "Go on."

"Honestly, I just wanted to go home, and Weston was taking off in an Uber. I shared a ride with him," I explain, but although it was only five weeks ago, it feels like a lifetime. I was in a totally different headspace then, and it's thanks to Weston that I feel as stable as I do currently. "I cried a lot, and he hugged me. We were both having a tough week. He left his phone at my place, so he came back to get it the next morning."

"That's kind of cute," Peyton says, relaxing back in her chair. "I'm not going to lie to you, Gracie, I was a big fan of Charlotte and I'm so disappointed in him for screwing things up with her. I'm still mad at him, and I'm also confused."

I nod, listening. My bond with Weston has strengthened incredibly fast, and I'm perfectly aware that it may not make sense to most of the people closest to us. I was so in love with Luca for seven years that I'd resigned myself to being single for a long, long time before I would ever be ready to date again, and I imagine Weston felt similar when it came to life after Charlotte. We can't help the timing of when we met, but we *did* meet, and now things are developing in a way I could have never imagined. New feelings don't invalid the feelings we once had for Luca and Charlotte.

"We *were* only friends at first," I promise Peyton. "But we just click. We get each other, and I have no idea how I would have survived the past month without him. He's making me believe that it's possible to fall in love again."

Peyton's lower lip juts out. "Aww," she says, and I own my vulnerability. I'm not playing games. What I feel for Weston is definitely real, and I need her to believe that. "Listen. Weston's the youngest of the three of us, and he's also the softest. He's sensitive. He has a good heart," she says. "So, I hope he learns from his mistakes and treats you right. If he doesn't, you let me know, and I will kill him with my bare hands."

I laugh as she scrunches up the empty chip bag and stands up. "I was worried you wouldn't like me," I confess.

"Don't worry. I already knew I'd like you when Weston told me you want to be an elementary school teacher," she says with a grin, offering out her hand to pull me up. There's a flicker of fondness in her gaze as she adds, "Teachers are the best kind of people."

WESTON

I glance at Bill out of the corner of my eye. "Can I ask you something?"

"Sure."

"You're my field training officer. You've been watching me for the past nine weeks. The weekly reviews you give me are acceptable. Not great, not bad. Average." I pause, staring at the road ahead as I navigate the cruiser through tight traffic. "Do you think I can do this job?"

I sense Bill watching me as he mulls over my question in silence. It's the final hour of a relatively quiet shift and I've taken charge with ease and confidence, but that's only because there have been no high-stake calls. Nothing I haven't seen before, nothing dangerous that's gotten our blood pumping. On days like these, I think maybe I *could* ride this out.

"I believe you're capable of being a great officer," Bill says at last, drawing out his words slowly so that they truly sink in for me. "Physically, you can do it. You are tactful and fair. You follow protocol well. But mentally?" He tuts pityingly. "You struggle. I'm planning on extending your training."

There are still another seven weeks of field training to go, and it comes as a surprise to me that Bill has already made the decision this soon to extend it. I've been struggling with the mental load of such a demanding, emotional job, but I thought I'd been hiding it well. I'd perfected my poker face, and I only let slip that *one* shift . . . But it seems Bill can see straight through me.

"You're giving me an extension?"

"Yes," he says simply. "We look after people, Weston, but we also need to look after ourselves. You need to work on that. There's no use saving anyone if it means losing yourself."

I flash him a cynical look. "You're being suspiciously nice to me. You don't have to be, you know."

Bill chuckles but says nothing more. He fiddles with the onboard computer as I drive, then sits up straight as our dispatcher crackles to life over the radio. She reports a call for a possible break-in. The full details are unclear, but the scene is secure. There's no need to throw on the lights, but I do kick things up a notch and increase our speed. Hayes Valley. An apartment community. Fourth floor.

My heart skips a beat.

It's Gracie's apartment.

"Responding," Bill confirms with dispatch.

"I know her," I blurt, stepping on the gas. We aren't far away. Our ETA is two minutes.

Bill looks at me funny. "Who? The dispatcher?"

"*No.* The girl who lives in this apartment. She's . . . a close friend of mine."

"Is that why you're speeding?"

I ignore him, because I'm the officer in charge. I decide how fast we arrive on scene, and when Gracie is the civilian who requires our help, I *need* to race there. It's a suspected break-in, but her apartment complex is secure, so I'm already racking my brain as to possible scenarios. It's also six in the evening. The sun is out. Break-ins almost always occur during nightfall. What the hell has happened?

I park the cruiser outside one of the entrances to Gracie's apartment building and buzz us inside with the access code provided by dispatch. It's a much easier method than my usual off-duty way of buzzing random apartments until someone lets me in. We ride the elevator to the fourth floor and Bill watches me intently the entire time. In this phase of my training, I do most of the work while he observes. He'll only step in when necessary.

"It's down here," I tell Bill as the elevator doors ping open. I'm always determined to arrive on scene as fast as possible no matter what the call is, but when there's a personal connection involved, *of course* the stakes are higher.

I march down the hall, Bill close behind, and I see her.

Gracie's waiting outside the open door of her apartment, wringing her hands together in distress. She's pale, her face white.

"*Weston*," she gasps, and she runs to me. She throws herself into my arms and I gather her into my embrace. I have a job to get done and I know Bill is watching, but Gracie needs my comfort first. She presses her face into my uniform and murmurs, "I didn't think it'd be you who showed up, but I'm *so* glad it is. I'm so scared."

My hands on her waist, I pull back and examine every inch of her. All I see is fear in her blue eyes. "Are you harmed in any way? Are you hurt?"

"No. No," she splutters, shaking her head and clutching my arms. "I'm just scared, Weston."

"You called and said there was a break-in? Tell me exactly what's happened."

Gracie casts a fearful glance at the open door of her apartment. "I just got home from another class with the driving instructor and the door was wide open . . . *Look*."

"Okay, stay right here with Bill," I command, exchanging a quick nod of confirmation with Bill. "I'll take a look."

I pry my arms out of Gracie's death grip and fix her with a reassuring look as I move toward her apartment.

Honestly, I don't know what I'm expecting here. Has she been robbed? She does keep a lot of expensive cameras and computer equipment in the apartment, and I've noticed most of her clothes *do* have designer labels. She's a prime target for criminals looking for easy goods to shift to make a quick buck.

My hand resting on my duty belt, I peer around the door.

The apartment is trashed. Absolutely raided.

I step one foot over the threshold, but my adrenaline is pumping. Gracie told dispatch the scene was secure, but is it?

"Gracie," I call out to her. "Have you actually been inside and looked around?"

"No," she admits.

Fuck. I hate securing the scene. The likelihood of the perpetrator hiding out at the scene of their crime is very slim, but it happens. There's always the rare chance of someone charging at me from their hiding spot in the corner of a room, wielding a weapon and determined to flee.

I ease inside the apartment, my hand resting on my holster for my firearm, ready to brandish it at any moment. The blinds have been torn down from the windows, the couch cushions have been knifed open, the huge TV has a gaping crater in the center of it. Scattered across the floor are the twenty-four roses I bought Gracie a week ago.

I kneel down, my head still on a swivel as I scan my surroundings, and pick up one of the roses from the ground. The bud is flattened, the petals torn. It's like it's been stomped on. I grit my teeth and toss it away.

The kitchen cupboards are flung open, but the contents seem untouched. The refrigerator, however, is a different story. Fresh groceries are smeared across the floor, and I wrinkle my nose at the sight of raw chicken touching the tiles.

Burglars don't usually search through the fridge.

I cross to the master bedroom, keeping my back shielded against a wall at all times as I scope out the room. It's clear in here, too, but Gracie's clothes are strewn all over the bed and floor. On the dresser, there's a jewelry box. I flip it open and further confusion settles over me. It's full of watches, earrings, bracelets, necklaces. Jewelry is *always* stolen. Why hasn't this been touched?

"Everything all good in there, Reed?" Bill calls into the apartment from outside in the hall.

"Working on it!"

I secure the bathroom, then move on to the second bedroom that's been converted into an office. As I poke my head around the door, I feel my shoulders sink. I take my hand off my holster and scratch my temple. There's definitely no one in the apartment, but God, I'm confused. The computers and cameras are all still here, but damaged. There's a crack on the desktop screen.

A laptop lies face-down on the ground. One camera is smashed into pieces.

This isn't a burglary.

As I head back out into the hall, I scrutinize the apartment door. Completely untouched, the lock intact.

This isn't even a break-in.

"Well?" Gracie whispers, her lower lip trembling and her eyes wide. Bill also awaits my verdict on the scene, but I just shake my head.

"This wasn't a break-in," I say, hands on my hips. "It also doesn't appear to be a burglary, but Gracie, I'll need you to do a full inventory check for me, okay?"

"Nothing's taken?" she squeaks, equally as confused as I am.

"No. It seems personal. And it seems like they had a key." I suck in a breath, because I can tell by the look in her terrified eyes that she hasn't yet considered what I'm about to propose. Domestic disputes are the calls I handle the most, and destruction of property is commonplace. "When did you last talk to Luca, Gracie?"

Gracie's brows rise. "You think Luca did this?"

"Fill me in, please," Bill says, clearing his throat. "Who is Luca?"

"An ex-partner who lived here previously," I say, and pull out my notepad and pen. "Gracie, you agree things have been hostile with him recently, yes?"

"He wouldn't . . ." she says, rapidly shaking her head as though she can't bear even the mere insinuation of it. "I know him, Weston. He would *never*."

I sigh, because it's so obvious to me yet not to her. Who else with a key to this apartment would have enough of a vendetta to trash the place? Things have been growing increasingly hostile between Gracie and Luca lately. He hates that I'm in the picture, and he especially loathes the fact Gracie deleted their social media accounts. Maybe this is how he shows his anger.

I point my pen at the security camera in the hall. "Your building has cameras. We'll go check them out with the building manager. Are both your names on the lease?"

"Yes."

I groan. It's not impossible to charge for property damage when it's the suspect's own fucking property they've damaged, but it makes things complicated. Gracie wells up with tears now, and I stop scribbling notes and reach out to touch her hand. Bill narrows his eyes at the gesture.

"Listen. There's thousands of dollars' worth of damage in there," I tell her gently. "If we find out it's Luca, he can be charged with felony vandalism. But it's your property too, so if you don't want us to file charges, then we won't."

"He wouldn't . . ." Gracie repeats, and I think she may be experiencing a delayed onset of shock. "We've been arguing more lately, but he wouldn't destroy our home . . ."

"It's not his home anymore, though, is it?" I remind her. Maybe that's another element. Maybe Luca's decided he doesn't want Gracie to be the one who gets to keep their luxury apartment anymore. "We'll get this sorted, Gracie. We'll check the cameras and I'll write a report."

"What do I do now?" she asks, her voice timid. She's so vulnerable right now, I can't possibly expect her to step foot in that trashed apartment alone.

I run my fingers from her wrist all the way up to her shoulder as I move in close to her. Lowering my voice, I tell her, "Stay with me tonight. There's a spare key under the mat. Go there now and I'll be home when I finish this shift in an hour. We can order takeout. Will you be okay until then?"

Gracie nods, but she's still shaky. I wish I didn't have to get back to work. She needs me right now, but the best I can do is give her somewhere to stay that's safe. It's also a damn good job Luca has left the scene, because I'd love to throw a set of cuffs around his scrawny wrists. Their breakup has been so toxic. Charlotte and I had a clean break, and at first, that was unbearable to me. There was never even a sliver of hope of us getting back together, which hurt like a bitch, but I realize now that keeping clear of each other was the mature way to handle things. We've respected each other this entire time and I still genuinely care for her. That's why I sent her those flowers. It's a nice, civil position to be in.

Gracie and Luca, however . . . They remained in the picture for one another, and now look at them. Luca has completely spiraled. Are criminal charges really worth it for a woman you wanted space from? As much as I hate to think it, Luca clearly still loves Gracie deep down. How couldn't he?

Gracie locks up her apartment, leaving the mess behind to deal with later, and I realize she'll have to walk to my place. The sooner this girl buys a car, the better.

"Actually, Bill," I say, "I think we should give Gracie a ride to a safe location."

"I agree," Bill says, even though we both know it's not necessary. If it was the middle of the night, then sure, we would never let a distraught woman walk alone in the dark. It's daylight. She'll be perfectly safe, but Bill can very clearly see that I care about her.

The three of us head down in the elevator and hunt down the building manager. We gather around a computer screen in the management office and examine the security footage from the camera in the fourth-floor hallway. Gracie claims she was only out for two hours, so it's easy to narrow down the timeframe we need to check, and it's of absolutely zero surprise to me when we witness Luca entering the apartment. Gracie, on the other hand, withers away into a state of betrayal, hurt, confusion, disbelief. She sobs on my shoulder as Bill requests a copy of the footage and I write out my notes, but it's a waste of time. In the end, she decides to leave it as a civil matter.

She continues to cry in the back of the cruiser as we drive by my apartment building to drop her off. There's now only thirty minutes left of my shift, so she takes comfort in knowing I'll be there with her again very soon. She thanks Bill and me profusely as she climbs out of the car. I don't move a muscle until she's safely inside my building.

"Close friend?" Bill says, watching me from the passenger seat with a knowing smirk. "You could just say girlfriend. It's easier."

I ignore his teasing and grip the steering wheel tightly as I start to drive. "That ex of hers is a real piece of work . . . I'd have *loved* being the one to arrest him if he was still around."

"Careful," Bill warns. "You're working on *not* letting your emotions get involved, remember? In this job, Weston, always go with your head over your heart. Never make split-second decisions based on emotions. That's how you get yourself fired."

GRACIE

I don't recognize the person Luca has become.

He's not the same Luca I loved. The one my mother adored. The one I wanted to raise kids with.

It's impossible to deny the cold hard facts when they're on video. Luca let himself into the apartment we shared together, the one that holds so many memories, and spent ten minutes inside destroying whatever he could get his hands on. I've had no contact with him since he barged into the apartment on Tuesday in a fit of rage over our social media accounts being wiped from existence, so what the hell could have possibly triggered this? Has his anger been manifesting all week and he needed a release? Was this his payback? Was it the roses from Weston that did it? At first glance into my apartment upon my arrival home, they were one of the first things I saw. The gorgeous red roses Weston had delivered were scattered ruthlessly across the floor, torn from their box. That hurts more than the fist-sized hole in the TV.

I hear a set of keys jangling and I sit up, holding my breath. It's almost seven-thirty now, and I've spent the past hour curled up in Weston's bed. I haven't even turned on his TV. I've been alone in the silence, giving myself time to process Luca's behavior now that the initial shock has worn off. I've texted Elena and Maddie to let them know what's happened and that I'm staying at Weston's tonight. I call my mom too, and she's just as aghast as I am, but feels better knowing that I'm not still at the apartment. No one says anything, but it's clear it crosses each of our minds, the haunting question: What if Luca comes back? What if he hurts *me?*

The door opens.

"Weston," I say, exhaling the breath I've been holding. I throw back his comforter and run to meet him at the door, overcome with relief that I'm no longer alone. If anyone can protect me, it's him. I wrap my arms around his waist and smoosh my face into his chest.

He holds me close and strokes my hair. "Are you okay? Are you okay, Gracie? I'm sorry I'm late. I had reports to finish up at the station, but I'm here now. You're safe here with me."

"I'm okay," I whisper, but he squeezes me tighter as if I wasn't.

"Here, sit down," he says, guiding me to the couch. He wraps a blanket around me, the same one I snuggled up under the first morning I visited his apartment, and then grabs me a glass of water from the kitchen. "You still look pale."

I take the water from him, but there's a tremor building in my hands again. Aftershocks. "I really didn't expect you to be the officer who got the call," I say, my voice hoarse from my sobbing, "but I'm so glad you were."

He sits down on the couch next to me, still in his uniform, and rubs his hand soothingly up and down my thigh. "I know you haven't had a look for yourself yet, but it's bad. All of your computer and camera equipment is wrecked."

"I figured as much," I mumble. My head pounds. Will I need to get a cleaner in to fix the place up? Will mine and Luca's home insurance cover damage to belongings if Luca himself destroyed them?

"Can I be honest with you, Gracie?" Weston asks. His hand pauses on my knee. "I think it's a dangerously stupid idea to keep living in that apartment when Luca's name is still on the lease. You need to move out of there and rent somewhere else. And it's none of my business how your social media thing worked, but I assume you guys need to split whatever money you made from that if you haven't already. Anything else you guys still share, separate it. Cut all ties."

In hindsight, Luca and I should have done exactly that when we first broke up, but I never thought for a second that our relationship would turn into *this*. I believed it would always be civil. I even believed, at moments, that we would get back together. Now? Now I realize how naïve I've been.

"Maybe I should go back to Santa Cruz for a few weeks until I get everything figured out with Luca," I say, staring blankly ahead, lost in my own thoughts. "Just as soon as I get my full license and buy that Mercedes I want." I focus back on Weston and manage the smallest of smiles.

"That's a good idea," he agrees. He lets out a weary sigh as he sinks back into the couch and undoes the top few buttons of his shirt. Being dispatched to a 911 call made by myself would have been the last thing he expected during today's shift, I bet. "You are more than welcome to stay here, Gracie. I know we'd be a little cramped, but . . ."

I reach out for his hand and lock my fingers around his. "Can I take you up on that offer, Weston? Even just for a few nights? I'll need to go back to the apartment tomorrow to pack a bag, but you'll come with me, won't you?"

"Of course," he says. He glances down at our interlocked hands and smiles. "Have you eaten dinner?"

"No. I was on my way home earlier to make myself some beef stir fry."

He laughs. "Will pizza cut it?"

We order a large pepperoni pizza to share. In the time it takes for it to be delivered, Weston hops in the shower and changes into a pair of sweatpants. He straightens up his studio apartment, tidying away some clutter and even lighting a candle.

"I went out and bought some after the night I cooked you dinner," he says sheepishly, but I think it's sweet. He wants me to feel comfortable here, but I would feel comfortable anywhere Weston is.

When the pizza arrives, we sit together on the couch with the blanket draped over our laps and the pizza box between us. We watch old reruns of *How I Met Your Mother* and it's *exactly* what I need tonight, something that doesn't require much brain function. Just eating junk food and watching comfort shows on TV.

"Gracie?"

My gaze flickers from the TV to Weston. "Yeah?"

"I think you have more reasons now than ever to go see the world," he says quietly. "Get your affairs in order here first, then go travel."

"But I'm scared, Weston," I mumble, pushing away the empty pizza box. I lie down, resting my head in his lap and staring at the TV screen. "What if I'm eight thousand miles away and realize I can't do it?"

Weston laughs and says, "Then you just book a flight home, you goofball. What's worse: Regretting giving something a shot that didn't work out, or regretting never trying it in the first place? Once you start your career, these opportunities won't come along so easily."

"It sounds like you want to get rid of me," I joke.

"Never," he says, stroking my hair, "but it'd be selfish of me *not* to encourage you to do the things that scare you the most, wouldn't it? And you know I've been working real hard on not being selfish."

I smile, even though he can't see my face. "It *would* make great content . . . vlogging my travels. *Gracie on the Move*. Or maybe *Wandering Gracie*."

"See? You didn't know what your theme could be if you wanted to start from scratch all on your own, but *this* . . . This could be your new niche. It's perfect. And it gets you eight thousand miles away from Luca."

"I'd need to buy a new camera, though."

"That's true," he says, and we laugh.

I lift my head from his lap and sit upright again. The TV plays in the background, but neither of us are paying attention anymore. Softly, I cup his jaw, his skin freshly shaven. "But you definitely won't come with me?"

Weston's smile is apologetic. "No, Gracie, I can't come with you. But I promise I'd watch your videos. I'll be your number one fan." He places his hand over mine on his jaw and whispers, "I already am."

My heart soars. He always, *always* says the right thing.

"I said something to Peyton the other night," I say, swallowing hard, "and it's something I should probably tell *you*."

Weston raises an eyebrow curiously, and I take a breath. As I gaze back into his dark brown eyes, he feels like home to me. I trust Weston with every fiber of my being. The past five weeks, he's become my best friend. He's kept my world from crumbling down around me, and no matter what happens between us, I'll always be indebted to him for that. Weston's stirred up feelings in me that I've only ever felt before with Luca, and that only reassures me that I'm going to be just fine. I'm going to move on. I'm going to find the second love of my life one day. Maybe that's Weston, maybe it isn't, but I'll have a special spot in my heart for him always.

I press my forehead to his and close my eyes, whispering, "You make me believe I can fall in love again."

Weston exhales. He touches the pad of his thumb to my bottom lip. "I already have, Gracie," he murmurs. And, as he kisses me, it's like I'm all he's ever known.

WESTON

When I slip out of my apartment at six-thirty, Gracie is still fast asleep in my bed. I don't wake her to say goodbye, because she's sleeping peacefully and she deserves all the peace in the world after last night's incident. The last thing I want to do today is head off to work and leave her, but I've filled Peyton in on what happened, and she's offered to drop by and keep Gracie company. The silver lining, at least, is that I have the next four days off. When I get home tonight at seven, I'll take Gracie over to her place to pack some clothes. Tomorrow, we're going to go shop for that Mercedes she wants.

She's going to be fine, because I'll make sure of it.

Bill's waiting for me at the station, swigging his usual cup of cold filter coffee and sifting through paperwork. He flashes me a grin as I cross to my locker.

"How's your girlfriend doing this morning?"

SOMEWHERE IN THE SUNSET

"*Not* my girlfriend," I mutter, grabbing my duty belt. I secure it around my waist and remove my firearm from its holster, giving it a quick once-over before tucking it back in place. I click my locker shut and turn to Bill. "She was much calmer last night, and she's going to stay at my place for now."

"Going above and beyond to protect the citizens of San Francisco, I see."

I laugh. I'd do *anything* to protect Gracie, regardless of this badge and uniform.

"I wish she wanted us to file charges. I'd have loved the judge to serve us an arrest warrant for that piece of . . ."

"Speaking of warrants," Bill interrupts before I lose my professionalism, sliding some paperwork in front of me and tapping his finger against the mugshot image on the front page. "First thing on today's agenda is picking up this guy. Wanted under suspected armed robbery, so let's keep our wits about us, huh? He's got a long history of fleeing arrest, so be prepared for a tussle. Ah." He chugs the dregs of his coffee and sets the mug down with a clink. "Nothing wakes you up more than a fight."

"Awesome," I remark sarcastically.

I skim my eyes over the papers as we head out to the cruiser together. Starting the day shift at seven isn't too bad on these gorgeous August mornings when the sun is already up. I'm dreading the winter, though. Dragging myself out of bed to a job I hate will be worse when paired with cold, dark mornings. And, by then, I'll be working solo. Hopefully. It depends how long Bill plans on extending my training by.

As we settle into the car, I let dispatch know we're actioning an arrest warrant, double-check the address, and pull out of the lot. Picking up folks under warrants always makes me antsy. Sometimes you catch the wanted person so off-guard, they immediately hold their hands up in defeat and comply with our commands as we transfer them to jail. Other times, we're sprawled out on the floor, wrestling cuffs onto hands that are determined to fight back. I roll out my shoulders. My muscles still ache from the gym on Wednesday, so I'm not sure how much strength I'll be able to muster.

As I drive, I grab the paperwork from the dashboard again and glance over the details. This guy is almost three hundred pounds. Bill may be taking a backseat currently while he observes my performance, but he's gonna need to help me out on this one. There's no way I'm getting this guy to the ground on my own.

"If he resists, you'll back me up, right?" I confirm.

Bill scoffs. "Only after I've watched you utilize every skill I've taught you when it comes to subduing a resisting person. *Only* then, if you're still struggling, will I help. When you're dispatched to calls on your own, you won't immediately have a second officer there to save you when things take a turn. You only have yourself to count on."

"Maybe he'll surprise us and comply," I say.

"Keep dreaming."

The address on file isn't far from the station, only five minutes, but ten in morning traffic. I keep my mind busy as I drive, holding the nervous adrenaline at bay. I wonder if Gracie is awake yet. I pray this shift passes quickly. The sooner I get home to her, the better.

"Bill, does your wife like that you're a cop?"

Bill narrows his eyes at me. Admittedly, it's a random question. "She's used to it. She's proud of it. But I don't think she *likes* it. Why?"

"Just thinking," I say.

My mom always hated my dad working the beat in his younger days, too. She used to joke that her increasing wrinkles were from teaching, but I always believed they were from worrying about Dad so much. When he became deputy chief and didn't work the streets anymore, she was thrilled. And not because of the thicker paycheck: She was overjoyed that his safety was no longer compromised.

"Does your girlfriend not like it?" Bill asks.

"Again, Bill. *Not* my girlfriend."

I don't know how Gracie feels about it. She tells me to quit, but that's because she knows *I* hate it. Does she worry about me while I'm on shift? If I show up home tonight with a busted lip from fighting this perp, will she be horrified?

"Hey, I think it's that one," Bill says, pointing to a house.

I park the cruiser up a few doors down, out of sight. Sometimes if a wanted felon spots the car first, they're gone before we've even knocked on the front door. I grab the papers and triple-check the details one more time, arming myself with the facts. I tell dispatch we've arrived at the address, and then Bill follows me out of the car.

"You're pretty solid when it comes to executing arrest warrants," he says, "so stop fidgeting with your belt. You know what you're doing, Reed, so act like it."

I instantly stop fiddling with my flashlight and lift my head higher, chest out. "Oh, a compliment? Geez, Bill. I need to have a breakdown on shift with you more often. You're a changed man."

"Ahh. Let's just say you're my favorite rookie." He smiles fondly.

"Don't lie to me."

Bill shakes his head. "I'm not. The rookies I teach are usually overconfident and they try to skip ten steps ahead because they think they know better. You're the opposite. You doubt yourself. Question yourself. That makes you the best kind of officer to teach. And you're Mark's son, so that kind of makes you feel like mine, too."

"You sure do ride my ass like a father would," I mutter, and we share a laugh. I didn't realize Bill held me in such high regard, but maybe with his continued mentoring, I *could* do this, after all. I'm perfectly competent, but my fear gets in the way. Maybe if I overcome that fear, I'd grow to enjoy the thrill of never knowing what my next shift at work will entail.

We approach the old Victorian home, painted yellow with a garage beneath and stairs leading to the front door. Bill waits at the foot of the stairs, his hands on his hips and his sunglasses shielding his eyes. He gives me the go-ahead nod.

I climb the stairs and knock on the door. It's just after seven, so our guy may still be asleep, or he may not even be home at all. I listen for any signs of life inside, but I hear no movement. I rap my knuckles against the door harder this time.

"Police department," I call loudly. "We're here to serve an arrest warrant for . . ." I trail off as there's a noise from inside the house. I step closer to the door, trying to hear better. The warrant stated no other persons lived at this address. "Mr. Jones, I can hear you. Please come to the door."

Bill sighs. Serving arrest warrants is seldom easy. If the door isn't answered immediately, then it's obvious our wanted person is choosing evasion, and evasion leads to resisting, and resisting leads to a struggle. I glance back at Bill and scowl. It also means I'm going to have to stomp my foot through the door.

"I know you're in there," I say, keeping my tone steady. "I need you to open up the door or we're going to have to bust it down. It's your choice, but I'd rather not damage your property, so c'mon. Let's not make things difficult for each other."

I wait patiently, hand on my duty belt. Sometimes the friendly act works, but most of the time, my attempts at establishing trust are futile. No one answers the door, still. I lean over the railing of the stairs and peer through a window, but I can't spot anyone lurking inside. Our guy is either hunkering down somewhere within the house as though we won't force entry and find him regardless, or he's fleeing.

"I'm going to check if there's a back door," I tell Bill as I climb back down the steps. "Keep your eyes on the front of the house for me."

I walk by the garage and turn the corner to head down the side of the house, but I jolt in surprise when there's already someone staring back at me. It's our guy from the mugshot, and clearly I've woken him, because he's wearing nothing but a pair of sweatpants. He's barefoot. He's attempting a getaway.

"Hey. Let's not do this," I say, holding one hand up in a non-threatening manner while the other instinctively moves to my holster. My blood starts pumping. I've caught him off-guard, and he stands frozen, eyes wide. But then his hand twitches toward the waistband of his sweats, and now I drop the nice-cop bullshit. "Hey! *Hey!* Don't you fucking dare!"

I grab hold of my firearm, but he's quicker. He whips out a pistol and points it straight at me. I scramble backward, diving behind a parked car as a gunshot pierces through such a peaceful morning. "Oh, fuck!"

I yank my gun from its holster and keep my back pressed against the car, shielding myself as I radio dispatch. Another shot rings out. I peek around the vehicle and try to get eyes on our suspect, but all I see is Bill crouched down low behind the stairs to the house. A third shot rings through my ears and I realize only at this point that our suspect isn't running. He's fighting, and Bill is the one caught in the crossfire. He gets off two shots of his own, and then he ducks fully behind the stairs as a returned shot whistles past him.

He doesn't have enough coverage behind those stairs. If our suspect advances on him, he's cornered.

Fuck. My hands are shaking. I'm precise with my shots when there's no pressure, but when every fleeting second counts, I don't have time to steady my hands and reset my focus. Still trembling, I rise from the ground and stretch my arms out across the hood of the car, gun pointed.

"Reed, stay *down!*" Bill yells at me, but it's too late.

Our suspect spots me. He swings his gun from Bill's direction to mine, but I get a shot off first. And it fucking misses! Dad will never believe me when he hears I had a clean shot at an armed suspect and I fucking *missed!* I line up for a cleaner second shot, but gunfire sounds before I pull the trigger.

A blinding pain spreads through me. It's like I've just been hit in the chest with a sledgehammer. It knocks the wind out of me and throws me backward to the ground. I suck in a breath and glance down, almost laughing out loud in relief when I see the torn patch in my shirt and my bulletproof vest poking through underneath. Jesus. Why did Bill never warn me that getting hit in your vest feels as though you aren't even wearing one? Damn.

I groan as I roll over, grabbing my gun from the ground, but there's more crossfire blazing around me. Bill is shooting back. Our suspect is persevering. This is getting messy. We need to bring him down before any civilians get hurt. Despite the ache in my chest, I struggle back to my feet. I'm going to have a gnarly bruise, that's for sure. Maybe even a cracked rib.

"Stay down, Bill!" I call out to him. I have more coverage behind this car than he does behind those stairs. "I've got this!"

Bill dips low behind the stairs. I edge my way along the car, stretch out from behind the tailgate, and aim.

I'm still not quick enough.

I hit the ground hard again.

Ouch. That hurt a little more. And not my chest this time. My thigh.

I reach down to touch where it hurts, but I can't feel anything. When I look at my hand, it's red with blood.

"Ah, fuck, Bill . . ."

I gasp for breath, but it hurts too much.

My gun has slid underneath the car, but I can't even move, let alone reach for it. Gunshots continue to sound, until they don't. A resounding silence settles over the scene and suddenly Bill is on his knees next to me. He tears open my shirt, unbuckles my duty belt.

"Weston," he pants, blocking the sunshine as he leans over me. He bundles up my shirt and presses it hard into my thigh, almost his entire bodyweight pushing down onto my leg. "Hang on, buddy. We'll get you fixed up, okay? Just hang on."

Everything feels so cold. Sirens blare in the distance, but they don't grow louder. They only fade. Every breath hurts. There's blood on Bill's hands now too. Lots of blood. Too much blood.

"Bill . . ."

I want to say: *Bill, there's too much blood, isn't there?*

I want to say: *Bill, I never wanted to be a cop in the first place.*

I want to say: *Bill, I'm scared.*

Fuck, there is so much I want to say.

There's just no time.

GRACIE

Weston never gets out of the station exactly at the end of his shift. There are always reports to finish, so when he isn't home by eight, I don't find it unusual. It's been a long day without him around, but I kept myself busy. I did some laundry for him, even put fresh sheets on the bed. I showered and borrowed one of his shirts, but he's so tall compared to me that I'm pulling off wearing it as a dress.

We're going over to my place soon, though. I'll pack some clothes. Maybe even attempt to clean up some of the mess Luca left, but I also don't know if I can face it yet. I loved that apartment. All of the good memories I've ever had there are all so tainted now, and Weston is probably right that I should move out and find a place that's mine and only mine. I need to cut myself off from Luca completely. That means starting afresh.

When it gets to eight-thirty, I call Weston's phone. It sends me straight to voicemail, and I figure it's shut off inside his locker. It must have been a pretty hectic shift for him if he's *still* at the station completing paperwork.

I flick through TV channels, but I don't care about watching much. I'm bored now. I ordered Chinese food for lunch earlier, but it's growing late and I'm becoming increasingly hungry again. Would Weston mind if I ordered dinner without him? He'd understand. It's almost nine!

Now that I think about it, Peyton hasn't shown up. Weston mentioned last night that she would be in the city today and she'd drop by at some point to check in on me while he was at work, but if she hasn't by this time, then I doubt she's coming at all. Maybe it's a good thing. I've only met her that one time at the hospital last week, so I imagine there's still a list of questions she plans on asking me before she heads back to base next week.

There's a thundering knock at the door and I think: *Finally!*

But it's very quickly followed by: *Wait, why is Weston knocking on his own door? He has a key.*

I jump up from the couch and straighten out the shirt of his I'm wearing. I notice again how it smells like the cologne he always wears.

There's more pounding at the door. Desperate pounding. A voice shouts, "Gracie? Gracie, are you still in there?"

At first, I think it almost sounds like Elena. She knows I'm staying here. But as I rush to the door, I realize the voice actually belongs to Peyton. She's come by, after all. I unlock the door and swing it open.

Peyton stands in the hall, her hand pressed to the doorframe for support as she pants heavily. Her skin is tanned from all those scorching hot months in Kuwait, but somehow, she seems pale as she stands under the flickering, dim lights of the hallway. "I'm so sorry, Gracie, I forgot you were here . . . I was going to come by, but then I drove back to Bodega Bay to be with my dad when I heard, and then I *just* remembered you'd be here all alone, so I drove all the way back again to be with you," she splutters, gasping for air between words. Her eyes are swollen, and I'm staring at her with furrowed brows, wondering why she's so upset about forgetting to visit me when she has only met me *once* before. It's not that deep.

"Peyton," I say, reaching out for her wrist and pulling her into the apartment. "I'm absolutely fine! Bored, but fine. Weston should be on his way home."

Peyton's hand flies to her mouth. "Oh my God. Of course, you don't know . . . How would you?"

"Don't know what?" I ask, but my throat tightens. An awful, overwhelming feeling of dread settles over me and leaves me cold. "I don't know *what,* Peyton?"

Peyton stares at me in horror, her eyes wide and bloodshot. "Weston was serving an arrest warrant first thing this morning . . . Things turned ugly, and there was a shootout," she says, her voice shaky. "He got hit, Gracie."

No.

My heart drops into my stomach. That's why he's late. He's hurt.

And I've been sitting here all day with no idea, when all this time he has needed me.

I dart across the apartment, grabbing my sneakers. "What hospital is he in?"

I pull on my jacket. Find my wallet. Slip on one sneaker. Then pause when I realize Peyton hasn't responded.

She remains by the door, unmoving. There is no sense of urgency about her; just a raw, all-consuming pain in her eyes as she watches me. Peyton is a soldier. She's mentally tough. She'll have seen some awful things during her deployment. Injuries in the line of duty are something she is used to, yet she stands in Weston's doorway, trembling. My other sneaker slips through my grasp and falls to the floor.

No . . . No, no, no . . .

"He's not at the hospital, is he?" I whisper.

Peyton's face crumples. "No, Gracie. No . . ."

And that tells me everything I never wanted to hear.

I drop to my knees as my vision blurs. Peyton runs to me. She sinks to the floor and wraps her arms around me, her body shaking against mine. She sobs into my hair and I scream, and scream, and scream, until I have no voice left at all.

GRACIE

"Gracie, can I make you something to eat?"

"No."

"Gracie, you need to take a shower."

"No."

"Gracie, please stop watching the news."

"No."

"Gracie . . ."

"No."

My mom hugs me tight. She's staying with me at my apartment.

We tidied the place up. We gathered the destroyed roses and had them freeze-dried. They're inside a glass frame now alongside the handwritten note from Weston. It sits on the coffee table, and I spend an awful lot of time staring at it, but it doesn't bring me comfort. It only cuts me deeper.

GRACIE

There are thousands of people inside the auditorium at the University of San Francisco. *Thousands*. Everyone stands. A procession of bagpipes and snare drums escorts the honor guard as they carry the flag-draped casket to the front of the auditorium, and Verity squeezes my hand.

Officers from all over California are here. They are all in uniform, and they stand in salute. On large screens, a slideshow of images plays. Photographs of Weston as a young kid, of him with family and friends, of him graduating from the academy, of him being sworn in as an officer. There's a photo of him with the Golden Gate Bridge stretching behind, taken by myself barely three weeks ago. I supplied it to Peyton to use.

Everyone sits. There are hundreds upon hundreds of members of the public who are here to show support.

Weston is the third officer to be killed in the line of duty in California this year. The first of San Francisco PD in years. It's been on the news. In the paper. The community has really come together. Local businesses have been raising funds for the Reed family. There are even news crews here.

A pastor leads the memorial service. On a stage full of wreaths, he speaks of the tragic day last Monday.

Elena and Maddie sit on my left. Verity and my mom on the right. Maddie takes my other hand. But I'm okay. I'm too numb to feel anything. Too numb to cry. Too numb to be present. I sit way back in the stalls, because I didn't know Weston long enough to justify sitting closer.

The first tribute is delivered by Weston's field training officer, Bill. His arm is in a sling. He took a bullet that morning, too. He talks of Weston fondly. Jokes of how tough he was on him. Says he was honored to be his partner for ten weeks.

His friend, Adam, delivers the second tribute. He can't finish it. His voice cracks and he chokes on his tears before the pastor escorts him down from the stage.

Peyton and Keaton stand up together to deliver a joint tribute. They both stay strong up there at the podium in front of all these people, but they're both so resilient. They're hurting, but they keep it together. They're tough. At one point, I spot Keaton's wife, Lily, way down at the front. She has Sophia next to her and her newborn in her lap. Weston's nephew is only eleven days old. He'll never know his uncle, but he'll learn about him as he gets older. He'll know Weston through photographs and stories. Through memories kept alive.

The final tribute is from Weston's father. Mark talks of how proud he was of Weston for following in his footsteps, and I have to just sit there in these stalls with my heart in pieces because I know . . . I *know* . . . Weston never wanted to. It's why he wouldn't quit. His fear of disappointing his dad was bigger than his fear of putting his life on the line. But Mark would have understood. Of course he would have. It's too late now.

My chest is so heavy. It feels like I'm carrying the weight of the world even though my time with Weston was so limited. In the five weeks I knew him, he became my best friend. He kept me afloat when it was so easy to drown, and I have to believe that during the past five weeks, I gave him the same friendship and care he gave me. His final few weeks weren't all heartbreak. There were good moments in there, and I take solace in the fact I played a part in that. It's the only way I can sleep at night. Knowing that maybe I made his life a tiny bit easier, even just for a little while.

The pastor closes the memorial with a prayer. He asks only the officers of the Northern District to remain. Weston's station. The rest of the auditorium filters outside in our thousands and the blazing sunshine seems unjust when my soul feels like storm clouds and thunder.

Crowds line the university campus, awaiting the beginning of the funeral procession from here to the cemetery. There will be a private graveside service. Peyton has extended an invite to me, but I can't be there. *Five weeks . . . I was only a part of his life for five weeks.* There are so many more people who deserve to be there more than me.

Mom grasps my hand tight as the procession passes us. It's led by two motorcycles, then the hearse. The Reed family follows in a limousine. There are so many police cruisers and motorcycles. *So, so many.* It's a constant stream of flashing blue, red and white lights. Cameras are broadcasting this live. Uniformed officers in salute line the route out of the campus.

Elena wraps herself around my arm. Maddie cries. Mom squeezes my hand harder. Verity watches me with concern. I'm not emotionless. I'm just empty. The past week has been rough, and after days of grieving, it finally sank in that he was really gone. I've reached a state of acceptance now. A state of determination, even.

Because I know exactly what I have to do now.

I bow my head and close my eyes as the end of the procession passes. I wish it were easier to recall all of the conversations Weston and I had, but in those moments where we spoke, I never knew they were numbered. I do have one thing, though.

I have his note he sent with the roses.

The one that reads, in his handwriting: *Flowers or bear hugs? I'll always give you both.*

And oh, what I would do for one more bear hug from Weston Reed.

GRACIE

There's a knock on my door. I already know it's him. I invited him here, even though it scares the hell out of me. He still has a key, but he doesn't barge in. I inhale a deep breath before I open the door to face him.

"Hi, Luca."

Luca stands outside our door, his features downcast with remorse. "I didn't think you'd want to see me."

"I don't," I say. I open the door wider. A sign for him to enter. As he crosses the threshold, my pulse rockets. The last time he stepped foot in our apartment, he destroyed it. I shut the door and turn to him. "Take me off the lease. I'm moving out. You want to trash this place? Fine. Go ahead. It's all yours now."

"Gracie . . ." Luca swallows hard. Guilty as charged. He is *so* lucky I didn't want charges filed. "Where are you going to go?"

"I'm moving back home for a while," I say with a curt nod at the two suitcases on the floor. I'm almost done packing. The only belongings left in this apartment are his. "And I'd like to close our joint account. We'll split everything fifty-fifty."

"Okay," Luca says. He is in no position to argue, and for once, he doesn't. He knows he's fucked up big time. He stuffs his hands into his pockets and says, "You were right to close down our accounts. I shouldn't have gotten pissed about that."

"And?"

"And I'm sorry for trashing the apartment. I was wasted." When I raise an eyebrow, he adds, "I've been such an idiot since I left. I'm not the same without you."

When I look at Luca, I don't feel anything for him. Not even hatred at this point. It's complete and utter indifference. I walk past him and return to my suitcases, kneeling to the floor and folding a pile of T-shirts.

Luca follows me across the apartment. He sits on the edge of the couch, his head hung in shame. "I know it doesn't matter now," he murmurs, "but I never stopped loving you."

"But I stopped loving *you*."

"I know," he says. As I lift my gaze to meet his, he reaches out to touch my hand. A flicker of sympathy crosses his soft features. "I heard about Weston. I'm really sorry, Gracie."

I look away and clear my throat. "I'm going to be in Santa Cruz for a few weeks, and then I'm going to be gone for the next six months. Maybe longer. I don't know. I'm trying not to have a plan for the future for once."

"What?"

"You remember those big plans of ours? How we'd spend this gap year exploring the other side of the world?" I pause, because sometimes I can't believe it myself. "I'm doing it. I'm going."

Luca's brows arch in surprise. "By yourself?"

"Yes."

And he seems genuinely sincere when he says, "Good for you, Gracie."

"I know." I flip both my suitcases shut and zip them closed before hoisting them upright. I reach into my pocket, then hold out my set of apartment keys. "Here. These are all yours now. And honestly? I think it's best if we stay out of each other's lives from now on."

Luca hesitantly takes the keys from me, his frown deepening. "I'm sorry for everything I've put you through."

"Ahh, water under the bridge," I say with a flippant wave of my hand.

Luca stands from the couch. "Can I at least help you take those out to your Uber?"

"You can help me take them down to the garage."

"Huh?"

I throw him a smirk over my shoulder. "Someone got their license."

333

Luca takes my suitcases for me. As we leave the apartment, I don't take a second glance. I was so over this apartment the moment Luca left, and I'm ready for the next chapter in my life now. New beginnings, new memories.

We ride the elevator down to the parking garage and I point out my car. A black Mercedes, of course. I bought it the day after Weston's funeral. He was going to shop around dealer lots with me, so I knew he wouldn't have wanted me to put that on hold. I rocked up at those dealerships on my own, and he would have been proud of me. I negotiated the deal all by myself. Even got some new tires thrown in.

Luca places my suitcases in the trunk, and I hop in behind the wheel. Before he walks away, he knocks on my window. I roll it down.

"Good luck, Gracie," he says with a smile I used to adore. "This might be the last time you see me."

"It better be," I say, but my smile matches his.

I start up my engine, pull out of the garage, and drive myself home to Santa Cruz for the first time in my life.

GRACIE

Four months later

The sun sets over Echo Beach in the small coastal town of Canggu. It's December in Bali, but it's still warmer than San Francisco in the heat of the summer.

I stretch out on my lounger, admiring the streaks of orange painted through the sky while I sip on a coconut through a straw. These are my favorite moments. The slowing down to enjoy gorgeous sunsets in beautiful countries.

I hold up my camera.

"Weston, I wish you were here to see this one," I say, then turn the camera around to film the black-sand beach and all of the colors in the sky above it. I let him know I'm going for dinner soon with some other solo travelers from my hotel. I'll probably have seafood. Maybe I'll get around to trying crab tonight.

I film most of every day, but sometimes it's nice to enjoy the silence. No camera, no sharing my day with Weston, no retakes. Just silence, a sunset, and a coconut. It's been an exhausting day. I took another surfing lesson this morning, but I still suck. It doesn't get any easier, but I'm trying my best. I'm trying a lot of new things.

I skydived in Singapore and cried with nerves as the helicopter climbed thousands of feet, but then grinned the entire fall. Weston would never believe I did that, but I've done a lot of things he wouldn't believe. I've kayaked down the Nam Song River in Laos. Scuba dived with bull sharks in Thailand. Ridden a hot air balloon in Cambodia.

And I've documented every second of it. For him, for Weston.

Dear Weston, Love Gracie is growing. My theme is solo traveling in memory of someone special, because that person once told me to do the things that scare me most. I only wish Weston had taken his own advice, but he didn't. That means I had to. I *had* to do this. These videos are for him. It brings me so much comfort, feeling like he's still around, watching over me. I like to think he's somewhere in the sunsets.

I surpassed fifty thousand subscribers last week. My Instagram engagement is growing stronger with each new post, but I'll always remember my first follower. I'm earning ad revenue again, but I donate every cent to the Weston Reed Foundation. It's a charity Weston's father started in the weeks after his death. It offers support for families of fallen officers, and I'm its biggest champion. Peyton sends me emails every once in a while. She's still on US ground for now, on base in Colorado, and she watches my videos religiously. She enjoys hearing me say Weston's name.

I enjoy saying it even more, and I think of him every single day. On the days I get scared, the thought of him keeps me pushing forward. The night before he died, he asked me what I would regret most: Giving something a try and having it not work out, or regretting never trying it in the first place? And I know what the answer is. For the rest of my life, I am *always* going to do the things that terrify me.

There's pink in the sky now, smeared through the oranges and blues. Every night, I watch the sunset, because I know they will always be there.

I pick up my camera again and point it back at myself. The colors of the sky shine in my eyes, my cheeks sunkissed with splashes of freckles, and I have one more thing I need to tell him.

"I like to think you're somewhere in the sunsets, Weston, so I'll chase them forever."

ACKNOWLEDGEMENTS

Some of my readers may already be aware that this is my first New Adult romance after being exclusively a Young Adult author in my writing career so far. Well, let me say one thing: I am TERRIFIED. Switching genres is scary, but it's been a very natural progression for me. A lot of my readers have grown up alongside me, and if you have read my YA works and are still with me here now, then thank you a million times over from the bottom of my heart.

I will continue to say this in every single Acknowledgements I ever write: I have the greatest publishing team behind me. And no, I'm not biased. They really are the best. Ali and Campbell, you changed the trajectory of my life by taking a gamble on me when I was just seventeen, and I'll forever be so thankful to you for making my biggest dream come true. Clem Flanagan, my fab editor, thanks for all the feedback and for giving me a real boost when you read my first draft. Thomas Ross, Hannah Walker, Tonje Hefte, Rachel Morrell – thank you. Also extra thanks to Emma Hargrave.

A massive shoutout to my local Starbucks, for being my second home every winter when I set up shop in the corner of the café and pump myself full of caffeine. Thanks for never kicking me out, even on the night before my deadline when I camped for eight hours, surviving on adrenaline and blueberry muffins.

To my besties – Heather, Rhea, Bethany. You guys are everything the friends you have in your twenties should be – a safe space. It's a testament to our friendship that every time we are together, we feel comfortable enough to offload all of the anxious thoughts in our minds and be completely understood.

Sherilyn, if I was ever asked to describe the best sister ever, it would be exactly you. You've been through so much and are the most resilient person I know. I wish I was so much more like you.

Anders and Jaxson, my nephews who are growing up way too fast, I love you both so much. I hope one day you'll proudly tell all your teachers you have a cool auntie who's an author.

Grandma and Granda, I hope you aren't reading this, because you have never been allowed to read even my YA books thanks to my abundant use of swear words, so you definitely aren't allowed to read my NA books. Still, you tell every stranger you meet that your granddaughter is the best writer in the world. Thanks for being so proud of me.

Mum . . . I need an entire book all to itself to put into words how much you mean to me. The older I get, the more our relationship strengthens. I am so, so, so lucky that I can turn to you with anything. I read something recently that said to go easy on your mother, because she's living life for the first time too. Sometimes I expect you to have all the answers, but that's not fair – you're still searching for them too.

Craig, I never thought that one day my car salesman would make it into my Acknowledgements! You were the biggest distraction in the world while I wrote this book, but in all the best ways. Whenever I've written about my characters experiencing butterflies because they were so in love, I thought I was writing for dramatic effect. I never knew just how real butterflies in your stomach could be until I met you.

ESTELLE MASKAME published the first book in her international bestselling *Did I Mention I Love You?* series when she was just seventeen. A word-of-mouth sensation, she is also the author of the Mila trilogy (2022), and the "highly addictive" standalone novels *Dare to Fall* and *The Wrong Side of Kai*. With over one million copies of her books sold, and rights sold in twenty territories, her fiction attracts countless passionate, loyal fans worldwide. Winner of the Young Scot Arts Award 2016, Estelle has been shortlisted for the Young Adult award at the Romantic Novel of the Year Awards. When she's not catching up with her international fanbase – or travelling to America to research her characters and their lives – Estelle lives in her hometown of Peterhead, Scotland.

𝕏 ⃝ ♪ @estellemaskame
www.estellemaskame.com

THE JOURNEY STARTS HERE

As a Young Adult imprint, Ink Road is passionate about publishing fiction with a contemporary and forward-looking focus. We love working with authors who share our commitment to bold and brilliant stories – and we're always on the lookout for fresh new voices and the readers who will enjoy them.

@inkroadbooks

INK-ROAD.COM